PAPERBACK TRADING CO.
27601 FORRES ROAD
LAGU...

P9-EDP-013

More praise for Janet Dawson and KINDRED CRIMES

"A satisfyingly complex and multilayered novel . . . A wonderfully told and compelling story from a writer who's in complete control—as is her heroine—from start to finish. We'll feel cheated if there aren't more Jeri Howard books to come."
The Denver Post

"Dawson keeps suspense and interest at high pitch."
Publishers Weekly

"An auspicious debut."
New York Daily News

PAPERBACK TRADING CO.
25571 MARGUERITE PKWY.
MISSION VIEJO, CA 92691
(714) 380-4007

KINDRED CRIMES

Janet Dawson

FAWCETT CREST • NEW YORK

Sale of this book without a front cover may be unauthorized. If this book is coverless, it may have been reported to the publisher as "unsold or destroyed" and neither the author nor the publisher may have received payment for it.

A Fawcett Crest Book
Published by Ballantine Books
Copyright © 1990 by Janet Dawson

All rights reserved under International and Pan-American Copyright Conventions. Published in the United States by Ballantine Books, a division of Random House, Inc., New York, and simultaneously in Canada by Random House of Canada Limited, Toronto.

No part of this book may be used or reproduced in any manner whatsoever without written permission except in the case of brief quotations embodied in criticial articles or reviews. For information, address St. Martin's Press, 175 Fifth Avenue, New York, N.Y. 10010.

Library of Congress Catalog Card Number: 89-70346

ISBN 0-449-22014-1

This edition published by arrangement with St. Martin's Press, Inc.

Manufactured in the United States of America

First Ballantine Books Edition: May 1992

To my parents,
Don and Thelma Dawson, with love,
and to my fellow mystery writers,
who have given me encouragement.

One

MAN, WOMAN, AND CHILD POSED IN FRONT OF A thick green Christmas tree, its branches laden with silver tinsel and gold balls. He stood behind her chair, hands resting lightly on her shoulders. Her blond hair fell in waves past the collar of her red dress. In her lap she held a cherubic toddler. They smiled at the camera, the image of a perfect middle-class nuclear family, caught forever in a five-by-seven glossy.

"When did she leave?" I asked.

"Wednesday morning," he said, his voice tremulous. He cleared his throat. "She left the baby with my mother, said she was going shopping. She never came back."

He was a slender fair-haired man of about thirty, well-dressed, with finely chiseled features. Now he put one hand to his pale face, as though to erase the lines etched by worry and strain. He sighed deeply. I waited for him to continue.

"I got home from work around six. Renee wasn't there, so I called Mom. She and Dad live just a few miles away. Mom told me Jason was there but she hadn't seen Renee since about ten that morning. Of course I was concerned."

He'd waited an hour, then two, concern giving way to worry, plagued by visions of car accidents and abductions. Finally he called the police. They asked if Mrs. Foster left on her own. Of course she hadn't, he said. Then he looked in the closet, the dresser drawers, the bathroom. Her suitcase was missing. So were clothes, shoes, the things a woman would take with her if she planned to be gone for a while.

The next day the bank called him about a bounced check. Mrs. Foster had emptied the joint account.

"Can you find her, Ms. Howard?"

"Are you sure you want me to?"

Philip Foster blinked his puppy brown eyes in surprise. "Of course I want you to find her. Why would you ask a question like that?"

"Your wife apparently left on her own. She may not want to come back." He winced. I felt as though I'd kicked the puppy. But he had to know and I had to tell him. "If I find her I can't make her do anything she doesn't want to do."

"I understand," he said. "But if I could just talk to her . . . I'm worried about her. I have to know that she's all right."

I looked him in the eye for a long moment as I thought about this case and whether I should take it. Did Mr. Foster drink, take drugs, beat his wife or child? If that was the reason Mrs. Foster left, why didn't she take the kid? And why did I feel that Philip Foster was holding something back?

"You're from Los Gatos," I said. That's a town in the hills southwest of San Jose. "What makes you think your wife is in Oakland?"

"She was born in Oakland. But mainly it's the phone bill."

"What phone bill?" The man wasn't making sense.

"The one that came in the mail yesterday." Foster scrabbled around in the leather portfolio he'd brought with him. He pulled out the bill and shoved it across the desk at me.

"See," he said, pointing at an Oakland number circled in pencil. "I thought at first it was a mistake. I don't know anybody in Oakland. But I went back through the phone bills for the last few months, and that number appears several times. The operator told me it's an antique store called Granny's Attic on Piedmont Avenue in Oakland. Renee called that number the day before she disappeared. It must mean something."

"Did you call it?"

"Several times. I got no answer."

I picked up my phone and punched in the number. I let it

2

ring for a full minute before hanging up. It was a quirky piece of evidence. But it was enough to bring Foster up here from Los Gatos and enough to pique my interest.

"All right, Mr. Foster. I'll take the case."

I got a copy of my standard contract from the filing cabinet. We went over the details and he wrote out a five-hundred-dollar retainer check. That out of the way, I extracted more information from Foster.

My quarry, Renee Mills Foster, was five feet five inches tall and weighed 110 pounds, with shoulder-length blond hair—courtesy of a bottle—and blue eyes. She had no distinguishing marks or features other than a small burn scar on her left forearm. She would be twenty-nine on April 3.

As far as her husband knew, Renee had no relatives living, in Oakland or elsewhere. He didn't know where she'd gone to high school, but he thought she may have attended college at California State University in Hayward. In fact, Foster didn't know much about his wife at all. It was as though she didn't exist until he met her five years ago, while she was working as a secretary in a Silicon Valley computer firm. After dating a few months, they eloped to Lake Tahoe.

Foster told me his wife didn't have any friends. When he realized how that sounded, he amended it to name a co-worker at the computer firm. Renee had continued working there until right before their child was born, and she occasionally met the co-worker for a drink after work. As for other interests, Renee took a dance class four afternoons a week. Her husband said it in a way that sounded like he resented her taking the time away from the family hearth.

I wrote down the numbers of the Fosters' credit cards, though I doubted Renee would create a paper trail. She'd gotten several thousand in cash from the joint account. The money wouldn't last forever, but if she was careful she could stay hidden for a long time.

"What kind of car was she driving?" I asked Foster.

"She doesn't have it. She left it in the bank parking lot. The other private investigator found it there."

"Wait a minute," I said. "You already hired an investigator?"

A man named Gerrity, Foster told me, but he was unsatisfactory. He dug the investigator's report out of the leather portfolio. I leafed through the pages.

After emptying the bank account, Mrs. Foster left her Volvo station wagon in the bank parking lot, where it was ticketed. Gerrity had checked local cab companies until he located a driver who picked up a fare near the bank Wednesday morning, a woman matching Renee Foster's description, carrying an oversized handbag and a suitcase. The cabbie took her to the nearest CalTrain depot.

It sounded like the unsatisfactory Mr. Gerrity had done a decent day's work. Still, there are a lot of shifty operators in this business. Maybe Foster had been justified in terminating the investigator's services.

Foster was staying at the Hyatt on Broadway, a block from my Franklin Street office. I told him I'd be in touch as soon as I had anything to report. As he got up to leave, I asked him how he wound up in my office.

"Sergeant Vernon at the Oakland Police Department recommended you."

After Foster left I picked up the phone again and punched in the number of the Oakland Police Department Homicide Section, asking for Sergeant Vernon.

"Thanks for the client, Sid."

"I thought it was right up your alley."

"Which alley is that?" As if I didn't know.

"The disappearing wife." His tone was barbed. "The one who walks out on her husband."

"We left each other, Sid."

"So you tell me. Thought I'd slide a little business your way. Got to keep you employed so I don't have to pay you alimony."

"I won't hold my breath. Tell me about Foster."

"Not much to tell. He came in early this morning. Missing Persons checked Homicide to see if we had any Jane Does matching the wife's description." The rest of Sid's informa-

4

tion matched what Foster had told me. "Foster came up here waving that phone bill like it was hard evidence. Waste of time, if you ask me. He wanted to hire an investigator in this area and the name Jeri Howard just popped into my head."

"I know why you gave him my number, Sid. You don't think I can find her."

"The woman took a powder and doesn't want to come home. But you private investigators have a different way of looking at things. A case is a case, right? I figured you'd give it a shot."

"I will."

I hung up on him without saying goodbye. Steering Foster to me was Sid's way of applying the needle. He was telling me exactly what he thought of private investigators in general and this private investigator in particular. Sid Vernon liked to push my buttons, and damn it, he still got a rise out of me. Trouble was, I read Renee Foster's disappearance the same way he did.

I called the number on Gerrity's letterhead and got his answering machine. After leaving a message to call me, I checked my Oakland phone directory, verifying the address and phone number of Granny's Attic. Then I locked my office and went downstairs.

I walked through the midmorning drizzle to the Alameda County Courthouse, several blocks from my office. It was March and the weather vacillated between rain and sunshine. This Monday morning offered a gray sky and rain, curling the ends of my red-brown hair and beading on my khaki raincoat.

At the courthouse I checked the Fictitious Business Names records and turned up Granny's Attic, owned by one Vera Burke, who lived at an address on Monticello Avenue in Piedmont. Then I looked through the microfilmed Alameda County birth records.

That's when I discovered Mrs. Foster either wasn't born Renee Mills or wasn't born in Alameda County.

* * *

5

Foster told me his wife had been born in Oakland, April 3, twenty-nine years ago. But I found no record of a Renee Mills born in Alameda County on that date or during the two months either side of that date. I spent the next hour checking the same four-month period for the years immediately preceding and following. Then I widened my search to all twelve months in a five-year span.

No Renee Mills. Either she changed her name or she was born somewhere else.

In addition to the phone bill and the photograph, Foster had given me a copy of an insurance form filled out by his wife. I took the form out of my purse and examined it, noting that Mrs. Foster had listed her place of birth as Oakland and the date as April 3. She must have changed her name. If I had, I reasoned, I wouldn't stray far from the truth. It was too easy to make mistakes.

Her signature was a casual scrawl that left room for all sorts of possibilities. If Mills wasn't her name, there was a good chance it was fairly close to the real one. People tend to do that. I might as well try being creative.

I flipped to a blank page in my notebook and wrote Mills at the top. I played with it, writing variations, all with double L's in the middle, names like Nillson, Miller, Gillis, and Williams.

I went through the records again, looking for names other than Mills. This time I came up with several, all girls born in Oakland on April 3. Andrea Irene Gillis was good. So was Renata Marie Hill. Renee Claire Millsey and Elizabeth Renee Willis I liked even better. Willis . . . A coal glowed briefly in my memory, then died as quickly as it had appeared.

Birth records in Alameda County list the mother's or the parents' names. Renee Claire Millsey's mother was Lois Millsey. I consulted an Oakland phone directory. There were lots of Gillises, Hills, and Willises, but only one Millsey, C. B., at an address in North Oakland.

Millsey was the name on the mailbox, but I knew I had the wrong house when my knock was answered by a stately black woman with salt-and-pepper hair. She confirmed that she was Lois Millsey. I gave her a story about looking for a friend from college and she told me her daughter Renee was married and living in Chicago.

Granny's Attic was near the intersection of Forty-First and Piedmont, its window and front door topped by a blue-and-white striped awning. Rain dripped from the canvas onto the back of my neck as I read the sign on the door that said the store opened at ten and closed at six. According to my watch it was eleven-thirty, but the door was locked and the gray March light didn't penetrate the dimness inside. When I looked past the spinning wheel in the window I couldn't see anything but the first row of furniture.

I walked into the bookshop next door and leaned over a counter spread with paperbacks. "I'm looking for Vera Burke, the owner of Granny's Attic."

The clerk looked up from her cash register. "The store's been closed for a couple of days." She finished ringing up the sale and bagged the book for her customer. "I don't know where she is."

I went back to my car and drove to the Monticello Avenue address. It was a two-story Tudor with a landscaped lawn and a shut-up look. No one answered the bell. I decided it was time to activate the Cal State connection.

California State University at Hayward is a collection of buildings scattered across the flat landscaped top of a ridge that overlooks the bay and the communities spreading south from Oakland. When it's clear, you can see San Francisco and the Bay Bridge. Today the fine curtain of rain masked everything, making the campus a quiet green-and-gray island.

I walked quickly through the rain to Mieklejohn Hall, a red brick building at the south end of the campus. On the top floor I made for an open doorway across the corridor from the History Department office. Pipe smoke permeated the book-lined room. An older man with thinning auburn hair sat at a cluttered desk, briar in an ashtray on his right, reading what looked like a research paper and writing remarks on the typewritten pages. He wore gray slacks and an argyle

7

sweater over a sports shirt. I'd given him the sweater for Christmas.

I walked into the office and planted a kiss on the top of his head, where the bald spot showed. "Hi, Dad."

My father looked up, horn-rimmed bifocals slipping down his nose. He grinned at me and pushed his glasses back into position.

"How's my girl?" he asked. He always says that. It makes me sound like I'm thirteen instead of thirty-three. "You want some coffee?"

He stood up, stretching his six-foot three-inch frame, and gave me an affectionate squeeze. A head taller than me, he smelled of pipe tobacco and dusty books. We share the same red-brown hair and blue-green eyes, with a faint sprinkling of freckles across our faces.

Dad picked up a red mug and led the way to the department lounge, where a coffee urn brewed all day. He opened a cupboard and handed me a mug.

"None too clean," I said, inspecting it.

"Don't worry. History Department coffee kills the germs."

I helped myself to the black brew and dropped a quarter into the change jar next to the pot. "Not many students around," I said as we returned to his office.

"Spring-quarter registration is next week. I'm just trying to get caught up before the onslaught."

Dad angled his chair away from his desk and sat down, stretching long legs out in front of him. I took the wooden chair close to his desk. Behind a stack of papers I saw a double frame with a picture of me on one side and of my brother Brian with his wife and two children on the other. Three of the office's four walls were floor-to-ceiling bookcases, and the fourth held a large cork bulletin board and several framed posters, one of them a colorful reproduction of Buffalo Bill Cody from a recent exhibition of Wild West memorabilia. Dr. Timothy Howard's field of expertise was American history, specifically that of the Old West.

8

"I was in Monterey over spring break," Dad said. "I saw your mother."

It's a cold-water shock when your parents split after thirty years of marriage. My brother and I were stunned when Mother left Dad. The divorce affected my relationship with both parents. I drew closer to Dad, feeling his need for companionship. Things are prickly between me and Mother. After the divorce she returned to Monterey, where she had grown up in a rambunctious Irish-Italian family. Always a gourmet cook, she opened a restaurant called Café Marie. It keeps her busy, with little time for visiting.

Dad took the breakup better than his children did. He bought a townhouse in Castro Valley, where he surrounds himself with his collection of Indian pottery, his books about pioneers and gunfighters, and a circle of academic colleagues. He and Mother are still friends, a state I don't seem able to achieve with my own ex-husband. Or my mother.

"I went to Monterey last Christmas," I said. "It was a mob scene. Brian, Sheila, and the kids, plus a houseful of Doyles and Ravellas. It took me days to recuperate." I sipped the coffee and set the mug on one corner of his desk. "I just took on a new case."

"That wouldn't have anything to do with why you're here, would it?" he asked, reaching for his pipe.

I laughed. "Now that you mention it, I could use some information on a former Cal State student. At least, I think she's a former student."

"What's the name?"

"I'm not sure. She's using the name Renee Mills, and there are a couple of similar names I'd like to check out. She's about twenty-nine, so I'm guessing she was here ten years ago. Can you help me?"

"Do you have a social security number for any of these people?"

"Just one. Renee Mills." I reached for my handbag and took out my notebook and the insurance application Foster had given me. Dad glanced at the names, then picked up the phone on his desk and punched four digits.

"Abdul, this is Dr. Howard. I need some information on a young woman who would have been a student here about ten years ago." Dad recited the names and the social security number. He hung up the phone and turned to me. "One of my graduate students works in Records. He'll punch the information into his computer and see what comes up. You owe me dinner for this."

"You're on, as soon as I wrap up the case."

Dad drew on his pipe and looked at me soberly. "Is it likely to be dangerous?"

"A simple missing-persons case? I doubt it."

"You know I worry. Ever since . . ." His eyes went to the scar on my forehead.

I was pistol-whipped in a parking lot in Oakland two years ago while working on a case. I spent four days in the hospital. Since then my mother suggests I find another line of work and my father worries about me. Dad and I had this conversation frequently, and I knew what he was going to say next.

"I wish you'd carry a gun."

"Sometimes I do. But the kinds of cases I take don't usually warrant it."

One of Dad's colleagues appeared in the doorway, a slender gray-haired woman. Dad introduced her as Dr. Kovaleski and me as his daughter, Jerusha. I was named after Dad's mother, but Jerusha suited her far better than it suits me; at an early age I shortened it to Jeri.

Dr. Kovaleski had a question about an upcoming graduate seminar, so I excused myself and carried my coffee back to the lounge. I leafed through a month-old copy of *Newsweek* someone had left there, then I put the magazine aside and went back into the corridor. I read notices on the bulletin board outside the department office until Dr. Kovaleski left Dad's office. He waved me back in as his phone rang.

"Yes, Abdul, I'm ready." He scribbled on a sheet of paper as Abdul talked. Dad thanked him and hung up the phone.

"Several students named Mills, but none of them Renee, none in that time period, and none with that social security

10

number. The closest is a Remy Mills, male, graduated seven years ago with a bachelor's degree in business.''

"What about the other names?''

"Four Hills and two Gillises. Several of those are male, and none of the social security numbers resemble the one you've given me. There is an Elizabeth Renee Willis, an English major who dropped out in her sophomore year, ten years ago. The social security number is very close.''

I compared the social security number with that on Renee Mills Foster's insurance form. They were the same except for three numbers. She could have changed a three to a five, a four to a nine, and vice versa. Changing Willis to Mills must have been as easy as dropping Elizabeth in favor of Renee.

It wasn't foolproof, but it had worked for at least five years. It might have continued working if Elizabeth Renee Willis hadn't walked out on Renee Mills Foster last week.

"Willis,'' I said. "That name sounds familiar for some reason. I don't know why. Did Abdul give you an address?''

"Yes. In San Leandro.'' Dad circled the address on the sheet of paper and handed it to me. "But that was ten years ago. A mighty cold trail.''

"At the moment it's the only trail I have.''

Two

"TEN YEARS AGO? YOU GOT TO BE KIDDING."

The apartment-building manager was replacing a light fixture in the laundry room at the rear of the building. He tightened the screws on the glass globe and came down from his ladder. The rain drummed on the roof and blew in the open door.

"I haven't been here that long," he said, shutting his toolbox. "How am I supposed to know who was in number twenty-two ten years ago?"

"Is there anyone here who was a tenant then?"

"Mrs. Dailey in the next apartment, number twenty-three. She's been here maybe twelve years. You could ask her."

"Who owns the place?"

"San Leandro Properties, on East Fourteenth near Davis."

Apartment 23 was on the second floor, near the front of the building. I headed for the stairs. The overhang of the roof offered little protection from the rain. I stood close to the door as I knocked.

The woman who answered my knock was in her early seventies, her face a fine mesh of lines crowned by silvery hair. She wore a blue shirtwaist dress covered with tiny red-and-yellow flowers. Her large brown eyes looked out at me through thick tortoiseshell glasses.

"Mrs. Dailey?"

"Yes. Earline Daily. And you?"

"My name is Jeri. I'm looking for someone I went to school with at Cal State ten years ago. Her name's Elizabeth

12

Willis. She lived in twenty-two, next door to you. The manager told me that you've been here quit a while. I wonder if you might remember her."

"Next door? That was Alice Gray's apartment."

"Who's Alice Gray?"

"A dear friend of mine," Mrs. Dailey said. "We taught together at Bancroft Junior High School. You're getting awfully wet, young lady. Come in out of the rain."

She unlocked her screen door and held it open. I went in gratefully, thinking she was a trusting soul and trying not to drip all over her carpet. The living room was furnished with a chintz-covered sofa and a matching armchair grouped in front of a television set. A bookcase stood against one wall, next to a desk. Framed photographs of people I took to be Mrs. Dailey's children and grandchildren crowded all the available surfaces.

"So you were a teacher," I said.

"Forty years," she said proudly. "Seventh-grade math. Alice taught English. She was at Bancroft fifteen years. So we had that in common, though she's about ten years younger than me. After Mr. Dailey died I sold my house and moved here. One of my daughters lives nearby. It was nice having Alice next door. We played bridge every week with Mr. and Mrs. DeloSantos on the first floor. I certainly do miss her."

"Where did she go?"

"She moved back to Stockton two years ago. That's where she was from. Her parents started failing and she went back to care for them. She'd just retired herself."

"Do you have an address?"

"Yes, I do. We've kept in touch." Mrs. Dailey went to the desk. She found Alice Gray's address in a leather-bound address book and wrote it down for me.

"Thanks." I took the sheet of paper and tried to steer Mrs. Daily back to my original question. "Did you ever see a young woman at Mrs. Gray's apartment? Living with her or visiting her? Her name was Elizabeth Willis. This is the address she gave the university."

Mrs. Daily thought for a moment, then she clapped her

hands together. "Of course. Alice's niece." She looked up at me over her glasses. "I'm not sure of the last name, but Alice called her Beth."

"What can you tell me about her?"

"A nice, quiet girl. A pretty little thing with long brown hair. She stayed with Alice for about two years, then she dropped out of school, got a job, and moved to her own apartment. She did come to visit Alice from time to time."

"Do you know where she worked?"

"No, I'm afraid I don't."

"What about the rest of the family? Do you know anything about them?"

"Alice has a sister living here in the Bay Area," Mrs. Dailey said, "but I don't know her name. Alice is a widow like me. She has two grown sons, one in Redding and the other in Fresno."

"Was this sister Beth's mother?"

Mrs. Dailey shook her head. "I seem to remember Alice saying the girl's parents were dead and she'd been raised by her grandparents. I don't know if she was Alice's niece by blood or by marriage, though. I do recall Beth mentioning that her father was a Navy man. We were talking about Hawaii, and she said her family had been stationed there. That's the only time I remember her saying anything about her parents."

According to the information I'd copied from the birth records this morning, Elizabeth Renee Willis had been born to George and Francis Willis. It didn't say which hospital. But there was a Navy Regional Medical Center in Oakland. I wondered about my chances of prying any information out of the administrative hierarchy there. Of all bureaucrats, military bureaucrats are the worst. They tend to invoke the Privacy Act or national security and clam up.

"You said Beth visited her aunt. When was she here last?"

"Five years or more, I think. That's all I can tell you about her. I'm afraid I haven't been much help."

"Actually, you have." I thanked her and went back out into the rain. I located San Leandro Properties on East Fourteenth. The woman at the front desk gave me Alice Gray's forwarding address, the same Stockton address Mrs. Dailey had provided.

I pointed the car back toward Oakland. By now it was afternoon rush hour, a misnomer, since the commute stretched from three to six P.M. Interstate 880, known as the Nimitz, was never a picnic, and it was worse in the rain, as though the weather brought out the lunatic in all the drivers. A big semi tractor-trailer bore down on my rear end as though we were at Laguna Seca.

I took the Oak Street exit and drove the few blocks to the parking lot near my office. Willis, I said, my tongue lingering on the L and S sounds. Memory flickered, then slipped away. I shook my head. There was no guarantee that Elizabeth Renee Willis was Renee Foster. But the birth date was the same, the social security numbers were close, and Elizabeth had attended Cal State Hayward. To be certain, I needed to connect Elizabeth with Vera Burke and the antique store.

My office is in a four-story building in downtown Oakland, in a neighborhood somewhere between urban renaissance and urban decay. The tenants are a mixed bag, including several law firms, an accountant, a computer consultant who keeps odd hours, a word-processing service, and an agency for office temps.

I unlocked the third-floor office of J. Howard Investigations and hung my raincoat on the wooden coat tree just inside the door. The mail had been pushed through the door slot. I picked it up and tossed it on the desk. My answering machine's red light blinked at me, but when I played the tape all I heard was a hang-up.

I sat down and sifted through the mail. Bills, advertising junk, and a long white envelope from a recent client, the security chief of a local corporation. He'd come to my office after a spate of equipment thefts, looking for an outside face no one would recognize. I spent two weeks undercover at the firm, working as a temp, until I nailed the culprits, both employees. The security chief was appreciative, which meant I could use him as a reference. My statement had been processed for payment, he wrote, corporatese for the check's in the mail. I hoped it would arrive soon so I could pay some bills.

I labeled a brown folder with Philip Foster's name and added the papers Foster had given me and the contract he'd signed that morning. Thanks to the consultant with the odd hours, I have a computer, which is more efficient than my old manual typewriter. I switched it on and made notes of my interview with Foster and the other information I'd obtained.

After I printed out the notes and added them to the file, I called both Granny's Attic and Vera Burke's home in Piedmont, getting no answer either place. Then I read through Norman Gerrity's report again. He'd written a terse account of Renee Foster's movements from the time she left the Foster home in Los Gatos. The cab driver who took the blond woman to the CalTrain depot said his passenger carried a big handbag and one suitcase. She told him where to take her and didn't say anything else, except that he should keep the change from the twenty she handed him. Gerrity noted that a train for San Francisco left the depot half an hour after Renee arrived.

At the end of the report I saw the sentence "Search terminated at client's request." If Foster was so hot to find his wife, why didn't he let Gerrity continue the search? Why get rid of one private investigator and hire another? Foster had described the San Jose investigator as "unsatisfactory," but what I'd just read told me Gerrity was competent. There had to be more to it than "search terminated at client's request."

I locked my office and went next door to the law firm of Alwin, Taylor, and Chao. My friend Cassie Taylor was at her desk, feet propped on an open desk drawer, a deposition transcript in her lap. She looked elegant as usual in a pale gray pinstriped suit with an apricot silk blouse that set off her creamy brown skin and pearls in her pierced earlobes.

"Does your wardrobe consist entirely of khaki pants?" she asked, assessing my slacks and olive green sweater.

"Only half. The other half is blue jeans. What's wrong with khaki pants?"

"They're so bland. You should wear brighter colors."

"Sorry I'm not up to your bird-of-paradise standards. In my line of work I don't need to be noticed. You should talk. The practice of law would founder without gray pinstriped suits."

"Probably." She recrossed her slender ankles. "I want you to do a background check on the plaintiff in a breach of contract lawsuit."

"Sure. Give me the details over dinner."

Cassie nodded. "I'll be ready in fifteen minutes."

As I went back to my office, the phone rang. "Howard Investigations."

"This is Norman Gerrity." The voice at the other end was equal parts gravel and South Boston. I wondered how he wound up in sunny San Jose. "I'm returning a call from Jeri Howard."

"I'm Jeri Howard, Mr. Gerrity. I'm an investigator in Oakland. I'd like to ask a few questions about a former client of yours, Philip Foster. He hired you to locate his wife, then he ended your business relationship."

"You're Howard Investigations?"

"Yes, I am." Gerrity had a short bark of a laugh. "You want to let me in on the joke?" I asked testily.

"Don't get me wrong," he said. "But it's funny. You know what I mean?"

"No, I don't. Why don't you explain it to me? Foster said he terminated your services."

"He fired me," Gerrity said, an edge of wounded pride in his voice. "No, his old man fired me. I'll bet he didn't tell you that."

"Look, Gerrity, I know the drill. Client confidentiality and all that. Foster gave me a copy of your report. I read it. Something's missing. I thought maybe you could fill me in."

"Well," Gerrity said, "you should know what you're letting yourself in for."

"What am I letting myself in for?"

"Foster called me last Thursday. He'd done all the right things, gone to the cops, filed a missing-persons report. Then he decided to hire a private investigator and pulled my name out of the phone book." Gerrity stopped and I heard what sounded like a cigarette lighter.

"She left the car in the bank lot. So I figured she must have either been picked up by someone she knew, or taken a bus or a cab. I struck out with bus drivers, but on Friday I found a cabbie who remembered her. He picked her up on the corner and took her to the depot. No one remembers selling her a ticket, but a train for San Francisco left thirty minutes after she arrived. I thought my next move would be a trip to the city. But I didn't get the chance."

"That's when Foster fired you?"

"You got it. I called Foster Friday afternoon to give him a rundown. He told me to meet him at his old man's place in Los Gatos that evening. After I told both of them what I'd found out, the old man said thank you very much, and here's a check. Goodbye, Gerrity."

"They dropped it? Just like that?" I'd been taking notes. Now I set the pencil down and frowned.

"Like a hot potato," Gerrity said. "Foster Junior hires me, then Foster Senior tells me to take a walk. Now you tell me Foster Junior's hired you. If he wants to do it that way it's his money. But if you ask me, he's just going through the motions. I don't think he wants to find her."

"My impression is that he wants to find her very much."

"That's what I thought, at first. When he walked into my office he was frantic to find her. When I went to Los Gatos it was a different story. Now Foster Senior, he definitely doesn't want to find her. And he's calling the shots."

"You're sure?"

"Positive. Every case I ever worked, my gut told me which way to go. You call it intuition or indigestion, whatever you like. But my gut is usually right. And it did a tap dance on this one. That's why I didn't argue with Foster Junior. I just took the check, closed my file, and sent the report over by messenger Saturday morning."

"Thanks for the information." I twisted the phone cord with the fingers of one hand. Gerrity's tale bothered me.

"You gonna go ahead? Try to find her?"

"I took the client," I said. "I intend to finish the job."

"Well, good luck, Howard. Watch your back. Foster Senior looks like a tough son-of-a-bitch who doesn't like to be crossed. My guess is he's not far behind Junior. If you're ever in San Jose look me up. I'll buy you a brew."

I thanked him and put down the receiver. Gerrity's story of his short-lived employment was his version. But if what he said was true, this was more than just a simple missing-persons case. I read through Gerrity's report one more time. It was crisp, to the point, professional, just like the man on the telephone. I was inclined to believe him. Which meant my client hadn't been completely honest with me. That didn't signal an auspicious start to our business relationship.

I called the Hyatt, but got no answer when the switchboard rang Philip Foster's room. Then Cassie opened my office door. She had switched from heels to running shoes and she wore a black raincoat over her suit.

"Let's walk down to Nan Yang," she said. "I've just got to have some curried prawns."

"How can anyone as skinny as you eat so much?" I reached for my coat.

"Genes. It's all in the genes," Cassie declared. "I come from a long line of skinny, hungry people."

I've known Cassie a long time, since we were both secretaries at a law firm here in Oakland. I have a degree in history, just like my father, but teaching doesn't appeal to me. After college I worked at a local repertory theater, acting and painting sets. When the company folded I worked as a security guard, a sales clerk in a bookstore, an office temp. It was as a temp that I figured out they always need someone who can type.

The temp agency sent me to Cassie's firm on a job that was supposed to last a month. But another secretary quit so I stayed. Cassie and I shared an office for several years, then

19

she went off to law school. I took a paralegal course and moved from typing legal briefs to researching them.

Six years ago I met Errol Seville. He was dapper and silver haired, as debonair as his name, and he seduced me away from the law library. Errol was a private investigator, one of the best in the Bay Area, with a clientele he'd built up over the years. Among his clients was the law firm that employed me.

I was aware of Errol watching me whenever he was in the office, a glint in his gray eyes, a hint of a smile on his foxy face. I felt sure he was going to make some sort of proposition, though I wasn't sure just what. One day he offered to buy me a cup of coffee.

"I've had my eye on you," he said, smiling over the rim of the cup.

"I noticed."

"You're too smart to spend your days slogging through *West's Annotated California Codes*. I need a woman operative. I think you'd make a good investigator. What do you say?"

I thought about it for maybe three seconds. Then I grinned and said yes. I was getting stale at the law firm, considering a change. Or maybe I saw Bogie in *The Maltese Falcon* at an impressionable age. Me, a private investigator. I couldn't resist.

I worked with Errol for five years, until a massive heart attack put him in the hospital, where his doctor gave him an ultimatum. The Seville Agency closed. Errol and his wife, Minna, retired to their weekend house in Carmel, the one Errol never had time to visit while he was working. Now Errol gardens. For amusement he reads detective fiction. When I call him he points out the mistakes the authors make.

After Errol, working for another agency would have been like driving a Ford when I was used to a Mercedes. So I went into business for myself. Being self-employed has disadvantages. You have to buy your own medical insurance and you don't have a pension plan. All those safety nets can be attractive, if you're into security. I'm not. Or at least I don't

20

think about it now. My mother worries that she'll have to support me in her old age instead of the other way around.

At Nan Yang, a Burmese restaurant in Oakland's Chinatown, Cassie and I grazed through platters of satay, Thai garlic noodles, and curried prawns, washed down with cold beer. We chattered like a couple of teenagers until Cassie stopped talking and looked over my shoulder at someone approaching our table. She composed her face and smiled briefly.

"Hello, Sid."

I glanced up at my ex-husband and felt the prickle of flesh newly grown over an old wound. It had been eighteen months since I moved out of his apartment. The feelings didn't go away just because the divorce was final. I wondered how my parents stayed friends after their divorce. Maybe it was because they had two grown children and so much history together. Maybe Sid and I hadn't given it enough time. Maybe . . .

Maybe doesn't count.

"Hello," I said.

He leaned over our table, his golden cat's eyes glinting above his mustache. I felt the same jolt of physical attraction I always had. Sid Vernon is a good-looking man, tall, with dark blond hair and broad shoulders tapering to slim hips. He walks like a tomcat, with an assured easy grace. The first time I saw him move I wondered how he'd be in bed, and made it my business to find out.

He grinned when Cassie asked him about Vicki, his only child, the daughter of his first marriage. "She graduates from high school this year. I guess you know how old that makes me feel." He turned his gaze on me, one hand playing with the end of his mustache. "Found Foster's wife yet?"

"I have a few leads." I took a swallow of beer, determined not to let him bait me. He stayed long enough to ask Cassie about her family, then left to join a group of fellow cops at a front table.

"You should see your face," Cassie said. "Don't let him get to you."

21

"Sometimes he does." I examined the check and took out my wallet. "Did I tell you he steered this new client my way? Probably because he thinks I can't find the woman."

"Maybe he meant it as a compliment." I shot her a look and shrugged. "Suit yourself."

We split the check and headed home through the rain. As I drove, my windshield wipers beat a slow pulse. The Necklace of Lights strung around Oakland's Lake Merritt shimmered and reflected in the water. I live on Adams Street near the lake, in a U-shaped white stucco building with a red tile roof. My back corner unit has a lemon tree next to the porch and a camellia bush in front of the window. On hot days I sit on the steps and look at the flowers and the little fountain in the middle of the courtyard. Birds wash themselves in the fountain, tantalizing my cat, Abigail, who sits on the window ledge, her tail twitching as she dreams about catching them.

Abigail heard the key in the lock and came to greet me, meowing that she was hungry and would expire very soon unless I gave her something to eat. Considering how fat she is, starvation is unlikely. The vet tells me she needs to eat less and exercise more. I've cut her food intake, but how do you exercise a ten-year-old cat who sleeps most of the time? When I try to get her to chase a tennis ball, Abigail looks at me like I've slipped a cog and stalks off to sprawl on the dining-room table.

In the kitchen, cat underfoot, I spooned some tuna into her bowl and set it on the floor. I went to the bedroom and put on my favorite after-work attire, a cranberry-colored sweatsuit with a baggy seat and frayed elbows. Back in the living room I stretched out on the sofa, my feet up. Abigail jumped onto my lap and began washing herself. I stroked her silky brown-and-silver coat and she purred, a rumbling sound deep in her throat. Turning her over, I tickled her belly. She grabbed my hand between two paws, washed it with her rough pink tongue, then nipped it gently with her sharp teeth.

Outside, the wind stirred the brass chimes hanging above my front door. City sounds crept through the windows: a car engine, the hiss of tires on rain-washed pavement, a siren in the distance.

I reached for the remote control and switched on the television set. Channel Two was showing *Key Largo*, but I fell asleep in the middle and woke up when the news came on, with Abigail curled into a deadweight ball on my stomach. I got up and went to bed.

Sometime before dawn I woke up and remembered who Elizabeth Willis was.

Three

WHILE MY MORNING COFFEE DRIPPED THROUGH grounds and filter I opened the door of my hall closet. Toward the back were several cardboard cartons full of what historians call ephemera, things I periodically consider throwing away but can't—theater programs, newspaper clippings, old letters. I sat cross-legged on the floor and sifted backward through the layers of my life until I reached high school. The binding of my senior yearbook crackled as I opened it and scanned the signatures of people I couldn't remember unless I checked their names against their photographs.

I carried the yearbook to the dining-room table and leafed through it while I sipped coffee and nibbled toast. I found the face I sought, along with my own, in the senior class roster. His name was Mark Willis. And he had a sister named Elizabeth. But that wasn't the only reason the name pricked at my memory.

Sid answered his phone on the second ring. "The Willis case," I said.

"What about the Willis case?"

"Fifteen years ago, in Alameda. Who was the investigating officer?"

"Hell if I know," Sid said. "Call Ben Montoya. He's the desk sergeant over there."

Sergeant Montoya at the Alameda Police Department told me Lieutenant Rolf handled the Willis case. Rolf had retired

24

last year, but I could probably find him at the Spinnaker Marina on the Alameda side of the estuary.

I washed my breakfast dishes and called the Hyatt, again receiving no answer when the switchboard rang Philip Foster's room. Where was my client? In a bar? Wandering the streets? Considering his apparent state of worry when he hired me yesterday morning, I thought he'd be waiting for a report on the status of my investigation. As I left my apartment, yearbook in hand, I recalled Norman Gerrity's words of the day before, about Foster Senior. Was Philip hiding from his father?

Alameda occupies a long narrow island separated from Oakland by an estuary. An island in more than geography, it feels like a small town, with wide, tree-lined streets, picturesque Victorian homes, and a sandy beach on the bay, the sort of place where people think they're safe from the urban problems that plague other towns in the Bay Area.

I grew up in Alameda. I was born in Berkeley while my father was in graduate school. Grandma Jerusha lived in Alameda, and my earliest memories include journeying from our little apartment near the campus to Grandma's big Queen Anne on Chestnut Street, the site of Sunday dinners and holiday celebrations. When Dad started teaching at Cal State, with my brother Brian on the way, he and my mother bought a house in Alameda.

I spent my childhood and adolescence with my parents, my brother, and a succession of cats in a two-story Victorian on Bay Street, a pale blue house with dark blue-and-mauve gingerbread trim and a stained-glass fan window above the front door. I walked to school and piano lessons along those pleasant tree-lined streets, went to the beach at South Shore, took the bus to San Francisco when I wanted some excitement. Dad surrounded himself with books and Indian pottery. My mother gardened and cooked and grew restless.

I pushed those memories aside as I drove under the estuary through the Tube, headed for the Alameda waterfront. A woman in the office at the Spinnaker Marina told me Rolf was on his boat at slip twelve. The sun was out this morning, the sky a washed-clean blue, but with enough of a chill that I was glad I'd worn a sweater over my shirt and slacks. As I made my way down the swaying deck between a row of boats, a loaded barge glided by, blocking the Oakland skyline and leaving two sailboats dancing in its wake.

Slip twelve held a good-sized sailboat with "Ivy—Alameda" painted on its hull. A small black dog napping on the bow jumped to its feet and barked, button eyes partly obscured by its shaggy coat. A man stepped out of the galley. He was solidly built and sixtyish, with thinning gray hair and a paunch hanging over the waistband of his denim pants.

"Pipe down, Pepper," he told the dog. He inspected me, eyes sharp in his jowly face. "Morning. You looking for me?"

"Yes, if you're Bill Rolf."

"I am. And you?"

"Jeri Howard. I'm a private investigator. I'd like to talk with you."

"What about?"

"The Willis case."

He frowned. "Got some I.D.?" I showed him my license. "Why do you want to know about the Willis case?"

"It relates to something I'm working on."

"But you're not gonna tell me about it, right?"

"Right."

He grinned. "Come aboard. We'll talk. I don't get many female visitors these days. Guess I won't be choosy." He held out a hand as I stepped onto the deck of the sailboat. Pepper snuffled at my shoes and the hem of my slacks. "You want some coffee?" Rolf asked.

"Sure. I take it black."

He disappeared into the galley and returned with two large steaming mugs. "Have a seat." Rolf pointed to a cushion in the bow as he handed me a mug. He sat down opposite me.

"Good-looking boat," I said, sipping the coffee.

"Thanks. Bought her last year when I retired. Ivy and me—Ivy's my wife—we take her out almost every weekend when the weather's good. Pepper goes with us, don'tcha, fella?'' The dog jumped onto the cushion next to Rolf and barked, his tail wagging rapidly. Rolf scratched him behind the ears.

"It's an expensive hobby."

He laughed. "Don't I know it. Like that old saying—a boat's a hole in the water that you throw money into. It takes a lot of work, too. But what the hell? I got nothing better to do, and it keeps me out of Ivy's hair."

"Sounds like you wish you were still working."

"No." He shook his head. "I put in over thirty years. It's time for me to work on boats." He paused and gave me a measuring look. "How long have you been in the business?"

"Six years. I used to work for Errol Seville."

"I've heard of him. What do you want to know about the Willis case?"

"Details, impressions. I plan to get a copy of the police report. But that's just words on paper. You were the investigating officer. I want your perspective."

He sipped coffee for a moment before he started talking. "It was pretty shocking, even for an old war-horse like me. The whole town was appalled. Alameda's a small town, never mind the population figures. Things like that are supposed to happen in East Oakland, not the East End. But they do. People are always surprised when the evil turns up in their own backyard."

"What happened?"

"They were a Navy family. George and Frances Willis. He was a commander, assigned to the air station."

Bingo, I thought. Mrs. Daily was correct in her recollection that Elizabeth's father had been in the Navy.

"Everyone said they were a nice couple," Rolf continued. "They lived on Gibbons Drive in the East End. They had three kids. The oldest was a boy, Mark. He'd just turned eighteen. There were two girls. Elizabeth was fourteen and Karen was nine. Karen wasn't there that night. She was at a slumber party."

"It was May, wasn't it?"

Rolf nodded and began to speak, his words crisp and

27

clipped, as though he were reciting his own police report. "Mark Willis was supposed to go to a party with some friends, but he never showed up. Shortly after nine P.M. a neighbor called the police. He said he heard something in the Willises' backyard. Then he heard gunshots. A patrol car responded and radioed for backup. I got there about ten minutes later." He stopped and took another swallow of coffee.

"When I entered the house I saw George Willis in the middle of the living room. Frances Willis was in the doorway leading to the kitchen. Both had been shot with a .38-caliber weapon registered to Commander Willis. The gun was on the floor between the bodies."

"Where were Mark and Elizabeth?"

"The girl was up in her room. She was hysterical. The boy was downstairs. He opened the door and let the uniformed officers in. He was pretty calm, considering he'd just murdered his parents."

"There was never any doubt?"

"He confessed," Rolf said. "He looked me right in the eye and said, 'I did it.' Besides, his prints were all over the gun."

"Did he ever say why?"

"No." Rolf shook his head slowly. "Nobody knows, except Mark. Maybe he doesn't either. I placed him under arrest and read him his rights, but he didn't say much else. His aunt and uncle got him a high-powered lawyer and had a bunch of headshrinkers look him over, but he wouldn't cooperate. He just said, 'I did it,' and took his medicine."

"What happened to him?"

"Pled guilty to two counts of second-degree murder. He was sentenced to life. Eighteen years old. They sent him to San Quentin."

"What happened to the girls, Elizabeth and Karen?"

"You're looking for one of them, aren't you?" I didn't answer. "I think they went to live with their grandparents. George Willis was from somewhere back east. But his wife's family was from California. I don't remember where. The newspapers covered the case like a blanket. Check the back issues of the Oakland *Tribune*."

I nodded and set the coffee mug down on the deck of the sailboat. "I've always heard you have a better chance of being murdered by a member of your own family than by a stranger."

"Yeah," Rolf said with a grim smile. "Makes you think, doesn't it?"

"Thanks for the information." I got to my feet and so did Rolf.

"Let me know if you find her."

"Maybe I will." I stepped from the boat to the floating deck. "How do I get a copy of that report?"

"Let me make a phone call." Rolf and I walked up to the marina office, the dog trotting alongside. At the office Rolf used the phone. When he hung up he told me a copy of the Willis report was waiting for me at the Alameda Police Department.

"Thanks again," I said, shaking Rolf's hand. "Just one more question. Is Mark Willis still over at San Quentin?"

Bill Rolf laughed. "You should know more about the California criminal justice system. He was paroled three years ago."

Why would an eighteen-year-old boy, with no apparent motivation, shoot and kill his own parents? I read the police report. It didn't have any answers. Neither did the microfilmed copies of the Oakland *Tribune*. At the Oakland Public Library I rolled the film through the reader, locating the first story, front page of the *Tribune*, the day after the murders.

SON SLAYS PARENTS, screamed the headlines. Photographs of George and Frances Willis accompanied the story. George's picture showed a fair-haired, stern-looking man in Navy service dress blues, the three gold stripes of a commander circling his sleeves. He looked foursquare, solid, and bland.

Frances was different. She had an arresting face, long and narrow, with a strong nose and eyes so light the newspaper reproduction barely caught them. Dark hair curled and tumbled, falling to her shoulders, and her lips curved in a half-smile. Not beautiful, but . . . I searched for a word and found it. Sultry.

Another face stared out at me, a familiar one. Mark Willis. The suit-and-tie photo was from the yearbook. He resembled his mother, with short dark hair, pale eyes, and a narrow intelligent face. The caption said he'd had a scholarship to the University of California at Davis. He would have started college that fall. Instead he'd matriculated at San Quentin.

I had always wondered about Mark Willis and what really happened that night, though I never joined the crowds of curiosity seekers driving past the house on Gibbons Drive. I couldn't believe it was true, or I didn't want to believe that anyone I knew was capable of such a crime. But I had known Mark Willis only briefly.

We were in a play together. In the fall of our senior year the Drama Club produced *You Can't Take It With You*. With his dark hair grayed and his face aged by greasepaint, Mark played Mr. De Pinna, the old man who helps Pa Sycamore make fireworks in the cellar. I twirled around the stage as Essie, the daffy sister who wants to be a ballerina.

What did I remember about Mark? I thought he was good-looking, with his wiry body and slow, gentle smile. But he never seemed to notice me. He was quiet, reserved, polite, agreeable, a good student. As far as I knew he never got into trouble until the night he was arrested for the murder of his parents.

I looked at the photos on the screen of the microfilm reader recalling Bill Rolf's words. Things like that don't happen in Alameda. But it did happen. And my fellow students had talked about it, not openly, but surreptitiously, as though words said behind hands would make it less real. Shocked whispers buzzed in the hallways and between the stacks in the library, ricocheted off metal lockers in the shower room after gym class.

The curiosity that had us reading newspapers about our classmate didn't last long. Tragedy is superseded by the motion of life and time, moving forward like an unstoppable train. The turning of the earth brought other things—graduation, the summer of freedom after high school, and the first semester of college.

As a Navy brat, Mark Willis was part of Alameda's transient population of military kids who came and went as their fathers transferred from billet to billet, kids who'd lived in exotic places like Japan or the Philippines, kids who moved every couple of years. They provided more spice in the East Bay stew. But sometimes they didn't fit well in a place like Alameda, where some of us had been going to school together since first grade. Maybe that's why Mark kept to himself.

Looking at the photographs of George and Frances Willis, I realized that I had seen the Willis family together once. After our opening-night performance at the Island High School auditorium, there was a reception in the school's lobby. The cast, still in costume and makeup, mingled with the audience, drinking coffee, eating cookies, and accepting congratulations.

As I stood with my parents I felt something strike me between the shoulder blades. I looked down and saw a cashew land at my feet. I turned to locate the source. The youngest Willis girl, Karen, stood at one of the tables, blond hair in pigtails, her hand in a bowl of mixed nuts.

She saw me watching her and grinned. Then she lobbed a Brazil nut into the air. It found its mark, the bald head of the principal. Karen's giggle pierced the drone of conversation. It caught the attention of the older girl next to her, who flushed and turned, long brown hair swinging. She whispered something to her parents.

Commander Willis looked as though he were dozing, his heavy-lidded eyes drooping as he stood with his legs apart. His wife had been talking with another couple. Now she turned toward her daughters and glared. Frances Willis raised her hand and words hissed from her wide red mouth. Mark, still in costume and makeup, crossed to the table and deftly moved Karen away from her ammunition.

31

Now I advanced the film, taking notes as I read. The newspaper's coverage fleshed out the story, from the initial investigation of the murders in those first days to the Willis funeral the following week in Stockton, a private service attended only by the family. The day after the funeral there was a memorial service at the Naval Air Station where George Willis had been assigned, the same day Mark Willis was arraigned for the murder of his parents.

According to the newspaper, George Willis was from Florida and had no surviving family other than his children. He was forty-three at the time of his death, and he'd been in the Navy nineteen years. Frances Willis was sketched in more detail. She was forty when she died. Her maiden name was Madison. She'd been born and raised in Stockton, in the San Joaquin Valley. She and George had been married eighteen years. In addition to her children, she was survived by her parents, Mr. and Mrs. Lester Madison of Stockton, and two sisters, Alice Gray of San Leandro and Vera Burke of Piedmont.

Vera Burke, the owner of Granny's Attic. That clinched it. The woman I was looking for was Elizabeth Renee Willis.

I put down my pen and took the photograph from my handbag, the one that showed the Foster family in front of the Christmas tree. I searched Renee's smiling face for a resemblance to George and Frances Willis, and saw it only in her fair coloring and blue eyes.

Earlina Dailey said Alice Gray moved back to Stockton to care for her elderly parents. Vera Burke wasn't home, and the clerk in the bookstore next to Granny's Attic told me the store had been closed for several days. What if there had been some family crisis in Stockton? Could that explain why Elizabeth called her aunt before she disappeared? Maybe. But it didn't explain her vanishing act. Or the fact that she'd altered her name and her social security number, a deliberate move to conceal her identity.

I looked at the photograph again and tried to imagine the fourteen-year-old girl who had been in her room while her brother committed murder. Did it mean she spent the next fifteen years attempting to escape the past? I was sure Foster didn't know anything about his wife's former life. I wasn't looking forward to telling him.

I backed up the microfilm reader and scanned the articles again, looking for information about Elizabeth and Karen Willis. Elizabeth had been treated for shock at a local hospital, then claimed by her aunt Vera. Her nine-year-old sister, Karen, had spent the night of the murders at a friend's slumber party. She too was taken in by Vera.

A later story about Mark's sentencing revealed that the girls were living with their grandparents in Stockton. Evidently this arrangement continued until Elizabeth returned to the Bay Area to live with Alice and attend college at Cal State. She'd dropped out after two years, according to the school's records. She would have been twenty then, I guessed. She was nearly twenty-nine now and there was a gap in what little I knew about her, a four-year gap stretching from her departure from school to her marriage to Philip Foster five years ago, two years before her brother's release from prison.

Newspaper sidebars discussed how the murders affected the community the Willis family called home, full of quotes from people who'd known them. The printed words reverberated with disbelief and incredulity that George and Frances could have been killed by anyone, much less by their son. Mark Willis, they said, such a nice kid. Bright, well-mannered, and friendly. The all-American boy.

I wrote down names of neighbors, classmates, work associates, and friends, remembering that Mark Willis spent a lot of time with a buddy named Leo. I leafed through the yearbook until I found his photo. Leo Mercer. Was he still in the area?

Joseph Franklin was. The next-door neighbor who had reported the gunshots to the police and given the eulogy at the Naval Air Station memorial service still lived in Alameda. Now a retired admiral, Franklin was running for the state senate in the June election, nearly three months away, running hard and running early as he attempted to unseat the incumbent. He had a large campaign fund and a political agenda with a right-wing cast.

The stories concerning Mark's sentencing in November of that year were almost footnotes, compared to the fire storm of coverage about the murders. He pled guilty, cooperating only minimally with the attorney hired by his aunt Vera, an Oakland lawyer named Lawrence Kinney. The last story I read dealt with Mark's arrival at San Quentin.

I'd been to San Quentin once, when I was working a case with Errol. From the Richmond–San Rafael bridge it almost looked pretty, its cell blocks spread over several acres of prime Marin County real estate, with a view of the bay and San Francisco. But it was a hard, harrowing place, a maximum-security warehouse crowded with human dynamite. Twelve years in that place would change Mark Willis. It would either make him strong or poison his soul.

I wondered where he was now. By the time he was paroled twelve years later, his release would not have rated much newspaper copy. There had been too many murders to report in the interim.

When I returned to my office the light on my answering machine was blinking, but none of the messages was from Philip Foster. The hotel switchboard assured me he was still registered and rang the room. Still no answer. I hung up and got out my Oakland phone directory. I wanted to see if Lawrence Kinney was still practicing law in the area.

He was. In fact, his office was on Harrison Street in downtown Oakland. I picked up the phone again. I talked to a receptionist and a secretary before I heard a man's voice say, "Lawrence Kinney."

I told him who I was and what I wanted. My words were met with silence. Finally he spoke. "What prompts your inquiry?"

"It has to do with a case I'm working on. I'd much rather talk with you face-to-face."

"You say you're a private investigator. Have you worked for anyone I might know?"

"Possibly. I've done a lot of prelitigation work." I gave

him the names of several local attorneys. "Check me out. I'm legitimate."

"Have you talked to Vera Burke?" Kinney asked.

"Not yet. Her shop's closed and she appears to be away from home."

"That presents a problem, Ms. Howard. I can't discuss the Willis case without Mrs. Burke's approval. Contact me when you've spoken to her."

I tried persuasion, but Kinney had me on client confidentiality and he knew it. I had to find Vera Burke.

Four

I KNOCKED ON DOORS IN VERA BURKE'S MONTI-
cello Avenue neighborhood. In a house across the street I
found a maid named Eloise who said she knew the Burkes'
housekeeper, a woman named Nellie Potter.

"Her father died. Mrs. Burke's father, I mean. He had a
stroke earlier in the week." I had interrupted Eloise in her
housecleaning routine, and she took advantage of the break
to light up a cigarette.

"Mrs. Burke left for Stockton last Wednesday. She called
Nellie Friday morning to tell her the old man died. She said
she wasn't sure when she'd be back, so it was OK for Nellie
to take some time off. Nellie's been wanting to go to San
Diego to see her daughter."

I asked her for Nellie's address and phone number,
and she obliged. "Is there a Mr. Burke?"

"Oh, yeah. He's a doctor over at Merritt Hospital."

I thanked Eloise and left her to finish her cigarette and
housework. I drove to Pill Hill, site of two hospitals and
innumerable medical buildings. Dr. Charles Burke was a
radiologist on the Merritt staff. He'd left Friday for a conference in Baltimore and was not expected back until next week.

I returned to my office and called Stockton information for
a phone number to go with Alice Gray's address. The phone
rang for a long moment, then someone picked it up and
didn't say anything. I heard a wheezing breath and a cough,
then a voice, an old woman's voice.

" 'Lo?"

"Is this Mrs. Madison?" No response, just the rasping

breath. "I want to speak to Vera Burke. Or Alice Gray. Your daughters. Are they home?"

The old woman laughed. "Dead and gone," she said. "Dead and gone." Then she hung up.

I stared at the receiver in my hand. This is getting weird, I thought, replacing it in its cradle. And getting me nowhere, at least as far as Vera Burke was concerned. I had to find someone who would talk to me.

One of my classmates was now a real-estate agent in Alameda. Except for his time at college, he'd never left town, the sort of guy who organized class reunions and kept in touch with people. After a couple of tries I found him at his office. I asked him about Leo Mercer, Mark Willis's friend in high school. He told me he'd sold Leo a house on Mozart Street years ago. He also told me Mrs. Mercer taught school in Alameda and Leo worked at Ritchie Produce in Oakland, on Franklin near Second Street.

The Produce District is an area along the Oakland waterfront. Broadway ends just past the Embarcadero at Jack London Square, where restaurants and a footpath border the estuary. The district mixes offices, shops, restaurants, and bars with light industry and the produce warehouses that lend their name. Railroad tracks run down the uneven pavement along the Embarcadero and along Third Street, and it's not unusual to find a train delaying traffic as it lumbers through on its way to the Oakland station.

It was nearly one when I parked my Toyota on Third Street and walked to Franklin. Crushed fruit and vegetables littered the pavement on both sides of the street. A pungent scent of onions and oranges mingled and lingered in the air. The produce warehouses start work at two or three in the morning; several were already closed for the day, but Ritchie Produce was open. I spotted a man at the back of the building. He was locking a door. He turned at the sound of my footsteps on the concrete floor.

"Help you?"

"Leo Mercer?" I looked him over. He looked like an older version of his yearbook photo, a tall, well-muscled man

37

with coffee-colored skin and a thin mustache, dressed in blue coveralls. A paperback book poked out of his breast pocket.

"Yes?"

"I'm Jeri Howard. We went to high school together."

"I don't remember you." He shrugged. "It was a big school. You go to that ten-year reunion?" I shook my head. "Me neither. I'm not into that stuff. So why are you looking me up? Just to talk over old times?"

"To talk about Mark Willis."

He frowned. "Why?"

"I'm a private investigator, working on a case." His eyes bored into mine. "Want to see my license?"

He waved a hand. "No. I believe you. It's just that I don't like to talk about it."

"It's important. I need some background information about the family."

He hesitated. Then curiosity won out. "All right. Let's get some coffee."

It was the tail end of the lunch hour, and the Oakland Grill was half empty. We sat down at one of the varnished pine tables and ordered coffee.

"You talk to the Franklins?" Mercer asked.

"Not yet." The waitress filled our cups and departed.

"You should talk to them." Mercer stirred some cream into his coffee, then raised the cup to his lips. "Of course, they don't know the whole story."

"Do you?"

He shook his head. "Nobody does. All I can tell you is what I know. The truth according to Mercer. It's liable to be different from the truth according to anyone else."

"Were you and Mark Willis good friends?"

"Mark was the best friend I had," Mercer said, a somber look on his handsome face.

I reached for my cup. "Tell me about him."

"We got to know each other junior year. Our fathers were both Navy. Mine was a chief gunner's mate. We transferred to Alameda about the same time Mark's family did. Mark

38

and I had a lot of classes together. We both ran the four-forty, so we went out for the track team."

"What about his family?" I asked.

"I didn't know them very well," he said hesitantly. "We were always over at my house. Mark was at our place so much Mom said she was gonna adopt him. I had twin beds in my room. He'd stay over. We worked on our cars. I had an old Ford, and Mark had this beat-up green Volkswagen he'd rebuilt." Mercer stopped. With his finger he traced a few circles on the table surface.

"There was more to it than that. Mark never would say anything, but he was always looking for an excuse not to go home."

"Why?"

"His parents, I guess. I thought they were kind of cold. Distant, you know? In my family we hug each other a lot. Over at the Willis house I never saw those people touch one another. You understand what I'm saying?"

"Yes." I thought of my own family. We hug each other a lot, too. "What can you tell me about the girls?"

"The kid sisters? I didn't pay that much attention to them." He thought about it for a moment. "Karen, she was a pistol. Lively, you know. Always into something. The other one, Beth, she was real quiet. Moody. A watcher."

"What do you mean by that?"

"Watching people. Like, I'd be doing something with Mark and I'd feel her eyes on my back. Put me in mind of a cat watching a mouse hole."

"Let's get back to Mark and his parents. From what you said before, I sense that they didn't get along. There's something you're not telling me."

"Well," Mercer said, taking a deep breath, "somebody was using Mark as a punching bag."

I put down my cup and leaned forward. "How do you know that?"

"I don't know for sure." His mouth tightened under the mustache. "I'm telling you what I think. One day in the fall of our senior year, after track, we were changing clothes in

39

the locker room. Mark had these bruises, on his back, his side, and his upper arm.'' Mercer pointed out the spots on his own torso.

"Places that would be covered by a shirt. He looked like somebody'd been beating on him. I asked him about it. He said he was moving some furniture at home and he fell. I said, 'Man, you're lying to me.' He shook his head, wouldn't say anything else.''

"Was that the only time you ever saw him with bruises?''

"I never noticed anything until that day in the locker room. He had a little burn scar on his wrist, but he said it was from a spark in the fireplace. I look back on it and I wonder. We were teenage boys, always into something. Hell, I walked into a porch swing once and ended up with a black eye. But those bruises I saw in the locker room . . . I've taken some punches in my day. I know what it looks like when someone's been hitting you.''

Mercer shook his head, then took a mouthful of coffee and swallowed. "From then on, the rest of senior year, I looked for more bruises. Mark knew I was watching him. But I never saw anything else. In April he started to get real tense, though, strung tight like a wire. He spent a lot of nights at our house, but he didn't sleep well. He tossed and turned so much he'd wake me up. Something was going on. I wish . . .'' He stopped and stared at the table.

"What do you wish?'' I asked him.

"I wish I'd been able to help him.''

The waitress stopped to ask if we wanted anything else. I shook my head, watching Mercer's face as he stared a hole into the table.

"Tell me about the night of the murders.''

"It was Friday evening. There was this big party, eight o'clock at the high school gym. Mark and I had dinner at our place. We left about ten past eight. I was going to pick up some other people. Mark said he had something to do first and that he'd meet the rest of us at the party. He took off in his VW. Me and the other guys got to the party about eight-thirty. About nine, nine-fifteen, I noticed Mark still wasn't there. By then I had this real bad feeling." Mercer rested his chin on his tightly laced hands.

"I went to a pay phone and called Mark's house. A cop answered. I hung up and flew out of there, headed for the Willis house. When I got to Gibbons Drive there were cops and red lights all over the place. I couldn't get near the house. I stood on the sidewalk across the street. I stood there a long time, until I saw them bring Mark out. In handcuffs."

Mercer sighed. "That was the last time I saw him. I saw pictures in the paper and on TV, the sentencing and all. I didn't go to the memorial service."

"You ever try to see him at San Quentin?" I asked.

"Yeah, once, about three years after. He wouldn't see me." The waitress laid the check on the table and we both reached for it.

"I'll get it," I said, but he refused, so we each paid for our own coffee and left the grill.

"Thanks for the information." We stood on the corner of Third and Franklin. I heard a whistle in the distance and saw a train several blocks up Third.

"I hope this helps," Mercer said. "I don't talk about it much. I know Mark's probably out of prison now. Sometimes I wonder where he is and if he's all right. I keep thinking there's something I could have done. To help him past whatever he was going through, whatever made him do it."

The truth according to Mercer, I thought. It was different from the truth related in Bill Rolf's police report. Both pictures were incomplete. Memory is faulty by nature. It's subjective, selective. What Leo Mercer and I remembered about Mark Willis were only pieces of reality. I wanted to know what happened that night in the Willis house. It was almost as important as finding Elizabeth. Maybe what happened fifteen years ago explained why she'd disappeared.

It was time to talk to my client, presuming I could locate him. For once Philip Foster was where he was supposed to be. He answered the door of his seventh-floor room, an anxious look in his brown eyes that turned to relief when he saw it was me. He wore blue corduroy pants and a blue-and-red knit pullover, but he carried himself as formally as if he wore a suit.

"You have something to tell me?" he asked eagerly.

"Yes, I do. I've been trying to reach you since yesterday."

"I've been . . . unavailable." I waited for an explanation but I didn't get one. He waved me toward a table and a couple of chairs near the window and walked over to a small refrigerator. "Please sit down. Would you like something to drink?"

"No, thanks." I sat down. He took a soft drink from the refrigerator and popped it open. Then he sat down in the other chair, leaning forward, waiting for me to speak.

"First of all," I said, "your wife's name isn't Renee Mills. It's Elizabeth Renee Willis."

Philip Foster's face barely had time to register amazement at my words when someone knocked sharply on the door. His expression shifted again, beyond anxiety to outright fear. The knocking continued.

"Are you going to answer it?" I asked.

He set the soft-drink can on the table and got to his feet slowly, stiffly. When he opened the door, a silver-haired man in an expensively tailored blue suit strode into the room and turned on him.

"Philip, what the hell do you think you're doing? Why aren't you at work? I had to cancel all your appointments, plus the meeting on the Interstate account, all because you're up here on some goddamn wild goose chase."

I stood up, and the older man noticed me for the first time. "Who the hell are you?" he snapped.

"This is the private investigator I've hired," Philip said. "Jeri Howard. Ms. Howard, this is my father, Edward Foster."

"Pleased to meet you," I said.

Edward Foster was about my height, five-eight, with a whipcord body like a retired jockey. He had eyes like hard brown pebbles in a creekbed and his tight-lipped mouth didn't bother with a smile. As I looked at him I chalked one up for

Norman Gerrity and understood why my client had been unavailable for the past twenty-four hours.

"I thought we'd dispensed with peepers," Edward Foster said contemptuously. "This is a waste of time, Philip."

"No, it isn't. Ms. Howard's already found out something. Something important. Renee has another name."

"I'm not surprised." The elder Foster fixed me with his unpleasant gaze. "Well?"

I looked at Philip. "You can talk in front of my father," he assured me. "Please, go ahead with what you were telling me."

"All right. I checked the birth records for your wife's birth date. There was no Renee Mills born in Alameda County on that particular day. I checked a wider range of dates, with the same results. Assuming she changed her name but not her birth date I came up with some other names. Student Records at Cal State Hayward says your wife did study there. She was an English major and she dropped out at the end of her sophomore year. Her real name is Elizabeth Renee Willis."

Edward Foster walked over to the window and looked down at the traffic on Broadway. Philip watched him move, like a dog that expects a blow, then turned his attention back to me.

"While she was at Cal State, she lived with an aunt named Alice Gray in San Leandro. I went to that address, but Mrs. Gray has moved to Stockton. A neighbor gave me her current address. The antique store your wife called the day before she left is owned by another aunt, Vera Burke. I haven't been able to contact her. She went to Stockton last week because her father had a stroke and died."

"It sounds like you've done a lot," Philip said. His eyes darted from my face to his father's, then back again. He took a nervous step toward the door. He wanted me to leave.

"I'm not finished," I said. "Your wife's parents were murdered. By her brother, Mark. Elizabeth—Renee—was in the house at the time."

Philip's face paled. He sat down on the bed, hands gripping the bedspread as I gave him a brief history of the Willis case.

"My God," he said when I finished. "My poor Renee. To have gone through that."

"It sounds like your wife's grandfather had his stroke about the time Renee left. It's possible she went to see her family."

"Bullshit," Edward Foster said.

Philip winced. "Dad, please don't."

"She didn't go to see her damn family." Edward Foster's mouth twisted, and his hard brown eyes bored into mine. "I know it and Ms. Howard knows it, even if you don't want to face facts."

"I don't know where she went," I said. "But Stockton is a logical place to start looking."

"Her family was in Los Gatos." Anger sharpened Edward Foster's words. "She walked out on him. She packed a suitcase, left her kid with my wife, cleaned out the bank account, and disappeared, without so much as a word to anyone. You can bet she didn't go visit her family. And you can bet she's not coming back."

"You don't like her very much, do you, Mr. Foster?"

"She's a bitch."

"Dad!" Two red spots appeared on Philip's pale face. He looked like an unhappy clown.

"She doesn't love you. She never did. You might as well face it and get on with your life." His son sat hunched on the bed. Edward didn't bother to soften his harsh tone. "You're wasting your money and jeopardizing your job. Give it up and come home."

"No." Philip shook his head. "I want to find her."

Edward Foster threw up his hands. "Why?"

"He loves her," I said.

"Then I guess they're right when they say love is blind." Edward's mouth tightened and he looked at me, his eyes glinting. "What are you going to do next?"

"That's up to my client." I addressed my words to Philip. "It's your money, Mr. Foster. What do you want me to do?"

"Find her," Philip said.

44

"I'll do my best. I'll call you tomorrow."

I could hardly wait to get out of that room. All the way back to the office I turned the scene over in my mind. Edward Foster loathed his daughter-in-law. As far as he was concerned she could stay missing. I wondered how far he was prepared to go in order to convince his son to drop the search. No doubt he was back in the hotel room trying to persuade his son to do just that. And Philip appeared to be a man who was easily swayed.

I could end up without a client. But until Philip Foster told me otherwise, I would continue my investigation.

Five

I TRIED TO REACH ADMIRAL AND MRS. FRANKLIN that afternoon and evening, with no luck. At some campaign function, I speculated. My guess was confirmed by a story in the next morning's *Tribune* about the admiral's fund-raiser at an Oakland restaurant. I finished my coffee and the newspaper and left my office a little before nine.

As I drove to Alameda I thought about Elizabeth Willis and how difficult it was to pull her into focus. I had seen her at that high school reception, yet I couldn't clearly recall her face. Neither could my brother. Four years my junior, he had been her classmate, just as Mark Willis had been mine. When I called Brian last night at his home in Sonoma I interrupted his dinner. He picked up the phone as his wife, Sheila, shushed my niece and nephew.

"So," Brian said, "when are you going to get a real job?"

"That's getting old, baby brother."

"I know. Besides, I can't recommend teaching, not these days. Were we this crazy when we were kids?"

"You were a pain in the ass until you were twenty. Listen, this is important. Think back to junior high. Do you remember a girl named Elizabeth Willis?"

Brian laughed. "That was a long time ago."

"Try."

"How much can you remember about junior high?" he protested.

"Acne and hormones."

"See what I mean? Kids are self-centered at that age. Other people don't register. Elizabeth Willis, huh?" The

46

phone line went quiet. I pictured my brother's forehead furrowing under his dark hair as he searched his memory. "Was that the girl whose brother killed someone?"

"Yes. The parents. Do you remember her?"

"Vaguely. The girl I'm thinking about was slender, with long brown hair. She was shy and sort of faded into the woodwork." He chuckled wryly. "Now I have students like that."

"You're no help."

"Sorry."

This morning I drove slowly along Gibbons Drive, which runs like a leafy tunnel through Alameda's East End, trees spreading their branches high across the street. Big houses sat comfortably on their lots, lawns lush and green from the recent rain.

The Franklins lived in a Spanish-style house of cream-colored stucco, with a red tile roof and red flagstones leading from the driveway to the front porch. A red-white-and-blue sign on the front lawn proclaimed FRANKLIN FOR STATE SENATE. As I went up the walk I looked at the two-story house on my left, where the Willises lived fifteen years ago. Its pale green exterior and closed blinds didn't reveal any secrets. Then I mounted the shallow steps of the Franklins' front porch and rang the bell.

The woman who answered was short, perhaps five-two. Her silver hair was curly and cropped close to her head. Laugh lines surrounded her warm topaz eyes. She carried a pair of gardening gloves in her left hand and held the door open with her right. I noticed a smudge on one knee of her blue slacks.

"Mrs. Franklin?"

"Yes?" She looked up at me curiously.

"My name is Jeri Howard." I held out my license and the topaz eyes examined it. "I'm a private investigator. I'd like to talk to you and your husband."

"Whatever for?"

"A case I'm working on. It relates indirectly to the Willis family."

Her eyes flicked to the house next door, then back at me. "How odd," she said. "I was thinking of them this morning."

"You were? Why?"

She shrugged. "No reason. I just was. Please come in."

Mrs. Franklin opened the door wider, and I stepped into a tiled entry hall, with more campaign signs leaning against one wall. She led the way though an arched doorway to the living room. The room was large, with a thick beige carpet that made me feel like I was walking on marshmallows. The furnishings were evidence of the Franklins' years in the Navy. Two oriental rugs in shades of blue and red covered the carpet in the center of the room, and a ship's bell hung on the wall next to a carved mahogany bar. The rest of the furniture was teak. Brass trinkets from the Philippines, cloisonné from China, and Japanese lacquer competed for space on the shelves of a boxy curio cabinet and on the low tables at each end of the sofa. Framed Japanese woodblocks and Chinese silk prints dominated the walls. On the mantel I saw pictures of another sort, photographs of the Franklin family, including one formal shot of the Franklins, the admiral in his dress white uniform, sword dangling at his side and several rows of medals on his chest.

"That was taken at Joe's retirement, two years ago," Mrs. Franklin said when she saw me looking at the photograph.

"Is your husband home?"

"No, he's playing golf. I expect him back soon, though. He's speaking at a meeting at eleven." She sat down at one end of the long sofa and I took the armchair facing her.

"Now what's this about?" she asked.

"I'm looking for Elizabeth Willis," I said. "She's missing from her home."

"I'm sorry to hear that." Mrs. Franklin frowned. "I haven't seen Beth since . . . it happened."

"No matter. I need some background information about

48

the family. It may help me find her. I understand you and your husband were close friends of the Willises."

"Yes, we were. For a long time." She stopped and looked past me out the front window. "There's Joe now." She got up and went to the front door, opening it. I heard the slam of a car door and brisk footsteps coming up the walk.

Admiral Joseph Franklin entered the house carrying a golf bag, which he stowed in a hall closet. He was a tall spare man with thinning gray hair, a long narrow face, and an uncompromising beaked nose. He radiated what Navy people refer to as military bearing. Wearing tan slacks and a short-sleeved pullover, he carried himself as though he wore a dress uniform. He looked at me and waited for his wife to introduce me.

"This is Miss Howard, Joe," Mrs. Franklin said as I stood. "She's a private investigator."

"Private investigator?" His opaque gray eyes went over me carefully.

"She's looking for Beth Willis. She's missing."

"Indeed. Get me a cup of coffee, will you, Lenore?" Mrs. Franklin looked at me inquiringly. I shook my head. As his wife went back to the kitchen the admiral fixed me with a narrow-eyed stare. "Are you really a private investigator?"

"Yes." I took out my license and showed it to him.

He glanced at it. "Who hired you?"

"My client's identity is confidential."

The admiral was not accustomed to insubordination. His mouth tightened. Mrs. Franklin came back, carrying his coffee.

"Sit down," she said. "Tell Joe what you told me."

"I have to get ready. We'll need to leave at ten-thirty," Franklin said, glancing at his watch.

"I won't keep you long," I said. He sat down with ill-concealed impatience, his wife next to him on the sofa. I resumed my seat in the armchair.

"I need some information about the Willis family."

"I don't know what good that would do," Franklin said.

"I'm looking for leads anywhere I can find them. The

49

more information I have about Elizabeth and her family, the easier it will be for me to trace her. People don't change the patterns of their lives that much, even when they are trying to conceal themselves.''

"It sounds like she left of her own accord," Franklin said. I didn't answer. "Then you'll have a hard time finding her."

"I'd like a clearer picture of whom I'm looking for. Anything you can tell me about the family will be helpful. Admiral, I gathered from the newspaper article on the memorial service that you'd known George Willis for a long time."

Franklin studied me for a moment. He didn't answer right away, considering whether to answer at all. Then he spoke, deliberately and carefully, as though he were addressing his political constituents.

"I met George Willis at the Academy. We were in the same class. He was from Florida. Some little town near Pensacola, where we both went through flight training. His parents were dead. We weren't close friends at first, but later we kept running into one another at duty stations all over the West Coast and the Pacific. When two officers are in the same career pattern, assignments often coincide. That's when we got to be friends, when our families were growing up. George and I would be stationed aboard the same carrier, and back in San Diego or Pearl our wives and kids would be holding down the fort."

"Our children, Kevin and Ruth, are the same ages as Mark and Beth," his wife added.

"You spent a lot of time together?"

"We did." She smiled. "Joe and Franny played golf constantly. They were both golf nuts. On Friday nights we'd make a foursome for bridge. Franny and I put in time in officers' wives clubs from here to Guam. We did a lot of things together, especially while the men were gone. Barbecues in the backyard, camping trips, picnics. We were stationed in the same places so often that as soon as the movers delivered our household goods I'd look around for George and Franny."

"I understand you heard the shots, Admiral, and called the police."

"Yes, I did." He reached for a pack of cigarettes on the coffee table, pulled one out, and lighted it. He gestured toward the back of the house. "It was shortly after nine o'clock. I stepped onto the patio to have a smoke. I heard something in the bushes. I walked over to the fence to investigate. Then I heard gunfire. I came back to the house and called the police."

"Did you hear anything, Mrs. Franklin?"

"I wasn't home," she said. "I'd gone to a movie with some friends. Sort of a ladies' night out."

I turned my attention back to the admiral. "Did they ever find out what it was you heard in the backyard?"

"No. It was dark. I imagine it was a stray cat. It's hardly important considering what had just happened." He made an abrupt dismissive gesture with his hand. "It was a difficult time for all of us. I don't think rehashing it will help find Beth now."

Or you just don't want to talk about it. The admiral was giving off unmistakable signs that he didn't care to continue this conversation. I wondered why.

"What was Elizabeth like?"

"She appeared to be a normal teenage girl. Nothing unusual about that."

"We lost track of the girls afterwards," Mrs. Franklin said. She gave her husband a quick sidelong glance, assessing his mood. "They went to live with their grandparents in Stockton. We transferred to San Diego in August of that year and we didn't keep in touch."

"Did Mark and his parents get along?"

"What the hell kind of question is that?" The admiral glared at me over his coffee cup.

"Did he fight with his parents? Did they yell at each other? Was there ever any indication of physical or emotional abuse?" With those words I nudged the hornet's nest. I got hornets.

"That is absolute nonsense," Franklin said angrily, his

51

eyes blazing. He got to his feet and leaned over me, punctuating his words with the hand that held the cigarette, railing at me as though he expected me to snap to attention, like some recalcitrant seaman recruit. "Complete and utter nonsense. Who told you that? It's slander and I won't listen to it, not then and certainly not now. You're poking around in something that doesn't concern you. I'm not even sure I buy this story about looking for Beth. Who are you, some cheap media hack looking for a sensational story? Trying to smear my campaign?"

"Thank you for talking with me." I reached in my purse, pulled out one of my cards, and gave it to Mrs. Franklin. Then I stood. "If you think of anything that might help, call me."

As I went down the front steps of the Franklin house I heard the admiral's angry voice from the living room. All I had to back up the child-abuse theory was Leo Mercer's story about seeing Mark Willis covered with bruises. But it was worth exploring. Since the Franklins and the Willises had been good friends, I expected the admiral and his wife to deny any possibility of abuse in the family next door. But the admiral's response was too vehement.

Not then and not now, he'd said. Had someone else raised the issue of child abuse fifteen years ago?

Six

SHORTLY AFTER NOON I WENT TO SEE MY CLIENT, to quell the uneasy feeling I'd had since leaving his hotel room the day before. Philip Foster had said he still wanted me to find his wife. But Edward Foster had the stronger will. He'd also had all night to work on his son.

Philip opened the door. I looked past him and saw an open suitcase on the bed, clothes folded neatly inside.

"Were you planning to tell me?" I walked into the room and saw Edward Foster standing on the other side of the bed. "Or maybe you hoped I wouldn't notice."

Philip's pale face flushed with embarrassment. "Of course I was going to call you. This afternoon. I intend to settle my bill."

"But you're leaving." I swept a hand toward the suitcase. "Without letting me finish what I've started."

"I don't think there's any point in it. Do you?"

"Of course I do. Or I wouldn't be here."

Philip shook his head, avoiding my eyes. "Renee left me and she's not coming back. Dad's right. It's time to pick up the pieces and go on with my life. We're going back to Los Gatos."

Edward Foster gazed at me with hard brown eyes and a smug twist to his thin mouth. He'd been running his son's life for so long that persuading Philip to drop the case must have been a cakewalk. I wondered what he'd used for leverage.

"I want to talk to Philip alone," I told him.

"I think whatever you have to say . . ."

"I don't give a damn what you think, Mr. Foster. Until Philip pays me off he's my client. This is between my client and me. You can get a full report later. Now get out."

Anger flickered over his face, but he kept it under control. He felt secure enough in his victory to smile tightly as he walked toward the door. "Call me when you're finished packing," he said, directing his words to me as much as to Philip.

When the door closed I looked at Philip. He sat down on the bed, looking drained, as though his father had sucked all the life from him.

"What the hell is going on?"

"I don't know if I can explain."

"Try." I narrowed the space between us. "Two days ago you hired me to locate your wife. You really wanted me to find her. That's what you said yesterday, right here in this room. Find her. Today you've changed your mind—or your old man changed it for you. I've put in a lot of time on this case. You owe me an explanation."

"I know. I intend to pay you."

"It's not about money. It's about unfinished business." I touched his arm. "I want to know why. I found out some things about Renee's past you didn't want to hear. But that's no reason to drop the investigation just when I've come up with some good leads. I believe you love her."

"I do," he whispered.

"Then let me find her."

"It's too late."

"Too late for what? Philip, you know your father's manipulating you. Don't let him do it." I examined his face to see if my words were having any effect. He stared at the suitcase on the bed, a man having a debate with himself. "If you're going to fire me, at least tell me why."

He was silent for a moment, then he raised his head. "My son. It's about my son, Jason," he said, his mouth working. I waited. Maybe he'd say something that made sense.

"My mother noticed a bruise on Jason's back. She was concerned about it, but in all the confusion after Renee left,

54

Mom didn't get him to her doctor until Monday. The doctor was suspicious, so he did a complete examination. Then he contacted Renee's doctor, the pediatrician who's been taking care of Jason since he was born. It turns out the pediatrician was suspicious too. After he talked to my mother's doctor and my parents, everybody was convinced."

"What are you talking about?" I knew the answer before the question was out of my mouth.

"My wife's been abusing my son. Our baby." A wave of pain swept over Philip's face. "And I didn't know."

"If something like that was going on, why didn't you know?" I said brutally.

"I've been asking myself the same question ever since my father told me. A couple of months ago I got home from a business trip. Jason had a bruise on his arm. Renee said he fell. He'd just started to walk, so I didn't think anything about it. Babies fall down, don't they?" I didn't answer. He wasn't really asking for one.

"Everything sounds like excuses. I work long hours. I'm not there enough. I've been willing to leave the responsibility to Renee. So it's as much my fault as anybody's."

"If it's true."

I wasn't sure what I believed now, especially after talking with Leo Mercer. But somebody had to play devil's advocate for the absent Elizabeth Renee whoever-the-hell-she-was.

"You haven't heard Renee's side of this story," I said. "Just your father's version. Besides, if it is true, it makes more sense to find the woman and get her some help. You say you love her. At least find her, so you can be sure what your next move should be. Don't leave her out there in limbo."

"I don't know what to do." Philip looked at me uncertainly.

"You're the only one who can decide. Not your father, not me. Think about it, Philip. Then call me and let me know what you want to do. I'll be in my office the rest of the afternoon." I got up and walked to the door.

"The bill . . ."

"You gave me a retainer. That should cover most of it. I have your address in the file. If I don't hear from you I'll send you a bill, along with a report and the papers you gave me."

He said nothing as I shut the door behind me. It didn't matter. I knew what he was going to do.

In the hard-boiled novels the private investigator always has a bottle in his bottom desk drawer. I didn't, so I stopped on the way back to my office and bought a six-pack of cold Anchor Steam. I was midway through my first when the phone rang. I set the bottle down and picked up the receiver.

"Howard Investigations."

It was my ex-husband. "Who did you piss off in Alameda?" Sid asked.

"What do you mean?"

"Somebody called the Alameda Police Department to complain about you."

"How did you find out?"

"Sergeant Montoya called me."

"Are you going to tell me what Sergeant Montoya told you, or do I have to drag it out of you?"

"My, aren't we testy this afternoon. A male civilian named Franklin, Joseph Franklin. Retired Navy admiral, prominent citizen, running for state senate. He called the Alameda Police Department this morning, said you were harassing him and his wife. He wanted to know what he could do to have your license pulled."

"He's been watching too many cop shows," I said, taking a long pull from my beer. "I barely scratched his surface. I ought to go back over there and really rattle his cage."

"What's going on?" Sid asked.

"What do you think's going on? I'm working on a case."

"The Foster case? It's got something to do with the Willis murders and it's getting complicated, right? Are you in over your head, Jeri?" I couldn't tell if he was concerned or delighted at the prospect.

"I'm just trying to find the guy's wife." Not anymore,

56

though. I'm sitting here drinking beer in the middle of the afternoon because my client changed his mind.

"Having any luck? Or are you just irritating prominent Alameda citizens?"

"I'm not in the mood to argue with you, Sid."

"That's a switch."

"Go to hell." I hung up on him. The phone rang again and I picked it up, ready to peel a layer of skin off Sid Vernon if he'd called again.

"Miss Howard? This is Lenore Franklin." She didn't give me time to respond. "I'm afraid my husband called the Alameda police to complain about you."

"So I hear."

"I had no idea he would react that way. He was extremely upset."

"I'm doing what I was hired to do, Mrs. Franklin."

"I know. And I'm sorry. I've been thinking about it since you left. About the Willises and some other things. I'd like to talk to you, privately. Can we meet tomorrow morning? There's a coffee shop called Ole's on Park Street."

"I know where it is. I can be there at nine." My case might very well be over, but I wanted to hear what Lenore Franklin had to say.

After Mrs. Franklin hung up, I unlocked the filing cabinet and pulled out the Foster file. Elizabeth Renee Willis Foster looked out at me from the Christmas photograph I'd clipped to the left side of the manila folder, her face revealing nothing as she smiled at the camera over the head of the child she had supposedly abused.

I leaned back in my chair and put my feet up on the desk, staring at the phone as I nursed the rest of my beer. Funny how things work out. Some afternoons I would sit here for hours without so much as a wrong number, and now I couldn't even drink a six-pack without interruption. I hoped the phone would ring one more time, though. I hoped Philip Foster would change his mind.

I finished my beer and set the empty bottle on the edge of the desk. I tuned my radio to a local jazz station. They were

57

playing a Billie Holiday set. "Gloomy Sunday" didn't exactly improve my mood, so I pulled a second bottle from the six-pack and twisted off the cap. The phone didn't ring at all, and the hands of the clock kept going around.

Midway through the second beer my stomach lurched and I put the bottle aside. I'd had no lunch, nothing since breakfast. I found a box of wheat crackers in my bottom desk drawer, and the little refrigerator at the back of my office yielded a hunk of salami and some Monterey Jack, a bit green on one side. I spread the feast out on my desk blotter, using my letter opener to scrape the mold off the cheese as I gnawed on the salami.

At a quarter to four the door to my office opened. Cassie came in, like some exotic bird in her blue linen suit and a silk blouse the color of raspberry sherbet.

"Won my case," she said triumphantly, then she stopped at the sight of me and the debris on my desk. "What's all this?"

"Have a beer. You'll probably save me from myself."

"A little early, isn't it?" She took a handful of crackers.

"It's a wake. For my latest case. Or maybe I should say my late case."

Cassie kicked off her shoes and settled into one of the chairs in front of my desk, her feet tucked under her. "What happened?"

"My client bailed out on me." I gestured toward the clock. "He went back to Los Gatos. I've spent the afternoon hoping he'd change his mind. But he won't."

"Why? Did he think you weren't doing the job? Did he pay you?"

"He wanted me to find his missing wife." I gave Cassie a rundown of the case. It didn't matter now. The Foster file was closed.

"He's afraid to look any further," Cassie said when I finished talking. "Afraid he might find out he's as much to blame as she is. Maybe it's better if you don't find her."

I shook my head. "I like to leave things a little less confused than the way I found them. Damn it, Cassie, I like to

58

finish what I start. And there's more to this case than a missing wife who may be a child abuser. Those murders fifteen years ago have something to do with the fact that she's missing. I know it. Ever since I talked with the investigating officer and read those articles in the *Tribune*, I can't shake the feeling it's all tied together.''

''You want to know why Mark Willis killed his parents,'' she said.

''Yes, I do. There has to be a reason.''

''There's always a reason,'' Cassie said. ''We've both heard lots of reasons.''

I nodded. After law school Cassie put in two years in the public defender's office, a great place to hear reasons. In my six years as a private investigator I'd heard reasons too, all kinds of reasons. Some were amusing, some heartbreaking, others made me shake my head at the twists and turns of human nature. Sometimes when I find out the reason I wish I hadn't, but anyone who turns over rocks for a living should be prepared to deal with whatever crawls out.

''Suppose what Leo Mercer says is true,'' I said, ''that the Willises were abusing their kids, or at least Mark. There's a pattern in abusive families, isn't there?''

''Yes.'' She sighed and shifted position in the chair. ''It doesn't necessarily have to be physical abuse. It can be emotional as well. It can be neglect.''

I swung my feet off the desk and leaned forward in my chair. ''If a child is abused, there's a good chance that child will become an abusive parent.''

''Is that what you think happened with Elizabeth Willis?''

''It makes sense. We learn how to be adults by observing adults. The nearest grown-ups are usually our parents. If the parent is an abuser, the child can learn the abusive behavior.''

''But it can go the other way,'' Cassie argued. ''The child can grow up saying, 'I'll never be like Mom or Dad,' and make a conscious effort to be a loving parent.''

''Granted.'' I moved one of the beer bottles to the right side of my desk and the second to the left. I pointed at one of them. "Here I have a missing woman who may or may not hurt her child. And over here I have a source who tells me her brother may have been physically abused. There's a connection. I think I'm looking at two generations of an abusive family. If I'm right—"

"She's still missing and you don't have a client."

"I know. But she's out here somewhere. I want to find her, Cassie."

"So you can fix her? Is that why you're in this business, Jeri? To fix all those broken people?"

"Maybe." Jeri Howard, I thought, people fixer, windmill jouster. "I think she needs help."

"I'm sure she does. But if she wanted help she could have gotten help in Los Gatos, or San Jose. They have shelters and counselors there, too. Maybe your client was right and there's nothing you can do. You're getting emotionally involved. Time to detach and let go."

I pushed back my chair and put the remainder of the six-pack in my little refrigerator. Despite the beer I felt sober. Self-reflection is always sobering. Don't get emotionally involved, Cassie said. But I always invest a piece of myself in my work. That's what gives me the edge, the impetus I need to see a case from start to finish. I'd grabbed the Foster case and I was running with it when Philip Foster untied my shoe-laces.

"I want to find her, Cassie."

"You don't have a client." She got up and put on her shoes. "And I need a background check, remember?"

"I'll start tomorrow. Do you want to get some dinner?"

Cassie shook her head. "I can't. I have some work to do."

"See you tomorrow, then."

When Cassie closed the door I tossed the beer bottles into the wastebasket. I switched on the computer and updated the Foster file, noting, as Norman Gerrity had, that the case had been terminated at the client's request. While the last page printed, I totaled a final bill and subtracted Philip Foster's retainer. Tomorrow I'd send a statement, along with the personal papers and the photograph Philip had given me.

As I carried the folder to the filing cabinet something slipped out and I knelt to pick it up. It was the phone bill, the one with that call to Granny's Attic in Oakland. I looked at the number, circled in pencil. One last shot, I thought, and picked up the receiver. If nobody answers I'll forget the whole damn thing.

I punched in the number of the antique store. The phone rang twice. Someone picked it up, and I heard a woman's voice say, "Granny's Attic."

Seven

JUST INSIDE THE FRONT DOOR OF GRANNY'S ATTIC
a woman with a shopping bag stood at an oak dresser, idly
examining an old album full of someone else's photographs.
The antique store was long and narrow, with a central aisle.
On either side I saw rows of furniture: tables, chairs, bookcases, dressers, all of them looking as though they'd spent
years in someone's attic.

A colorful patchwork quilt was displayed on the wall to
my left. The other wall held a framed collection of samplers.
The wooden floor creaked as I walked toward the glass-
fronted counter at the rear of the shop. It contained jewelry,
cigarette cases, and other small items, illuminated by a floor
lamp with a fringed fabric shade.

The store's proprietor was showing a customer a bracelet.
I stood to one side and watched her. She was of medium
height and sturdy build, in her late fifties. I saw hints of
Frances Willis in her round strong-featured face. Curly dark
hair streaked with silver fell to her shoulders, unfettered by
combs, permanents, or sprays. She wore a bright turquoise-
colored caftan and several strands of cloisonné and cinnabar
beads around her neck. The beads clicked together musically
as she leaned over to clasp the bracelet around the customer's
wrist. After a moment of holding the bracelet up to the light
at various angles, the customer said she'd think about it. She
removed the bracelet and handed it back, then walked up the
center aisle to join the woman with the shopping bag.

"Vera Burke?" I asked as the proprietor put the bracelet
back into the display case.

"Yes?" Her eyes were bright and intelligent, and matched the blue of her caftan.

"My name is Jeri Howard. I'm a private investigator."

"Really?" She smiled. "I've never met a private investigator. What can I do for you?"

"I'm looking for your niece."

"Which one? I have several."

"Elizabeth."

The smile disappeared. "Beth. What do you want with Beth?"

"She left her husband and child in Los Gatos last week. She hasn't been seen since."

She frowned. "How do you know that?"

"Her husband hired me to find her."

Vera Burke looked me over, the sharp blue eyes taking in my rumpled slacks and shirt. She could probably smell beer on my breath. She thought about it for a moment, then she nodded.

"Please, come in and sit down. Tell me everything."

I stepped behind the counter and saw a sagging sofa with a long tear on one of the flowered cushions. Opposite the sofa an oak desk stood with its surface three inches deep in paper. A small table at one end of the sofa held a hotplate and a simmering teakettle.

As I settled onto the sofa, she offered me tea. It was a strong spice-scented brew in a chipped china cup. My hostess poured another cup for herself, pulled out a straight-backed chair, and sat down.

"Mrs. Burke," I began.

"Call me Vee," she said, waving her hand. "Everybody does." Then she looked past me at the back door and whistled. I followed the direction of her eyes. The door was ajar. An elderly Yorkshire terrier, gray at the muzzle, walked stiffly through the door, coming from the alley behind the shop. The dog solemnly inspected my foot, then climbed into a wicker basket on the floor nearby and settled with a pleasurable groan onto the cushion.

"Tell me about Beth," Vee Burke said.

"Her husband hired me a few days ago." I sipped the steaming tea and burned my tongue. "He drove up here because there was an Oakland phone number on his last bill, the number of this store. He told me she'd been born in Oakland and she went to Cal State Hayward. I've been trying to reach you since then."

"I was in Stockton, burying my father. He died Friday."

"I'm sorry. Why did Elizabeth call you?"

"To ask about Dad. I called her when he had his last stroke." Vee sipped her tea, then set her cup and saucer down on the little table. "He wasn't expected to live. I asked if she could come back to Stockton. None of us has seen her in five years."

"Why?"

Vee sighed. "Beth always wanted to get away. From her memories, her family. She's drifted all her life. The girl needs an anchor. I thought when she married Philip things would change. The way she described him, he seemed a steady young man. But Beth is terrified that people will know about what happened to her parents. As though it were her fault." She shook her head and lifted her cup to her lips.

"When she moved to the Peninsula she changed her name. No more Elizabeth Willis. She was Renee Mills. And no contact with the family. I'm the only one who knows how to get in touch with her. I had to promise not to tell anyone else. I told her it was absurd, but I went along with it. I'm always careful. I write to her at a post office box." She waved her hand in a distracted gesture of frustration. "She doesn't want Philip to know anything about her. It's ridiculous. If he really loves her it shouldn't matter."

"He knows now. I told him. I got the details of the murders from the investigating officer. I gave Philip a full report."

"How did he take it?" Vee's eyes were anxious.

"He was concerned about her," I said, choosing the words carefully.

"I knew it wouldn't matter to him. Not if he loves her. What happened wasn't her fault. She was an innocent bystander. I suppose she was afraid he would find out about the psychologist she saw afterwards."

"Philip fired me this afternoon. He told me my services were no longer needed and went back to Los Gatos."

"Why?"

I swirled my cup and looked at the tea leaves floating in the water. "There's some evidence that Elizabeth abused the child."

Vee Burke's mouth rounded into a shocked circle, then clamped shut. Indignation colored her face. She got up in a blur of turquoise cloth.

"That's outrageous. Absolutely outrageous. I don't believe it. How could he believe it?"

"When Philip hired me he seemed eager to find his wife. Then his father showed up, apparently to tell him about the alleged abuse. That's when the weather changed. Philip seems to be firmly under Papa's thumb, and Papa definitely doesn't like his daughter-in-law."

"He's lying. She wouldn't hurt her own child. She loves that little boy. How dare he carry tales like that to Philip?" Her jaw tightened and her eyes burned with anger. I would have given anything to see a confrontation between Vera Burke and Edward Foster.

"You've got to find her," Vee declared, "and straighten this out."

"Philip fired me."

"I'm hiring you. Right now."

She reached into the desk drawer and pulled out a checkbook. "What do you charge? You need a retainer, don't you? How much?"

"Are you sure you want to do this?"

"Of course I'm sure. My mind's made up." She scribbled out a check, tore it from the book, and held it out to me. "Here's five hundred dollars. Do we have an arrangement, Ms. Howard?"

"I didn't come over here looking for a client."

"Why did you come?"

"I've been asking myself the same question. It boils down

65

to one thing. I started an investigation and I'd like to see it through to the end."

"I'm giving you the opportunity to do that. I want you to find my niece," Vee Burke said. "And I'll pay you to do it."

We stared at each other. I reached for the blue paper rectangle she offered. "All right. I'll hold the check in the file. If I find her I'll cash it and bill you for my fees and expenses. If I don't find her, you just pay the expenses. Fair enough?"

"Fair enough."

I put the check in my wallet. "When did you call Elizabeth to tell her about your father?"

"The week before he died. A week ago Friday."

"Did she say she'd come to Stockton?"

"She said she'd think about it. I knew it would be hard for her to get away, with a baby. And how would she explain it to her husband?"

"Then she called you Tuesday, the day before she disappeared. What did she say?"

"Beth asked if there was any change in Dad's condition. I said he'd gotten worse. She wanted to know if her sister, Karen, was coming to Stockton. I said I didn't know. I asked her again if she could come. She said she didn't think so, that it would be very awkward. I didn't hear from her again. I went to Stockton Wednesday night, and Dad died Friday morning. I called Beth in Los Gatos, but I didn't get any answer. I tried again that afternoon. I hoped it meant she was on her way to Stockton, but she didn't come. Neither did Karen."

"Elizabeth left the baby with her mother-in-law last Wednesday and said she was going shopping. She took a suitcase and some clothes, and withdrew several thousand dollars from the joint account. She left her car in the bank lot and took a cab to the train station. No one's seen her since."

"That's odd," Vee said, running a hand through her unruly hair. "She disappeared before Dad died. But where is she? Why hasn't she contacted me?"

66

"How long were you in Stockton?"

"A week. I got back late last night."

"You mentioned that Elizabeth saw a psychologist after the murders. Did she have some sort of breakdown?"

"I don't know if you could call it a breakdown," Vee said. Her left index finger beat a nervous tattoo on the thin china cup. She stared into her tea as though she were trying to read the leaves swimming at the bottom.

"Beth was a moody child, even before the murders. And afterwards she had trouble dealing with it. My God, who wouldn't? Her parents killed while she was in the house. By her own brother. All those questions from the police. Seeing it splashed all over the newspapers and television. It was awful." She shuddered.

"When we took the girls to Stockton to live with the folks, they went through the trauma of being uprooted and having to adjust to a new place. Karen was only nine. She wasn't sure what was going on. She was always more resilient. But Beth—well, being a teenager is difficult enough without having to contend with murder. She seemed all right during the summer. But in September school started. Mark was sentenced in November. We had to go through it all again. Beth started acting out at school."

"Acting out?"

"She exhibited all sorts of odd behavior. She accused people of staring at her and talking behind her back. Maybe they were. Stockton isn't that far from the Bay Area. People knew who she was and what happened. She didn't make any friends and her grades slipped. My mother is rather old-fashioned. She thought Beth just needed more discipline. Finally my sister Alice and I took Beth to see a psychologist. He said what she was going through was part of the normal grief process. She saw him for several months and it seemed to help."

"I'd like to talk with your sister."

"She's living in Stockton now, with Mom and Dad—with Mom."

Mom must be the old woman who'd answered the phone

when I called Stockton yesterday. I sipped my tea, my tongue encountering a bitter tea leaf.

"Elizabeth lived with your sister in San Leandro when she went to Cal State. She dropped out after two years. Why?"

"I don't know why," Vee said. "She enjoyed college, or so she said. Then she seemed to lose interest. After she dropped out of school she moved over to San Francisco. She had this thing about wanting to be a dancer. She worked part-time as a secretary to make ends meet and worked with this little dance troupe at night. Then six years ago she suddenly gave it up. She moved to Sunnyvale and changed her name. That was the last I heard of dancing. She got a good job, secretary to the head of one of those computer firms in the Silicon Valley. Then she met Philip and they were married."

Vee stopped and poured more tea into her cup. She offered to freshen mine but I shook my head. "Why the abrupt change?" I asked.

"I think she was in a relationship that didn't work out. I don't know for sure because she didn't talk about it. Maybe she just wanted to get away from here, from the memories. I suppose changing her name and cutting herself off from the rest of us was the only way she could do it."

Elizabeth's deception had worked, I thought, until she left. She must have known Philip would look for her. By looking for her he was bound to find out the truth. It was as though she wanted him to find out. What triggered her departure? News of her grandfather's illness? But Vee Burke said her niece never showed up in Stockton.

"What about Karen?" I asked Vee. "Were they close?"

"Not when they were growing up. There's a five-year age difference. Now that they're adults, I don't know. I doubt it. Karen isn't close to anyone. She stands alone. I suppose you want to talk to her."

"Yes, I do."

"She moved to Berkeley a few months ago. When I call I rarely find her at home."

"Does her job keep her busy?"

"It must." Vee reached across her untidy desk and pulled

68

her Rolodex close. She flipped through the cards, wrote an address and phone number on a notepad, and handed the sheet to me.

"She works as an actress and model. She makes commercials. I haven't seen any of them, but then I don't watch television. When I called her last week to tell her about Dad she said she'd be shooting all this week."

"Do you know where I can find her?"

"She usually works at a studio over in San Francisco. The Folsom Studio, near Eleventh and Folsom. She told me about it once when I complained that I could never get in touch with her. Evidently they don't like for her to get calls or visitors when they're in the middle of a shoot, unless it's an emergency."

"And Mark?"

"What about Mark?" Shutters dropped over her eyes and her voice was guarded.

"He was released from prison three years ago. Where is he? I want to talk to him."

She was silent for a moment. A grandfather clock at the front of the store whirred and bonged six times. It was closing time, but Vee Burke made no move to lock the front door.

"He lives in Cibola," she said finally. "It's a little Gold Rush town up in the Sierra foothills. He has a shop on Main Street." She flipped to another card in the Rolodex and wrote down the addresses and phone numbers for Mark's apartment and shop.

"Thanks." I tucked both sheets of paper into my wallet. Then I handed Vee one of my business cards. "Here's my number in case you want to get in touch with me."

"What will you do next?"

"I called Lawrence Kinney yesterday. He said he wouldn't talk to me without your permission."

"That's no problem," Vee declared. She picked up the phone and found Kinney's card in the Rolodex. "He works late."

"I'd like to see him as soon as possible."

When the attorney answered his phone, Vee told him Elizabeth was missing. "I've hired a private investigator named Jeri Howard. She'd like to talk with you right away. Tell her anything she wants to know."

Kinney's voice was indistinguishable on the other end of the line. Vee thanked him, hung up, and turned to me. "He's expecting you."

"Thanks. I'll see if I can locate Karen in the morning."

"I don't have children of my own, Ms. Howard," Vee said. "I have to love other people's children. I'm counting on you to find her."

"I will," I said. It felt good to be back on the hunt.

Eight

KINNEY'S BUILDING WAS AT NINETEENTH AND Harrison, one of the new high-rises near Lake Merritt. A security guard posted at the reception desk signed me in and called Kinney's office to announce my arrival. On the tenth floor a double door and a brass nameplate marked the law firm's entrance. The door was locked, so I pushed a buzzer on the wall next to it. A moment later a woman in a gray dress opened it.

"Jeri Howard," I said. "Lawrence Kinney is expecting me."

Kinney's office had a view of Lake Merritt, but he wasn't looking at it. He sat at a big mahogany desk, several law books piled to one side, writing on a yellow legal pad. When I entered he came from behind the desk, crossed an expanse of burgundy carpet, and shook my hand in a brief, economical movement. He was a slender, dapper man a few inches shorter than me, with close-cropped white hair and a neatly trimmed Van Dyke beard. He wore a dark blue suit with a vest over a pale blue shirt. A round gold pin anchored his striped tie.

"Have a seat, please." He indicated a pair of wing chairs in front of the desk. I took one and he sat in the other, crossing his legs.

"I checked you out," he said.

"I'm sure you did."

"The attorneys I spoke with were pleased with your work. One told me you are capable and discreet. Another said he recommends you highly. That is, if you are who you say you are."

I showed him my investigator's license. He examined it closely, then nodded.

"So Vera Burke hired you. When you called yesterday, you hadn't talked to her. You had a different client. Am I right?"

"Yes. My client was Elizabeth Willis's husband. He changed his mind about finding her."

"I assume he had his reasons."

"He claims she's been abusing their son. Vera doesn't believe it."

"Interesting." Something flickered in Kinney's eyes, but I couldn't tell what he was thinking. He laced his fingers together and rested his hands on his knee. "What do you want from me?"

"Background information on the Willis family. Maybe if I know where Elizabeth came from I'll have a better idea of where she went."

"That's one way of going about it," Kinney said. "I take it you know the details of the murders."

"I spoke with the investigating officer yesterday, and I have a copy of the police report. I also read the coverage in the *Tribune*. That's how I got your name. How did you come to be Mark Willis's attorney?"

"I've known Charles and Vera Burke for years. Charles called me the morning after the murders. He asked if I would talk to the boy. When I saw Mark and got the details of the case, I agreed to act as Mark's counsel."

"What can you tell me about George and Frances Willis?"

"When people are dead, other people generally say good things about them." Kinney favored me with a tight smile. "What I can tell you is hearsay. Not admissible in a court of law, but perhaps suitable for your purpose. Most people spoke of George Willis with affection. He was called a man's man, a good officer. Frances did volunteer work with the

72

officers' wives club and she played a lot of golf. Everyone said they were nice people."

"But . . ." I said. "Your impression?"

"My impression was that the family was fragmented. George Willis seems to have been less interested in the role of husband and father than he was in his Navy career. He was away a lot. That forced Frances Willis into the role of family leader. I'm not sure she was up to it."

"You said most people spoke of George with affection. What did they say about Frances?"

"Not much at first," Kinney said. "Then little bits of information that helped me form a picture. She was a striking woman—from all accounts, a fun-loving one as well. One of her friends told me she liked to party. Another hinted that Frances slept around. She didn't seem to be close to her children. In fact, several people reported that she was impatient with them. I detected an undercurrent in the accounts of Frances Willis, one of restlessness, frustration, dissatisfaction. Of course I never met the woman, so I'm speculating."

I asked Kinney the same question I'd asked myself. "Why did Mark Willis murder his parents?"

"He didn't like them very much." Kinney shifted in his chair. "He didn't exactly say that, but he didn't have to. As for a specific reason, I don't know. Mark was polite and cooperative, up to a point. But he never retracted his so-called confession. He never offered an explanation or an excuse. I had nothing on which to base a defense. It's difficult to defend someone who seems determined to go to prison."

"Why do you think he did it?"

He was quiet for a moment, staring out the window at the lake. Then he spoke. "Policemen, lawyers, and psychologists will tell you that when a child kills his parents there's usually a history of child abuse, both physical and psychological. There have been a number of well-publicized cases over the past few years."

"You're the second person to bring up the subject," I said. "Do you think that's what happened in the Willis family?"

73

"No evidence of it." Kinney stroked his beard. "My probing in that direction was met by disbelief and outrage from friends and family alike. Remember, they were nice people. The consensus was that George and Frances Willis would never do such a thing. Of course, these were the same people who couldn't believe that a nice kid like Mark Willis killed his parents. Without input from Mark, I never got anywhere with that line of questioning."

"What about input from Elizabeth?"

"Minimal. I had very little access to her."

That surprised me. "But she was in the house when it happened. That makes her a material witness."

"Elizabeth told the police she was upstairs in her room when she heard the shots," Kinney said. "It was never clear to me whether she came downstairs to investigate. I wanted to question her right after the murders, but she was hysterical. After the hospital released her to Vera, she spent the next few days lying in a darkened bedroom at the Burkes', crying when she wasn't sedated. Her aunts wouldn't let her or Karen go to the funeral." The attorney stopped and shook his head.

"When I finally talked to Elizabeth she told me all she could remember was hearing shots. The police couldn't get much else out of her either, and I must say they took her statement at face value. Why shouldn't they? Mark's fingerprints were on the gun and he'd confessed."

"What's your guess?"

"I think she saw something," Kinney said. "I don't know what. Maybe she blocked it out. Or she's lying. I wish I knew which. It was a traumatic experience for a young girl. That's why her aunts were hesitant about my pressing Elizabeth for details. It meant that Mark's statement was the only version of the facts available."

"Vera Burke hired you to defend her nephew. I would think she'd have been more cooperative."

"Things always look different in retrospect," Kinney said. "I was in the middle of a tug-of-war between Vera and her sister. Vera wanted to help Mark. Alice Gray was primarily interested in protecting her nieces. At the first opportunity she whisked them off to Stockton to live with the grandparents.''

"What was your impression of Elizabeth?''

"A troubled young girl.''

"In what way?''

For a moment Kinney seemed to grope for words, an unusual condition in a lawyer. "I can't quite put my finger on it,'' he said finally.

"When I talked to her she seemed a bit sullen, resentful of my questions. Of course she'd already been questioned by the police. I told Vera and Charles at the time that they should see the girl got some counseling. That fall, as I prepared for Mark's sentencing, Vera mentioned that Elizabeth was seeing a psychologist. I was glad to hear that she was getting some help.''

"Vera says Elizabeth saw the psychologist for a few months,'' I said. "That doesn't seem like sufficient damage control for a teenager who may have seen her brother murder their parents.''

"I doubt that it was. The whole episode was frustrating, from start to finish.'' Kinney was talking about his Willis case. I knew how he felt because I was thinking about mine. And it wasn't finished.

"Given the circumstances, I'm sure you did the best you could.''

"My best would have been keeping Mark Willis out of prison.'' Kinney shook his head slowly. "Whether he deserved to be there or not. That's how the game of criminal defense is played.''

It was after seven when I left Kinney's office. Outside, the streetlamps cast pools of light on the dark pavement of Harrison Street. As I came down the steps to the sidewalk I felt a chill that had nothing to do with the March evening. It felt like the scrutiny of someone's eyes.

I swept the dark street with a glance and saw a man and a woman walking down the opposite sidewalk. I thought I glimpsed someone sitting in a parked car to my left, face in

75

shadow. Under one light pole a shaggy-haired derelict scavenged in a trash can. He stared at me for a long moment, his eyes intense above a thin face shadowed by stubble, his frame lost in his baggy gray clothes.

How young he looked, I thought, guessing he was a runaway. I turned to the right and walked back to my car. I couldn't shake the sensation that someone's eyes bored into my back.

The front door of my building was propped open as two men in coveralls carried cleaning supplies into the lobby from a white van marked BUILDING SERVICE. The woman who ran the maintenance crew was in the lobby, going over the checklist she carried on a clipboard.

We exchanged greetings. "There's a light burned out in the hallway, right in front of my office," I told her, punching the up button. She said she'd take care of it, making a note on her checklist.

The outer door of Cassie's office was locked, but I saw a light burning inside. I knocked. A moment later I heard Cassie's voice. "Who is it?"

"Jeri."

She opened the door. She was shoeless and jacketless, the cuffs of her raspberry-colored blouse unbuttoned and rolled up her arms.

"I thought you'd gone," she said. "I was just about to order a pizza. Feel like sharing one?"

"Order a big one, with extra cheese and pepperoni. I'll get the beer from my refrigerator."

"What have you been up to?" She cocked her head to one side. "You look wired."

"I'll explain in a minute."

In my office I unlocked the filing cabinet and slipped Vera Burke's check into the Foster file. I pulled out the bits of paper I'd tucked in my wallet, the addresses and phone numbers Vera Burke had given me.

Mark Willis lived in Cibola. The name of the town was familiar. I took a California map from my desk drawer and scanned it. Cibola was a tiny speck on Highway 49, between

Jackson and San Andreas, in Calaveras County. When I was a kid we'd spent lots of summers in the Gold Country. Dad's mother was born in Jackson and she had a brother there, so we used the town as a base while we explored the towns of the Mother Lode. We'd probably driven through Cibola, but I didn't remember the town. No doubt it was just another collection of tired old buildings in a dusty street, a remnant of the gold frenzy of 1849.

I picked up the phone. Mark Willis's phone in Cibola rang several times. He didn't answer. Neither did Karen Willis in Berkeley. Maybe I'd have better luck locating both of them at work tomorrow, after I kept my appointment with Lenore Franklin. I fetched a couple of beers from my refrigerator and locked my door.

"The pizza will be here in about twenty minutes," Cassie said as she let me into her office. "I told the guy who took the order that we'd pick it up at the front door." She took one of the beers and twisted off the cap. "You look more cheerful than you did this afternoon."

"The Foster case has been reactivated."

"Did the husband change his mind?"

"No. After you left my office I called the antique store again. This time someone answered."

"The aunt?"

I nodded. "Vera Burke. I went to the shop and talked to her. She doesn't buy the child-abuse story, and she wants me to find Elizabeth."

"So you've got another client," Cassie set her beer bottle on her desk, which was piled with law books and file folders. "I guess that background check will have to wait."

"I'll finish it as soon as I can."

"That's okay," she said with a wave of her hand. "It looks like we may settle before the hearing. Besides, I know you wanted to continue this investigation. Now you've got a client, so do it."

"I may be out of town for a couple of days. If I give you my extra key will you look after my cat?"

"That bottomless pit with legs?" Cassie laughed. "Sure.

Just let me know when you're leaving and when to expect you back." I gave her the key. She put it in her purse and took out her wallet. "You go get the pizza and I'll clean off my desk."

Upstairs in her office Cassie and I devoured the pizza as though we hadn't eaten in a week, tomato sauce and strings of cheese dribbling down our chins and fingers. I grabbed a couple of napkins and mopped at my mouth, then reached for my beer. As we ate, Cassie told me about the case she'd won in court that afternoon. We finished the pizza and tidied up Cassie's desk. Then I heard something that made me come out of my chair.

"What is it?" Cassie asked.

"I'm not sure."

Wiping my hands on a napkin, I headed for the darkened outer office, Cassie at my heels. I heard the noise again, the dull thunk of a solid object striking wood. I pulled open the door, wide enough to look into the hallway.

The figure was clothed in black, wearing a turtleneck sweater and a knit cap with not much face visible in between. Those features I could see were obscured in the shadows left by the burned-out light fixture. Gloved hands held an iron crowbar, which was jammed in the crack between the frame and my office door.

I slipped out the door, moving quickly toward the intruder. Then he heard me and turned. Beneath the cap a pair of pale eyes widened in a narrow face. He swung the crowbar at me. I dodged the blow and heard another thunk as the bar hit the wall behind me. I kicked him on the knee. A voice hissed a curse, then he swung at me again. This time I caught the bar with my hands. We struggled, neither of us making a sound. Between the cuffs of the sweater and the glove of his right wrist I saw the blue lines of a tattoo.

He kicked me several times on the left shin and ankle. It hurt like hell. I fell against the wall, still clinging to the bar. His grip loosened. I wrenched the crowbar away from him and shoved one end into his abdomen. I heard him grunt in

78

pain, but the blow didn't slow him. He aimed a fist at my face. I twisted away from the wall, and the blow landed on my shoulder. I circled, limping slightly, but he kept moving too.

Over his shoulder I saw Cassie at her office door. "The police are on their way," she called, her voice shrill with tension.

The intruder rushed me, knocking me to the floor. He kept going, headed for the fire escape at the back of the building. I jumped to my feet and ran after him. He hit the door and his footsteps clattered down the metal stairs. By the time I got out to the landing he was in the alley, running toward the street.

"Are you all right?" Cassie asked as I walked back to my office, favoring my right ankle.

"I'm okay." I looked at my office door and the frame near the lock, examining the gouges and scratches left by the crowbar. "Guess he couldn't wait till office hours."

My left leg ached. I sat down on the floor and pulled up the cuff of my slacks to inspect my shin and ankle. A couple of angry red spots were already swelling, the skin hard and painful.

Fred, the building security guard, appeared from the stairwell. "I thought I heard something," he said, his face furrowing as he saw me sitting on the floor. "What happened?"

"Someone tried to break into Jeri's office," Cassie said. "I called the police."

"Damn." Fred hurried over to my door. "Did he get in?"

"No. This is as far as he got."

Two uniformed Oakland cops arrived a moment later. I stood up to greet them. I knew one of them, Glen Lee. His partner was a woman I didn't recognize. Her name tag read Alvarez. She took out a notebook and started asking questions.

"Ms. Taylor and I were in her office." I pointed toward Cassie's door. "I heard something in the hallway, looked out, and saw a man attempting to force my office door. We struggled, and he kicked me several times. I took this crowbar away from him, but he got away. He went down the fire escape at the back of the building and ran down the alley in the direction of Eleventh Street.''

"Description?" Lee asked.

"Male caucasian, slight build. I'd say five-six or five-seven, maybe a hundred forty pounds. He was wearing black pants, a black turtleneck, black gloves, and a knitted watch cap pulled down to his eyebrows. All I could see were his eyes and nose. The eyes were light blue or gray, and I didn't see any facial hair. Heavy shoes, maybe steel-toed. He had a tattoo on his right wrist. I only caught a glimpse, but it looked like a butterfly.''

"Any idea who might want to break into your office?" Alvarez asked.

I'd been asking myself the same question. Who wanted to get into my office badly enough to break in?

"No," I said, shaking my head. "I have no idea.''

That wasn't exactly true. I recalled the sensation I'd felt earlier on the street outside Lawrence Kinney's office. Someone had been watching me. Was it that kid I'd seen, rummaging in the trash can? Our eyes had met for just a few seconds, a brief period, but enough to make a connection. Had he followed me back to my office, wearing dark clothes under his rags, his hair stuffed into a cap? It would have been easy to get in, since the cleaning crew had the door propped open. Maybe he'd hidden in the stairwell with his crowbar until I left my office. But I couldn't be sure. It had been dark on the street, and equally dark in this hallway. The tattoo I'd glimpsed made me think of the Navy. There were a lot of sailors stationed in the Bay Area, some of them retired—like Admiral Joseph Franklin.

After the police left, Cassie and I looked at each other, then at Fred, who'd been hovering around, watching the excitement.

"Well, I've had enough drama for one night," Cassie said. "Let's go home." I waited in the hallway while she fetched her briefcase and locked her office. Fred assured me he'd keep a close eye on things in case that joker returned.

"Thanks, Fred, but I don't think he'll be back."

Cassie and I headed for the stairs. "Okay, Jeri, tell me what you really think."

"He was an amateur. He made a lot of noise. A pro would have picked the lock—quietly."

"What was he after?"

"Computer equipment, maybe. But there are easier ways to make a score. Smash a car window and grab the stereo, for instance. Eliminate the computer, and the only thing in my office worth stealing is information."

"That's what I thought. Now all you have to do is figure out what. And who's after it."

I went home to my warm bed and my hungry cat. The burst of energy I'd felt earlier in the evening after talking with Vee Burke had disappeared, leaving only exhaustion. Then, as I was spooning cat food into Abigail's dish, replaying the incident in my mind, something occurred to me.

The black-clad figure with the crowbar could have been a woman.

Nine

ABIGAIL WOKE ME THE NEXT MORNING. SHE PAD-
ded from the foot of the bed to my pillow and began her
campaign to get me up and out to the kitchen to feed her.
She poked at my face with her paw, claws in, and I shoved
her away. She returned, nose to nose, and began a rumbling
purr as her rough tongue sandpapered my cheek.

My eyes flew open and I grumbled at her. I shifted position in bed and she moved to my stomach, kneading the
blanket rhythmically. Her purring increased in intensity when
I scratched her ears. So did the kneading. When a claw went
through the blanket and pricked my stomach I sat up and
dislodged the cat.

"All right, I'm up," I muttered, with a lack of enthusi-
asm.

I pushed back the covers and examined my left leg. A
purple-black bruise ran up the calf from my ankle. I poked
at it and felt a twinge of pain. I crawled from my warm bed,
shivering in the oversized T-shirt that served as a nightgown.
Abigail trotted ahead of me as I walked barefooted to the
kitchen. I dished up her food. Through my kitchen window
the sky was gray, promising rain.

I looked at the kitchen clock and swore. No wonder Abigail had been so persistent. I'd overslept. If I didn't hustle
I'd be late for my meeting with Lenore Franklin.

I showered and dressed warmly in a pair of green corduroy
pants and a plaid flannel shirt. By the time I crossed the Park
Street bridge into Alameda, the rain had started, a steady
curtain of drops that required windshield wipers.

I parked on a side street and walked to Ole's Waffle Shop, a homey place with Formica tables, orange vinyl booths, and a steady morning trade. As I entered I saw Lenore Franklin sitting at a booth near the back, a coffee cup on the table in front of her.

"Good morning," she said, "though it's kind of dreary." Her face, so animated yesterday, matched the bleak day.

"I don't mind the rain." I slid into the seat facing her. A waitress handed me a menu and asked if I wanted coffee. I nodded and glanced at the menu.

"I like the sun, so I can work in my garden." She took a sip of her coffee, then put the cup down, her mouth twisting into a half-smile. "I feel awkward meeting you like this. Like I'm being disloyal to Joe by going behind his back."

The waitress returned, pen poised over her order pad. Mrs. Franklin ordered a cinnamon roll. "I'll have the same," I said, handing over the menu.

"It's just that he was so angry after you left," she continued. "He was . . . ranting. I worry about his blood pressure. He's been so preoccupied with this campaign, even though the election's three months away. I know he doesn't like being distracted, but his reaction was way out of proportion. I heard him on the phone, calling the Alameda chief of police to complain about you. I'm sorry he did that. After all, you're only doing your job. Trying to find Elizabeth."

"I suppose he didn't like my questions." I sipped my coffee.

"You implied that George and Franny Willis abused their children," Lenore Franklin said.

"The possibility of abuse was mentioned by several people I spoke with." Mrs. Franklin and I regarded each other over the table. "What can you tell me?"

She took her time answering. "I've been thinking about it since you left yesterday." She stopped as the waitress set the rolls in front of us and freshened our coffee. "About George and Franny and the children. I've been trying to recall something I may have missed. You asked whether Mark got along with his parents. There may have been some friction, but I

83

don't remember anything specific. He was a teenager.'' She shrugged, as if that explained everything.

"Parents and teenagers have problems. If there was anything unusual going on I didn't notice it. They seemed like a normal family, Miss Howard. They really did. Mom, Dad, and three bright, attractive children. Then one of those children picked up a gun and killed his parents. Things like that aren't supposed to happen.''

"But they do. More often than any of us would like to admit.''

She looked as though she wanted to disbelieve me, but couldn't quite manage it.

"I even got out the old photo albums to go with the old memories.'' She shook her head. "I don't recall ever seeing George or Franny strike any of the children. But . . .''

"But . . .'' I repeated.

"I suppose if you're going to beat your children you won't do it in front of the neighbors.''

"Maybe not. Just tell me about Mr. and Mrs. Willis. Give me a sense of the kind of people they were.'' I picked up my fork and cut into my cinnamon roll. "What do you remember about them?''

She sipped her coffee. "George and Joe were friends, but they were an unlikely pair. George was a farmer's son from the Florida panhandle. Joe's father was a well-to-do banker. They both got their Academy slots due to an influential relative. I don't think they had much in common besides the Navy.'' She took a bite of her roll, chewed, and chased it with some coffee.

"George wasn't ambitious. No, I take that back. He wasn't as ambitious as Joe. You have to be ambitious to get anywhere in the Navy. The whole structure is based on upward movement, at least for officers. Up or out, they call it. If George Willis had lived, he would have retired a captain, not an admiral. If he'd made it to captain at all.''

"I'm not sure I understand. He was a commander when he was killed.''

"He'd been passed over once for promotion to captain, at

the same time Joe made it," Lenore Franklin said, with the sagacity of a Navy wife. "The promotion boards were coming around again. If George had been passed over a second time, his career would have been over. Franny wouldn't have liked that."

"She was the ambitious one?" I asked.

"Franny enjoyed being a senior officer's wife. She was the pusher, the aggressive one. I think George liked being in the Navy. It's just that he didn't care about playing the kinds of games it's necessary to play to get ahead. But I thought he was a good officer, dedicated to his work. He was the kind of man who focused on his job, without paying attention to other things."

"Was his family one of those other things?"

She thought about that for a moment. "Maybe. He was always rather formal with the children. Sometimes even with Franny. They were an oddly matched couple. George was—well, I guess the only word for it is stolid. And Franny was so alive."

"How did they meet?" I asked, picking up my coffee cup.

"In a bar in San Francisco. George was at Treasure Island going through a school, and Franny worked in the city. They dated off and on for several months, even when George came down to San Diego to report to his duty station. Joe and I were in San Diego too. We'd been married about a year." She smiled, remembering.

"I was pregnant with Kevin. We lived in a little apartment. George stayed in the Bachelor Officers' Quarters. He came over for dinner about once a week. One weekend he went to San Francisco to see Franny and brought her back with him, by way of Las Vegas. They'd eloped. So we became a foursome. Almost from the start."

"Sounds like you spent a lot of time together."

"We did." She poked at her roll with her fork. "When Joe and George were gone, it was just us wives and kids. I appreciated Franny's company." She looked at me, then down at her cup. "They were good friends. I liked the Willises. Joe was always fond of Franny. And George."

I nodded, noting the pause. "They played golf together. Your husband and Mrs. Willis."

"All the time. I never cared for the game, hitting a little white ball around a green. Franny played a lot, especially when the kids were in school."

"What do you recall about the Willis children?"

"Normal kids, I suppose. Into things. Fun to watch." She smiled. "I remember Kevin and Mark building a tree house in our backyard in San Diego. Ruth and Beth playing on a beach in Hawaii when we were stationed at Pearl Harbor. The Willis kids were the same ages as ours, as I told you yesterday."

"Except Karen. She was younger."

"Karen," Lenore Franklin said, her tone chilly. "Yes. Five years younger than Beth."

"You act as thought you didn't like her."

"Of course I did." She looked startled and her words came too quickly. "She was a little hellion, though, compared to Beth. Beth was a sweet child, shy, unsure of herself, usually quiet and well behaved. Karen was always into something." A troubled look came over her face.

"No. I really didn't like Karen. She was a brat." Lenore Franklin stopped and looked at me, perturbed at her own admission. "My God, listen to me. I'm talking about a nine-year-old girl."

"Some kids are more difficult than others. I've been told Elizabeth was a moody child."

"All teenage girls are moody," Mrs. Franklin said with a smile and shake of her head. "It goes with the territory."

"You haven't told me much about Franny Willis, except that she played golf and she was ambitious. What was she like away from her husband and the kids?"

The waitress brought the check and refilled our cups. Mrs. Franklin stirred some cream into her coffee, then picked up the cup with both hands and took a sip.

"Franny drank a little."

I looked across the table. Her words had been spoken in a calm tone, but I saw something else in her eyes.

"I think you mean she drank a lot."

Her topaz eyes widened. "All right. She drank a lot. She had flirtations with men while her husband was gone."

"Affairs?"

"I don't know," she said, but her face gave her words the lie.

"What do you mean by flirtations?"

"Talk, gestures. Paying attention to men at the club, drinking with them, dancing close to them. The kind of playfulness between men and women that has an undercurrent to it. She was an attractive woman. Sensual, I guess you would call it. People used to talk about her. Just like I'm talking about her now, gossiping about a woman who's been dead for fifteen years." Lenore Franklin laughed, a short, unamused sound. "You're really good at this, aren't you? I wasn't going to tell you this much."

"I just let people talk." I sat back in the orange vinyl booth and looked at her soberly. "When you called me yesterday I assumed you wanted to talk. Something happened to cause people to gossip about Franny Willis. Tell me what it was."

"An incident at the officers club," she said, taking a deep breath. "Late summer, the year before the murders. It was a Hail and Farewell. That's a Navy party where you hail the newcomers and say farewell to the people who are leaving."

Her mouth thinned into a tight line. "One of the new officers was a young lieutenant in his twenties, unmarried, very attractive. Franny flirted with him quite openly, even though George was at the party. The lieutenant reciprocated. They danced like they were glued together. Someone took offense, only it wasn't George. It was one of the departing officers, a lieutenant commander. One of Franny's previous conquests. His wife was there, but the two men had words over Franny. She'd been drinking steadily all evening. While the men were arguing, she got up on a table and started taking off her clothes. She was down to her slip before Joe and George got her out of there. People talked about it for months."

"I can imagine. What was Franny like afterwards?"

"Our relationship cooled," she said slowly. She looked down at the table then raised her eyes to mine. "I was disturbed by her behavior. So I didn't see her as often as before, even though we lived right next door to one another. She kept her distance too. I think she knew how I felt." She laced her fingers together tightly and rested her hands on the table.

"Besides, Joe and I were having some problems of our own. Nothing major, just one of those bad patches you go through in a marriage. What went on at the Willises' became less important than what was happening at the Franklins'. After the murders, I regretted that. I wondered if there was something I could have done. We transferred to San Diego that August. I was never so glad to leave a place in my life."

"Now you're back, living in the same house."

"Fifteen years is a long time. It creates distance. A young couple with two small children live in that house next door. It's not the same place." She sighed. "You're right. I wanted to talk." She pushed away her cup and reached for the check, but I covered it with my hand.

"It's on me."

She stood up and buttoned her raincoat. "I told Joe I was going shopping. I guess I'll go buy something. Will any of this help you find Beth?"

"Maybe."

Lenore Franklin walked away from me without saying goodbye. I watched her go past the front window of the coffee shop and wondered how fond of Franny Willis Joe Franklin had been.

Ten

KAREN WILLIS'S ADDRESS WAS A TWO-STORY brown-shingled house on Virginia Street in North Berkeley. Four mailboxes lined the porch rail, with the occupants' names embossed on strips of red plastic tape. Karen lived in apartment C, and she hadn't picked up her mail for a few days. I went up onto the porch and tried the front door. It was unlocked.

I stepped into the hallway, wiping my feet on a woven mat. Ahead of me a staircase led up to a landing, then turned left. I took the stairs to the second floor. Apartment C was on my left, D on my right. A door at the end of the upstairs hallway opened onto a small deck with a set of back stairs leading down to the driveway.

I walked back to apartment C and knocked on the door. I waited and heard nothing but the sound of rain pattering on the deck outside. A moment later the door to D opened. A young woman peered out, wearing gray sweatpants and a UC Berkeley T-shirt, her long black hair pinned in an untidy roll at the back of her neck. She carried a thick hardbound book in one hand, her finger marking her place as she looked me up and down, suspicion in her eyes.

"She's not there."

"That Karen," I said with a quick smile. "I can never catch her at home. Do you know where she's working now?"

"I have no idea." Karen's neighbor brushed a strand of hair off her forehead. "She hasn't lived here very long and she works a strange schedule. Sometimes she's here during the day and sometimes she's gone for a couple of weeks at a

89

time. She takes a suitcase with her. I guess she travels. Her boyfriend comes over and picks up her mail. He's got a key to the apartment.''

''Is she still dating that big blond guy, the one that drives the Corvette?''

''Blond? Her boyfriend's dark, with a mustache. He rides a motorcycle.''

''Are you sure?''

''Of course I'm sure,'' the neighbor said, sounding miffed. ''He was here last Wednesday. That's when Karen left.''

''On the motorcycle?''

''No. She took her own car. A brand-new white BMW.'' The young woman sounded a bit jealous as she described the car. ''Whatever she's doing, it must pay well.''

The deck held a couple of lawn chairs with rain puddling in their seats. I went down the back stairs and out to the street. Evidently neither the front nor the back door of Karen's building was kept locked. If I had to come back and check out Karen's apartment, I could at least get into the building.

Getting into the apartment itself might be a problem, with Karen's vigilant neighbor across the hall. As I unlocked the car door, once again I felt eyes on my back. I looked up and saw the woman from D staring at me from her second-floor window. She saw me looking and stepped away from the glass.

The feeling didn't go away, after I started the car. I looked around me. There was a lot of foot traffic in the neighborhood because it was close to the university. Further down the street I saw a mail carrier, a woman with an umbrella, and two young men with small backpacks. A woman wearing a tan raincoat glided along the opposite sidewalk, short brown hair visible under a matching hat.

I shook my head, wondering if I was getting the whim-whams. My instincts were usually correct, though. As I drove down Virginia Street a blue car fell in behind me. I turned left on Sacramento, then right again on University. The car was still behind me, several lengths back. Was it following me? University Avenue was heavily traveled, the main access to Interstate 80. Anyone headed for the freeway would be following me.

Ahead of me an AC Transit bus angled to the curb to pick up a passenger, its rear end still protruding into my lane. I swerved into the left lane to avoid it. While I waited for the light to change at San Pablo Avenue I looked for the blue car I'd seen earlier, but it had disappeared.

I concentrated on driving as I continued down University and took the ramp onto the interstate. Cars in the heavy midday traffic jockeyed for position on the wet pavement as we approached the maze where several freeways came together in a knot. I kept to the right lanes, leading to the Bay Bridge. I waited my turn to pay the toll, then headed across the span to San Francisco, my windshield wipers trying to keep ahead of the rain.

I took the Ninth Street exit off the freeway and drove into San Francisco's South of Market district, maneuvering through traffic until I found a parking place near the intersection of Eleventh and Folsom. I got out and locked my car, then I walked along Folsom Street, looking for a building that might be a studio. Midway down the block I saw a van parked in a driveway across the street, with the name of a catering firm painted on the side.

I jaywalked over to the van and looked up at the building. In a previous life it had been a warehouse like its neighbors, but a foot-high sign above the garage opening said "Folsom Studio."

The back of the van was open and so was the door to the studio. I watched the doorway for a moment, looking for a guard, but I didn't see anyone. Then a young woman in coveralls hurried out, grabbed a covered tray from the van, and slammed the door shut. She hurried back through the doorway. I followed her. Once through the vestibule I was in a long hallway, its linoleum floor dark and scuffed. The girl in coveralls disappeared into a stairwell on my left. At the end of the hall I saw the security guard, his back to me as he talked on a pay phone. I dodged up the stairs.

The second-floor hallway was a bustle of activity. To my right I saw a set of double doors with a light overhead. Must be the studio itself. To my left I saw a series of doors lining the corridor.

"I'm looking for Karen Willis," I said to a man in blue jeans and a sweatshirt. He shrugged and kept walking. I worked my way down the corridor, asking my question until someone told me he'd seen Karen Willis in Wardrobe. Up on the third floor, he told me, second door on the left. I doubled back to the stairs.

In the third-floor hallway I stopped at the sight of a half-naked man examining his reflection in a full-length mirror. He was tall, about six-three, with a shaven head, a black handlebar mustache, and broad muscled shoulders. He wore baggy white trousers, riding low on his torso, and carried a black leather whip in his right hand. He preened for a moment, unaware of my presence as he tweaked the end of his mustache with the whip. Then he caught sight of me and grinned. He strolled past me to the stairs, his muscles rippling.

Second door on the left, I muttered. I walked toward it with the growing awareness that Karen Willis wasn't making commercials, despite what she'd told her aunt. If Vee Burke wanted to see her niece work, she'd have to catch Karen's act at the Pussycat Theater.

Two girls who looked about sixteen came out the door of Wardrobe, both brunettes in gauzy pink harem outfits that showed nipples and pubic hair. I let them pass and walked into the room, a small rectangle with costumes hanging from a bar along one wall and a cluttered counter on the opposite wall. I saw a dark-haired woman bent over a sewing machine at one end of the worktable in the middle of the room.

"Put that damn thing out," she said in a harsh voice, looking up. She was Asian, in her thirties, her short black hair sculpted into New Wave art. She glared at the tall, long-legged blonde who'd just fired up a cigarette. The blonde, dressed in a short blue-and-white kimono and a pair of slippers, sat on the counter, a phone receiver in her hand.

"There's a pay phone downstairs. Get off my line."

"Jesus, Lila, you're a bitch," the blonde said, hanging up the phone. "What's the matter? Aren't you getting any? I'm sure any one of the guys would be happy to oblige."

Lila nailed the blonde with a withering look. She finished whatever she was doing at the sewing machine and held up the costume, spangles on diaphanous muslin. Then she threw it at the blonde and glared at me.

"What do you want?"

"Karen Willis."

"That's her." Lila jerked her chin in the direction of the blonde. "This isn't a lounge. You want to talk, go someplace else."

Puffing defiantly on her cigarette, Karen Willis jumped off the counter and strolled toward the doorway, her costume over one arm. I followed her. In the hallway we looked each other over. The kimono, barely concealing a spectacular figure, was loosely belted at the waist and stopped an inch or so below adequacy. Her long blond hair owed more to peroxide than to nature. A baby face and a pair of wide blue eyes made her appear younger than twenty-four. She didn't look anything like her sister. Or her brother.

"Who the hell are you?" she asked.

"Jeri Howard. I'm a private investigator."

"No shit? As in Sam Spade?"

"Something like that."

"So what do you want?"

"I'm looking for your sister, Elizabeth. She's missing."

"Dizzy Lizzie? Well, well," Karen Willis said, her full red lips curving into a smile. "That is indeed interesting."

She led the way to a makeshift lounge, a small room with several worn sofas and a coffee urn on a table near the door. "Coffee?" she asked. I shook my head. She helped herself to a cup from the urn.

As she stirred cream into the coffee a man with dark, curly hair and a bushy mustache came through the doorway, his muscular frame clad in tight blue jeans and a knit shirt. He leaned over her shoulder and put his hand on her waist, whis-

93

pering something in her ear. She shook her head and gestured toward me. His eyes met mine briefly, then darted away. He nodded quickly to Karen and disappeared into the hallway. Karen's boyfriend, I guessed, the one who rode a motorcycle.

Karen strolled across the room to where I stood. "Have a seat." She sprawled comfortably on an orange-flowered sofa, set her coffee mug on a box that served as an end table, and scratched one long bare leg with her red-tipped fingers. She positioned her cigarette on the side of an already full ashtray.

"How'd you find me?" she asked, picking up her coffee.

"Your aunt Vee. She said you made commercials at the Folsom Studio."

"That's just a little story I tell Vee. I think she knows. She just doesn't want to admit it. So we pretend I'm respectable."

"How long have you been in the business?"

"Five years. I make a lot of money. I suck a lot of cocks, get fucked in a variety of ways by a variety of people, and then I go home." She stole a glance at me to see if I was shocked, decided I wasn't, and blew smoke rings with her cigarette.

"Beats the hell out of selling lingerie at Macy's, which is what I did when I dropped out of college. I may not be in the business much longer, though."

"Why?"

"The flesh peddlers like young flesh, the younger the better. Fifteen-year-olds with firm boobs and tight asses." She looked down at her breasts and legs. "I'm almost twenty-four."

"What would you do instead?" I asked.

"I'm considering my options." Her eyes narrowed and she didn't elaborate about any of the options. "So what do you want, Jeri?"

"Information that might help me find your sister."

"I haven't seen Lizzie in years. Auntie Vee informs me she got married and produced a baby. What'd she do, walk out on the guy and leave him holding the kid?"

"Something like that. She went shopping last week and didn't come home. Her husband hired me to look for her. I thought she might have gone to your grandfather's funeral in Stockton, but Vee says she didn't show."

"Me neither. I was working."

"You haven't been home in a while, according to your neighbor."

"Nosy bitch," Karen said. "We're at a hotel over on Ninth. We stay in town when we're making a movie. Makes it easier to find the cast and crew at six A.M."

"So you haven't seen Elizabeth."

"Lizzie wouldn't come to see me," Karen said, shaking her head. "We never had more than three words to say to one another."

"She changed her name."

"Yeah. Vee said something about that. What did she change it to, Mary Sunshine?" When I didn't respond, Karen blinked her blue eyes and blew smoke rings.

"Bet she didn't want her husband to know the sordid family history." An inappropriate giggle bubbled from her, masking some other emotion. "I was only nine. From the way everyone acted, I thought the Navy had transferred my parents overseas. Can you believe it?" She shook her head and picked up her coffee mug, her long red fingernails clicking against the ceramic surface.

"It took me a couple of months to figure it out. Nobody explained it to me, that's for damn sure. Nobody wanted to talk about it. I saw pictures of Mark in the newspapers and wondered why. Shit." She ground out her cigarette in the overflowing ashtray, then fished in the pocket of her kimono, pulling out a pack of Marlboros and a butane lighter.

"When we went to school in Stockton that fall, Lizzie started acting weird. Vee and Alice hauled her to a shrink. I don't think it did her much good. By that time some of my wonderful little classmates had informed me that my brother blew away Mom and Dad." Karen grimaced, but she kept talking.

"Grandma Madison was crackers. She used to give a party

95

on my mother's birthday, even though the birthday girl was dead.'' I wondered if Karen was exaggerating for my benefit. Behind the grimace I thought I saw another Karen, one who enjoyed telling this tale. She ran one hand through her blond hair and leaned back against the sofa.

"Grandma was into religion. She told me God was punishing the whole family. For what, I was never sure. One week it was because Mom and Dad had to get married because Mark was on the way. The next week it was Dad's fault for being in the Navy and moving us around so we never had a stable home. Reason of the week, you know what I mean? Grandma's been going to some crackpot preacher for fifteen years, trying to figure it out.''

"Have you figured it out?''

"I don't know and I don't care,'' she declared, her mouth turned down at the corners. "It just happened. He killed them. They're dead, and nothing's going to bring them back. Why should I spend the rest of my life speculating?''

"It affected your sister a great deal.''

"Oh, poor Lizzie.'' Karen's sarcasm stripped any sympathy from the words. "She was in the house when Ma and Pa got killed. So she spent the next five years having vapors and being fragile.''

"She got all the attention.''

"You bet,'' Karen said with a tight smile. "And she loved it. She ate it up with a spoon.''

"Did you resent that?''

"Of course I did. Who wouldn't?'' She picked up her coffee and took a swallow. "But then I realized I could do anything I damn well pleased. They were all too busy worrying about Lizzie to notice me. She gave me a lot to worry about.''

"Such as?''

Karen considered me with a malicious glint in her blue eyes. "Lizzie had hysterics at the drop of a hat. She really honed it into an art. She fainted very stylishly, draped limbs and all. And she could produce these two perfect teardrops, one in each eye.'' Karen put a finger under each of her eyes and made a face. "She accused people of talking about her behind her back. Of course they were talking about her. She was loony tunes."

"So she used it to gain sympathy," I said.

"Hell, yes. If Grandpa asked her why her grades were so lousy, Lizzie would put her hand on her forehead and her eyes would get teary."

Karen's right hand moved to her forehead, palm out, and she fluttered her long lashes in a parody of her sister's actions. "Oh, Grandpa, I'll do better next time. I promise. It's just that I can't concentrate." Then she laughed, a raucous bawdy sound. "Shit. Worked every time. Probably still does. I'll bet she uses it on her husband."

"I wouldn't know," I said, fascinated by Karen's own performance. "What about afterwards? Your aunt said something about a dance troupe."

"If you could call it that," Karen said, lighting another cigarette. "A bunch of leftover hippies from the Sixties. I saw them perform once. Black leotards, bare feet, and sitar music. She lived in the Haight with some guy who played the guitar. I think he was pretty heavy into drugs. He used to hit her."

"How do you know?"

"She showed up at my high school graduation with some major-league bruises on her arm. Told everyone she'd fallen down the stairs at her apartment. Of course I didn't buy that. Finally she told me they'd had an argument and he hit her. I said she ought to dump the creep, but she gave me this song-and-dance about how she loved him."

"Know where I can find this guy? Or any of the other members of the dance troupe? What did they call themselves?"

"Lizzie's old boyfriend is dead. Overdose. She took it hard, but I thought she was well rid of the creep. The troupe broke up about the same time. They called themselves *Invitation* or some such thing. Anyway, that's when Lizzie dumped the dance crapola and got into the nine-to-five routine. Nothing like a regular paycheck to make a convert. She went to Sunnyvale to work. Next thing I know Vee tells me Lizzie got married and she's living somewhere down by San Jose. I don't know when. I don't keep track.''

"You haven't seen her since?" I asked, watching her face.

"Hell, no," she said, looking straight into my eyes. "We've got nothing in common."

I wasn't sure I believed her. I switched subjects.

"What about Mark? Have you had any contact with him since he got out of prison?"

She shook her head. "Vee's the only one of my relatives I can tolerate. And vice versa, I suppose. I don't know where Mark is."

"How do you feel about him?"

"My brother was nine years older than me," she said slowly. "Sometimes he was nice, sometimes he teased me, sometimes he just ignored me. So did Lizzie. I used to feel like an only child. He and LIzzie were close, though."

"Would she seek him out?"

Karen tilted her head to one side, running her hand through her hair. "I think so. Yes, I believe she would."

A large bulky man poked his head into the lounge and zeroed in on her. "Hey, Karen, we're ready for you. Shake a leg."

She stretched out one long leg and shook it. Then she put out her cigarette and stood up, the spangled costume over her arm.

"If she gets in touch with you, call me." I gave her one of my cards. She barely glanced at it before tucking it into the pocket of her kimono.

"See you in the movies." She tossed her mane of blond hair and strolled out of the lounge.

As I drove back to Oakland in the rain, I wondered about the difference between Vee's fragile Beth, in need of nurturing care, and Karen's Dizzy Lizzie, who manipulated the sympathy others felt for her. How did these versions of Elizabeth fit with Philip Foster's wife, Renee? Was I looking at different pieces of the puzzle, or three different personalities superimposed on the same woman?

I thought about the Willis family and how things had turned out. One child a murderer, another a porno actress, and the third a possible child abuser.

Would things have been different if Mark Willis hadn't shot his parents that night in Alameda? Maybe, maybe not. Something had to be terribly wrong in that family to make him pick up a gun. Random violence happens. But sometimes when you look at it long and hard, random violence isn't so random after all.

Eleven

I WENT BACK TO MY OFFICE AND PUT OUT SOME feelers to a former theatrical colleague, asking if she'd ever heard of a dance troupe called *Invitation*. She hadn't, but assured me she would ask around. That done, I picked up the phone and tried Mark Willis's work number in Cibola. This time he answered.

"Mark Willis." His voice was clipped, neutral.

"I'm trying to locate your sister Elizabeth."

"My sister?" His voice turned wary as he realized this wasn't a business call. Then the phone line crackled with tension. "Who is this? What the hell do you want?"

"Elizabeth is . . ." The receiver slammed down in my ear before I could get out the word "missing." I broke the connection and dialed again. This time the line buzzed with a busy signal. I suspected Mark Willis had taken the phone off the hook.

I tried to match the harsh voice with the pleasant, self-effacing boy I remembered from high school. That's what time and a prison sentence will do. But I wasn't the same teenager either. Mark Willis was touchy about his past. That meant I'd have to approach him indirectly, instead of coming right out with the reason for my visit to Cibola. I planned to drive up there tomorrow. It was too late in the day now. Besides, I was feeling guilty because I hadn't finished the work Cassie had requested. I spent the rest of the afternoon working on the background check. When I gave it to her I let her know I'd be out of town, so she could check on Abigail.

100

Saturday morning bits of blue sky peeked through clouds as I ate breakfast and read the newspaper. I left plenty of dry food and water for the cat, who looked huffy at the sight of my overnight bag. After filling my Toyota with gas I got on the freeway and headed east across the flat cropland of the broad San Joaquin Valley, toward the Sierra Nevada. The Bay Area and the valley were poised on the edge of spring, but as I climbed into the foothills it was the tail end of winter. I could see snow on the peaks to the east. The black oaks along the highway stretched bare branches toward a sky that became overcast, pale gray darkening to the east.

I stopped in Jackson for lunch, feeling a chill breeze blow through the twisting downtown streets. Over corn bread and lentil soup in a hole-in-the-wall café, I heard the waitress and a customer speculate on the possibility of snow. I sipped my coffee and watched Saturday shoppers scurrying along the sidewalk.

We used to visit Jackson when I was a kid. My Grandma Jerusha had a brother named Woodrow, an engineer at the Kennedy Mine. He lived in a log house on a back road north of town, as full of old mining equipment as his head was full of Gold Rush lore. Once he outfitted Brian and me in coveralls and miners' hats and took us down the shaft into that dark world where men dug for gold.

I finished my lunch and paid my tab. At a nearby bookstore I checked a book on California inns to see if there was a hotel in Cibola. It listed a bed-and-breakfast place called the Murdock House, its address simply Main Street.

I headed south on Highway 49, across the Mokelumne River and into Calaveras County. The two-lane ribbon of asphalt stretches north and south along the Mother Lode. Each town along its length is really two towns, superimposed on one another, one for the locals, who need groceries and hardware, and one for the tourists, who come on the weekends and in the summer seeking contact with California's rowdy Gold Rush past. The towns are a jumble of the nineteenth and twentieth centuries. Old hotels like the National in Jackson, the Leger in Mokelumne Hill and the City in

Columbia coexist with art galleries and restaurants. County historical museums full of Victoriana and mining equipment sit next to gift shops that sell T-shirts and ceramic doodads and dispense ice cream and soft drinks.

Cibola was like that, set in a picturesque little valley between Mokelumne Hill and San Andreas. The twentieth century was evident in the gas station and the supermarket on the highway, but when I turned off the highway I felt the presence of the past.

Main Street climbed a gentle hill, past a two-block business district and into a residential area. The street ended, forking into two smaller streets. At the base of this V I saw a sign swinging on a post, reading THE MURDOCK HOUSE— BED AND BREAKFAST—1857.

I parked on the street and carried my overnight bag down a sidewalk lined with gaslights. The house was a two-story Victorian, painted pale yellow with blue trim, surrounded by a hedge and a wide lawn of winter-brown grass. The bushes hugging the foundation had not yet budded, but I saw a crocus or two poking up from the flower bed.

Another sign directed me to a side porch, where a bell on the screen door tinkled musically as I stepped into a hallway and looked around. To my left I saw a small parlor that served as a lobby. A woman sat at a writing desk, streaks of gray in her short hair and large gold hoops in her pierced ears. She looked up as I entered.

Her name was Nancy Coulter and she liked to talk. As she checked me in she told me that during the summer I'd need a reservation for a Saturday night, but March was off-season. She and her husband had bought the place eleven years before, and they'd done most of the restoration themselves. The house was registered as a historical landmark, she said proudly.

She gave me a brief tour. The front parlor had a fireplace with a long mantel of creamy marble that held a Seth Thomas clock and two lush African violets in matching brass pots. Above the mantel hung a massive oil portrait in an ornate carved gilt frame, a stern-looking Victorian gentleman with gray in his black beard, his hand resting on his watch chain.

On either side of the fireplace were recessed floor-to-ceiling bookcases, painted white and filled with books. An old piano sat in an alcove next to the front door. In another corner I saw a game table with a deck of cards on it. A low shelf nearby held a collection of board games and a carved wooden chess set. An ivory moiré paper decorated the walls, and white lace curtains hung on the tall windows. Several comfortable-looking old sofas with high backs were grouped around the fireplace under a crystal chandelier that had been wired for electricity.

Mrs. Coulter led me back through the lobby to the kitchen and dining room, full of trestle tables and plain ladder-back chairs. "Breakfast is at nine," she said. "We have coffee set out at eight and all through the day. In the afternoons and evenings we have lemonade and cookies."

I followed her out the back door and past several cottages on a path made of worn red brick. She pointed out a small guest parking lot and the access road that led from the street. Beyond the parking lot I saw a white frame church with a yard full of gravestones.

Mrs. Coulter showed me to a second-floor room with a slanted roof, a window with flowered curtains, and a double bed covered with a colorful patchwork quilt. She told me the doors were locked at eleven P.M., and if I planned to be out later than that I should let her know so she could give me a key. I left my overnight bag in the room, then went outside and moved my car to the parking lot. When I returned to the inn, Nancy Coulter invited me to join her for a glass of sherry.

"This is very pleasant. The inn and the town." I sat down in an oak rocking chair. The sherry warmed me as I sipped it. I relaxed against the rocker's padded cushion, savoring the beauty of the room and the afternoon quiet of the little mountain town. I could almost forget that I was here for a reason other than a weekend's interlude.

"We love it here," Nancy Coulter said, seated on the rosewood sofa. "My husband and I are refugees from the city. We decided we wanted to run an inn. This place is a dream come true. Of course, inkeeping is very seasonal. We're always busy in the summer, though we've had more off-season business since *Sunset* magazine did an article on us last fall. But that's only the weekends, when people can get away. When the winter comes we generally have the place to ourselves during the week. The whole town's like that.''

"How do people survive financially?"

"After the tourists leave, you mean? A lot of people work at the sawmill up in Jackson. Or they have two or three jobs. My husband's an accountant. I substitute teach during the school year. So does the woman who runs the bookstore. The guy who has the framing shop also works as a handyman, fixing things, doing some carpentry on the side. Then spring comes and the season starts again. Business is starting to pick up now, but the busy time is between Memorial Day and Labor Day. What brings you up here?''

"Exploring the Gold Country," I said. "Right now I'd like to explore Cibola."

I thanked her for the sherry, carried my glass to the kitchen, and left the inn by the side door. As I walked through the front gate I heard water rushing over stones. I looked for the source. To my right I saw a bridge spanning a creek. The water ran down the hill, behind the buildings on Main Street, then through a little park. I saw a gazebo in the distance, looking like the top of a wedding cake.

Cibola on a Saturday afternoon in March didn't exactly bustle, but there were people entering and exiting the shops. Some of those businesses sought the tourist trade, selling ersatz miner's gear, postcards, and shot glasses with CIBOLA printed in gold letters. I strolled past a couple of gift shops and a bakery, then stopped to peer into the window of an antique store. Further down Main Street I passed a red brick building with "1859" carved into its cornerstone. A big wooden sign proclaimed the structure the Cibola Odd Fellows Hall, home of the town's historical museum.

Just past the museum there was a break in the line of buildings. A waist-high iron railing looked down on the little park, accessible from a staircase on my left. The Victorian gazebo stood on the opposite side of the creek. I saw an elderly couple sitting on the bench inside. I watched a couple of kids skylarking on the wooden footbridge, then I turned and crossed the street.

Just inside the door to a bookstore I saw a yellow Labrador retriever sprawled on the carpeted floor. She looked up at me, tail wagging, so I knelt and scratched her ears. The dog groaned and rolled onto her back for a belly scratch.

"You've made a friend." The woman at the counter was short, with a long, nut brown ponytail and wide green eyes behind her glasses. "Daisy loves to have her stomach scratched."

"I can see that." Daisy's head was thrown back and she looked as though she could remain in that position the rest of the day. I gave her one last tickle and stood up.

The frame shop was next to the bookstore. It was empty when I entered, though somewhere in the back I heard the beat of vintage Rolling Stones. I looked around me. One wall held a collection of paintings, from watercolor land-scapes to abstract oils. Beneath them stood several racks of unframed prints. The opposite wall was dominated by a large textile piece in vibrant primary colors, woven with yarn, rags, beads, and strips of leather. Under the wall hanging a long two-tiered shelf displayed an assortment of pottery and sculpture. Each item had a small card with the name of the artist, as did the wall hanging and the pictures on the walls.

A large wooden table at the rear held a telephone, but was otherwise bare. Samples of mats and molding hung on the wall behind the table, next to a door leading to what looked like a workroom. I circled the room slowly, then stopped to look at a serigraph of the Murdock House.

"That was done by a local artist," a voice behind me said. "She has a studio outside town."

I turned. A pair of electric blue eyes moved over me, giv-ing nothing, taking measure. He stood in the doorway at the back of the shop, a pack of Marlboros visible in the pocket of his red-and-yellow plaid shirt. A scar slashed down the left side of his face, from the corner of his eye to his mouth. It made him look like a pirate.

The same face had looked out at me from the yearbook, and across the stage in *You Can't Take It With You*. The same, yet different. We'd been teenagers then, and fifteen years had passed. Greasepaint and lines drawn on his face aged him for our theatricals. Now life had aged him for real, streaking gray through his dark hair, etching lines at his eyes and mouth. There was something else, despite his grin and the flirtatious glint in those blue eyes. Something dangerous, a knife edge honed by twelve years in prison.

"I like it." I pointed at the serigraph. "You did the framing?"

"Yes." He moved toward me, graceful in faded jeans and sneakers. He smelled faintly of smoke.

"Nice work."

"Framing is an art in itself." He gave the words a sardonic spin and laughed. "I read that someplace. Are you looking for anything in particular? Or just looking?"

"Just looking." My eyes were on him instead of the print and he knew it. "I'm sure you hear that a lot."

"All the time." He smiled and reached out to straighten a painting on the wall. "I have a few bread-and-butter customers. Everyone else is just looking."

"You're the handyman."

"That's me. I fix furnaces, mend wiring, replace broken windows, and build kitchen cabinets. Who are you?"

"Jeri Howard." I stuck out my hand. He took it. His own hand was calloused, though his touch was gentle. His grin was hard to resist.

"Hello, Jeri. I'm Mark Willis."

Twelve

"I'M IN THE MIDDLE OF SOMETHING BACK HERE," he said, releasing my hand. "Come talk to me."

I followed him through the doorway to his workroom. The music I heard came from a radio on top of a wooden cabinet. The Rolling Stones gave way to the Beatles as he reached to turn down the volume. A table, about six feet square, stood in the center of the room, pieces of a wooden frame scattered on its surface. All around me I saw a chaotic jumble: sheets of matting and lengths of frame stacked against the wall, another cabinet spilling tools, bits of debris on the wooden floor.

"When was the earthquake?" I asked.

"This is creative clutter."

"It looks more like a fire hazard."

"Very funny. There's some coffee on that table back there. Help yourself."

I stepped over a box filled with wood scraps and made my way to the rear wall, where a spindly-legged table stood next to an old white icebox and a deep stainless-steel sink. The table held a percolator and a tray with several ceramic mugs, three mismatched spoons, and a restaurant sugar container. I poured myself some coffee, then looked up at Mark Willis.

"How about you?"

He nodded. "Black." I poured a second mugful and carried it back to the worktable.

"Thanks," he said, taking it from me. He looked me over thoughtfully. I wondered if he remembered me from high school, but I saw no recognition in his eyes. "Are you here for the weekend?"

"Just tonight." I found a wooden stool of uncertain sturdiness and perched on it, my back against the wall. "I'm staying at the Murdock House."

"Exploring the Gold Country?" His hands fitted together the mitered corners of the frame, fastening them with glue and clamps.

"I've been up here before. My grandmother was from Jackson."

"A lively town. Livelier than Cibola. This is where you come for a restful weekend." He put the frame aside and took a sheet of paper from the drawers of the wooden cabinet. It was a watercolor landscape of a lake. He spread it on his worktable and placed several mat samples next to it, trying to pick up the blues in the watercolor. "Have dinner with me. You can tell me all about your grandmother."

"I don't even know you," I said, smiling behind my coffee mug. It wasn't entirely a lie. I'd never really known him.

"Sure you do. I just introduced myself."

"That's not what I mean."

"How will you get to know me if you don't have dinner with me?"

I hadn't counted on liking him so much. I had to ask him questions about his sister and the crime that put him in prison. I had to watch my step.

"All right. Dinner."

He smiled. "I'll pick you up at six-thirty."

"I didn't bring any dress-up clothes."

"This isn't a dress-up town."

He made me laugh as he told a yarn about the Cibola Volunteer Fire Department, then we were interrupted by a series of tourists, all of them just looking. I rinsed the coffee mug in the sink and left it on the table, telling Mark I'd see him later. I looked at my watch. I'd spent more than an hour with Mark Willis. He had told me about life in Cibola but nothing about himself. And I hadn't told him I was a private investigator looking for his sister—or that we'd encountered one another in a past life.

I walked back to the Murdock House. The gray sky had

darkened and the chill in the air increased. I helped myself to a glass of lemonade and went to the front parlor, where I rummaged through the shelves until I found a slender volume of Cibola history. I settled on the sofa and read for a while. A cinnamon-colored cat strolled into the room. She rubbed against my legs and jumped into my lap, positioning herself between me and the book. I gave up reading and stroked the cat, which is what she had in mind.

"She's not supposed to be in the main house," Mrs. Coulter said as she came into the room a moment later. "She thinks she owns the place."

"I don't mind. I like cats."

"She had kittens two months ago. Want one?"

"I have one. I don't think she'd take kindly to interlopers in her apartment."

"They're at the under-foot stage. I don't think I'll have any trouble finding homes for them. Say, if you're not doing anything there's a chili supper tonight at St. Anselm's Church."

"Thanks for the invitation, but I have a date."

"Really? Who with?"

"The man at the frame shop. Mark Willis."

"Mark's a nice man," she said, with a lift of her eyebrows. "Good-looking, too."

I nodded, wondering if she knew Mark Willis had done time for murder. She scooped up the cat and carried it away. I finished the book and my lemonade.

Upstairs, I changed my knitted pullover shirt for a coppery sweater that complemented my hair. At six-thirty I met Mark Willis on the side porch of the Murdock House. He too wore slacks and a sweater. His jacket was black leather, the kind with zippers and studs.

"Where are we going?" I asked as we went through the front gate onto Main Street.

"A place called Ballew's." It was on a cross street, past the block where Mark's shop was located, in a one-story Victorian cottage. The parlor and bedrooms had been converted to dining space, with oak tables covered by white cloths and mismatched wooden chairs. Each table held a crockery jar containing fresh

109

flowers. The tables in the front room were filled. A middle-aged woman with a blue apron over her dress greeted Mark by name and escorted us to a small square table in a room that had once obviously been a bedroom.

I scanned the selections on the menu. When the waitress returned, we ordered grilled trout for me, rack of lamb for Mark, and a bottle of rosé. During dinner I told him about my Grandma Jerusha, who left Jackson in the Twenties for Hollywood. She once had a small part in a deMille picture. Mostly she had a good time, until the Depression put a damper on things and she met my grandfather.

Mark listened and drank most of the rosé as I talked. Instead of loosening his tongue, the wine made him quiet. His blue eyes watched me, as though he were looking for something. It was disconcerting. Over coffee and dessert he pulled out his cigarettes, asking me first if I minded. I shook my head and he lit one, drawing in the smoke. He moved the ashtray close to him, taking pains to keep the stream of smoke away from me. I watched him watching me and I was fascinated.

I'd done most of the talking, I thought as I finished my coffee. He hadn't asked me what I did for a living, a natural question for one person getting acquainted with another. Maybe he wasn't curious, or he didn't care, or he figured I'd tell him. I would, after dinner. I had to.

When the check came we both reached for it. His hand was quicker than mine and he whisked the check out of my reach.

"It's on me. I invited you, remember?"

"I can't let you pay for my dinner, Mark."

"Why not?" He smiled, prepared to brush aside my objection.

"I'll explain it to you on the way back."

He studied my face for a long moment, then he ground out the cigarette in the ashtray at his elbow. "All right." He put the check down on the table so I could see it. I pulled some bills from my wallet to cover my portion and he did the same.

It was quiet outside, so quiet I could hear the gurgling of

Cibola Creek. We crossed Main Street to the gap in the buildings and stood at the railing, looking down on the little park. A pair of gas lamps on either side of the footbridge left pools of light in the deserted park.

"You were going to tell me something," he said. He stuck his hands in the pockets of his leather jacket.

"I came up here for a reason." I felt moisture in the air surrounding us. Then a tiny snowflake drifted down onto Mark's dark hair, lingering for an instant before it vanished.

He raised one eyebrow and his mouth curved in a tentative smile. "What reason?"

"Looking for Mark Willis."

His face hardened as the smile vanished. A pair of steel shutters dropped down in his blue eyes. The contrast was almost frightening. When he spoke again his voice had a chill that matched the night air.

"Why?"

"I'm a private investigator."

"You should have told me," he said harshly. "This afternoon in the shop."

"So you could get your guard up?"

"I like to know who I'm dealing with. Especially when I ask that person to dinner."

"I had dinner with you because I wanted to. It had nothing to do with business."

"How did you find me?"

"Your Aunt Vee told me where you lived."

"What do you want?"

"I'm looking for your sister Elizabeth."

"Betsy?" His eyebrows drew together and he stared at me. "Did you call the shop yesterday?"

"Yes. You hung up on me before I had a chance to tell you why."

"Tell me now."

"Elizabeth disappeared. Ten days ago. I thought she might contact you."

"I haven't seen Betsy in fifteen years. I don't understand. Why are you looking for her?"

"It's a long story and I'm cold." A few more snowflakes floated lazily in the air, glittering as they caught the light. I drew my jacket tighter around me. "I'd like to tell you if you'll listen. But I want some answers too."

"Suppose I don't have any to give?"

"Then I enjoyed having dinner with you."

I turned and started up the sidewalk. I'd gone about twenty feet when I heard him move behind me. He caught my arm. I stopped and faced him, meeting his cold eyes.

"That's quite an exit line," he said. "And it's having the desired effect. All right, Jeri Howard. That is your name, isn't it, or do you have another surprise to spring on me?"

"I'll show you my investigator's license."

"Save it. I'll make us some coffee. If you don't mind coming to my place."

Mark lived in a Victorian house that had been converted into flats. It was on the other side of Cibola Creek, past the Murdock House and the church I'd seen earlier. We went around the house to the back, where there was a staircase to the second floor. He unlocked his door and switched on the light, motioning me into a small living room.

"Have a seat," he said, walking to a kitchen separated from the living room by a counter. On this side of the counter was a small drop-leaf table with two chairs. Across from me, between the windows, a shelf held some stereo equipment and a television set. I took off my jacket and settled on one end of an old sofa upholstered in blue and brown. To my left I saw a tall narrow shelf jammed with books and a door leading to the bedroom.

"So talk," Mark said, his voice level as he scooped coffee grounds into an electric percolator. "What's Betsy done now?" He made it sound as if Betsy had done a few things in the past.

"She changed her name to Renee Mills and married a man from Los Gatos. His name's Philip Foster. They have an eighteen-month-old son named Jason. A week ago Wednesday she left the kid with her mother-in-law. She said she was

112

going shopping. Instead she went to the bank and cleaned out the joint account. She didn't come back."

I watched him as I spoke, looking for some reaction, but I didn't see one. He looked controlled, guarded, as he filled the percolator with water and plugged the cord into a wall outlet.

"Did Philip Foster go to the cops?" Mark asked, coming into the living room, a glass ashtray in one hand. He set it on the table, pulled out a chair, and sat down, lighting a cigarette.

I nodded. "Yes. Then he hired me. It's gotten complicated since then."

I stopped. Mark didn't react. His face was a mask as he drew in smoke and exhaled. The silence stretched as we listened to the percolator pump water through the coffee grounds. He stubbed out the cigarette, stood, and walked to the kitchen, filling two mugs with coffee.

"Black, right?" he said.

"Yes." I walked to the counter and took the mug he offered.

"What made you think I'd know where Betsy is?"

"Karen told me you and Elizabeth were close. She said Elizabeth might come to you if she were in trouble."

"Is she in trouble?"

"I think so." I sipped the strong black coffee.

"So Karen thinks I might know where Betsy is. Just out of curiosity, how did Karen turn out? Vee never mentions her."

"She makes porno movies."

His head went back and he laughed, the sound filling the small apartment. I watched him. He was amused, but there was something else behind the laughter.

"Interesting reaction," I said.

"If Karen wants to screw in front of a camera, it's her business. Somehow I find it appropriate."

"Why?"

"Karen's the cuckoo in the nest. She's not my father's child."

113

"Are you sure?"

"Even at the age of nine I could count." His mouth twisted. He stared past me at the wall. "My father was on a carrier out of San Diego when Karen was conceived. He managed to ignore the fact that she was born two months after he got back from a nine-month cruise."

"Who is her father? Or do you know?"

"I suggest you ask Joe Franklin. He and my mother were fucking each other regularly for years." His words were ugly, filled with contempt. They fell into the charged air between us and lay there glittering and dangerous, like a razor-sharp blade.

"Leo Mercer told me about the bruises."

He looked at me over his coffee mug and didn't say anything. He was wary, at bay behind the barrier of the counter.

"Betsy's husband didn't know any of this?"

"No. He was upset when I told him."

"But he wants you to keep looking."

"He fired me. He went back to Los Gatos."

"Why?"

"By the time I found out Renee was really Elizabeth, Philip's father showed up in Oakland. He was pressuring Philip to drop the whole thing, forget about his wife, and go home. He told Philip Elizabeth had been abusing their child."

Mark's hand tightened on the handle of his mug and some of the coffee sloshed out onto the counter. He stared down at it. Then he picked up a dishrag and mopped up the spill. The silence in the room grew and stretched between us.

"I don't want to talk about this anymore," he said finally.

"I need some answers, Mark."

"I don't have any."

"I think you do."

He shook his head. "No. Not tonight."

"When?"

"I don't know."

I set my coffee mug on the counter, buttoned my jacket, and crossed the small apartment to the front door. As I reached for the door handle, he spoke.

"Wait. I'll walk you back to the inn."

"You don't have to."

"I want to."

While we were inside, the drifting snowflakes had marshaled themselves into an orderly snowfall. Swirling white crystals crowded the air. Most of them melted into oblivion when they hit the ground, but some clung tenaciously to the grass and bushes outside Mark's apartment. We moved out of the range of the porch light into the darkness. I shivered, partly from the cold and partly from the emotions which left me unsettled.

"Why are you doing this?" Mark asked as we passed the churchyard, its gravestones silvered by snow.

"Vee wants me to find Elizabeth. And I'd like to hear her side of the story." We walked on in silence. When we reached the Murdock House I saw a light burning in the parlor and heard someone playing the piano.

"Besides . . ." I didn't finish. He stopped and turned to look at me, more questions on his face. "We've met before. Island High School. *You Can't Take It With You.* You were Mr. De Pinna. I was Essie."

He stared into my eyes. In the glow from a nearby streetlamp his somber face was light and shadow, the scar standing out in relief. "I thought you looked familiar," he said finally, his voice quiet. "But I don't remember things or people. I don't want to."

"Will you talk to me tomorrow?" I asked. "Or am I wasting my time?"

He didn't answer. Instead he pulled me close and put his mouth on mine. I tasted coffee and cigarettes, and my arms twined around his neck as I kissed him back.

"Maybe," he said, with just a hint of a smile. Then he stuck his hands into the pockets of his leather jacket and disappeared into the falling curtain of snow.

Thirteen

SUNDAY MORNING NANCY COULTER SERVED HER Murdock House guests an enormous breakfast: omelets with cheese, bacon, and vegetables, big enough to cover a plate and cut in wedges, accompanied by home fries and baskets full of blueberry muffins. On this off-season weekend the dining room was half full. I shared a table with two middle-aged sisters from Eureka and a divorced father from Los Angeles whose teenagers were on spring break. The kids, boy and girl, looked bored, but their father was full of Gold Country lore. The Angelenos planned to go north to Jackson and Sutter Creek, while the two sisters were headed south for Murphys and Angels Camp.

I listened to the buzz of conversation and ate too many muffins. Gradually the dining room emptied of people and the clean-up began, with two helpers ferrying dirty dishes to Nancy Coulter, who stacked them in the dishwasher. I reached for the insulated coffee pitcher and poured another cup, telling myself I would not eat the remaining muffin in the basket.

I hadn't slept well. It was too quiet up in the mountains for someone who was used to the city sounds of Oakland. But it was more than a strange bed in a strange town that kept me awake. The Willis case was fast becoming an obsession. I wanted to know what happened fifteen years ago and why. Mark Willis was the only person who could tell me, but he wouldn't answer my questions. Suppose I got my answers and I didn't like them? Was it better not to know?

There was an invisible line there. I wasn't sure I wanted to cross it.

I had to face something else. I was attracted to Mark Willis and that bothered me.

"Hi, Mark," I heard Mrs. Coulter say from the kitchen. "You hungry? I've got half an omelet here."

I looked up and saw Mark walk into the kitchen, dressed in blue jeans, a work shirt, and the leather jacket. He gave me a guarded smile.

"Sounds good. Thanks." Mrs. Coulter handed him a plate, a fork, and a mug. He carried the plate into the dining room and sat down next to me.

"Any coffee in that pitcher?" he asked.

"Sure." I handed it to him, along with the muffin basket. "Eat that muffin before I do."

"Saving you from yourself?" He broke the muffin apart and buttered it. Then he dug into the omelet and finished it before speaking. "I have some work to do at the shop. I talk better when my hands are busy."

Cibola on a Sunday morning was quiet and placid, its empty streets washed with sunlight and its air cool and clean. Remnants of last night's snowfall lingered in the shadows where the sun had not yet melted it. The town had an early-morning look about it, as though it had just gotten out of bed and was stretching before that first cup of coffee. The loudest noise was the peal of bells from St. Anselm's Church, and the only other people we saw on the street were an elderly man and his wife headed up the hill to Mass.

Neither Mark nor I spoke as we walked down Main Street. He unlocked the door to the frame shop, then locked it behind us, leaving the closed sign facing the street. I followed him back to his chilly workroom, where he switched on the light. His worktable was clean and bare, and the room looked as though he'd tidied it up before leaving last night. He reached under the table, pulled out an electric space heater, and plugged it into a wall outlet. Then he straightened and looked at me across the table, his hands on his hips.

"I have to explain something," he said. "I've worked

117

hard since I got out of prison, trying to be Joe Citizen. I support myself and I stay out of trouble. I've never had so much as a traffic ticket since the day I walked out of San Quentin. People up here accept me, even if they know who I am. I don't look back. I look forward. It's a balancing act. When the past comes up, it upsets my balance. I get defensive.''

"Do I upset your balance?''

The smile crept back onto his face. "Oh, yes. You do.''

I opened my purse and pulled out the five-by-seven photograph Philip Foster had given me, the picture of Mark's sister and her family in front of last year's Christmas tree.

"This is what she looks like now,'' I said, handing it to him.

Mark studied the photograph for a long moment. Then he set it on the table and pushed it toward me. He went to the cabinet against the wall and pulled out a sheet of art paper, a pen-and-ink drawing of a derelict old house. He placed it in the middle of his worktable and reached for his tape measure.

"None of us looked alike,'' he said, bent over the sketch. "I thought maybe it was because we had different fathers.''

"Did you?'' I put the picture back in my purse and perched on the stool, leaning against the wall.

"I don't know. I'm positive Karen's father is Joe Franklin. She looks like him, in the planes of her face. Besides, I know Franny was screwing Franklin. They were careful to keep it from Lenore, but they acted like I didn't have eyes or ears.'' He shook his head and laid several mat samples next to the sketch.

"I don't know about Betsy. I was only four when she was born. It wasn't until later I realized Franny was sleeping around. With anything in pants, every chance she got. Franny didn't like being married to George. But they had to get married, you see. I was born eight months after they hit the justice of the peace. She never let me forget it.''

"Franny resented you?''

"I'm not making excuses.'' Mark fixed me with a somber

118

gaze. "I never have. I'm just telling you so you'll understand about Betsy." He selected a charcoal gray mat and put the rest of the samples away. Then he went to a piece of equipment mounted on another table and carefully cut the mat.

"Home was hell," he said when he was finished. "I stayed away as much as possible."

"Did your parents beat you?" My words hung in the workroom like a malevolent presence. I saw his hands tighten on the mat cutter.

"George was away a lot," he said finally, his voice calm and steady. "When he was around his idea of discipline was to treat us kids like recruits. He used to punctuate his orders with a smack across the face. He used his belt too." He smiled at me but there was no humor in it.

"You see, Jeri, I was a wimp and a fuckup. I knew that because he told me repeatedly. I couldn't do anything right. So I quit trying. For him, anyway. I did things to suit myself."

"And your mother?"

"I hated her." He set the newly cut mat on the worktable. His bright blue eyes blazed, then turned to ice.

"She enjoyed it. She used to get this look on her face when she was hitting me, like she was having a goddamn orgasm. Sometimes she'd burn me with the butt of her cigarette. I'd break away, run and hide. When I was older I'd stay away and wouldn't come home. The last couple of years I spent a lot of nights sleeping at Leo's house."

"Why didn't you tell someone?"

"I did, once." Bitterness laced his voice. "When I was in junior high school. We were in San Diego then. The gym teacher asked me about some bruises on my arm. I told him Franny hit me. When he checked it out she told him I'd fallen down the stairs, that I was lying. He believed her. After that she was careful not to hit me where anyone would see the bruises. I just tried to stay out of her way as much as possible."

"What about Betsy and Karen? Did she hit them too?"

He shook his head. "No. When George was around he

119

would smack us indiscriminately. He even hit Franny now and then. But she left the girls alone. It was all directed at me. Until . . ." He stopped and bent over the picture he was framing. His jaw tightened. He seemed to vibrate like a wire.

"Until April?"

His head shot up. "What about April?"

"When I talked to Leo Mercer he said you started to get tense around April of that year, like something was bothering you."

He sighed. "Leo saw more than I thought. Maybe I should have confided in him. I don't know. Life's full of maybes and should haves. You can spend your whole life wondering about them."

"What happened in April?"

"Betsy turned fourteen in April. A few days after Betsy's birthday, Franny burned Betsy's arm with a cigarette. I figured it was a sign."

"What do you mean?"

"Betsy was a late bloomer," Mark said. "A skinny little kid. Then she changed overnight into this teenaged girl with hips and breasts. Franny started to pick on her."

"Competition?"

"Maybe. I think it was something else, though. I was going away to college. I got a scholarship to UC Davis. I even had a summer job lined up on campus." There was a wistful note in his voice as he considered the lost opportunity.

"God, I couldn't wait to get out of there. I was leaving the day after graduation. And I was never coming back. Of course that meant I wasn't going to be around to take all of Franny's shit. She knew it too. That's why she started in on Betsy. It was subtle at first—arguments, raised voices, a slap or two. Then Franny burned Betsy's arm. It left a little scar. Just like these."

Mark unbuttoned the cuffs of his work shirt and pushed up the sleeves. I saw several little circles of scar tissue on both forearms, just like the burn scar Philip Foster had described on his wife's left arm.

120

"When Franny burned Betsy I knew she'd picked another target," Mark continued, rebuttoning his cuffs. "I didn't know what to do. I started worrying, wondering how I could protect the girls."

"What made you think you could protect them when you couldn't protect yourself?"

Mark's eyes burned at me for a moment, and I knew I had touched a particularly sensitive nerve. Then his emotion cooled.

"I thought I could protect them by being there. By getting between her and them. But things just went downhill. George got passed over for promotion. He and Franny argued about it, so he stayed away, at work, or in the bar at the officers club."

He positioned the mat over the pen-and-ink sketch. "I saw what was going to happen. Franny would make Betsy her punching bag until Betsy was old enough to leave, then she'd start in on Karen. And George would just let it happen, like he had all along. I didn't know what to do."

"Is that why you killed them?"

He looked up from his work, his eyes boring into me. "Not many people ask me that question," he said softly.

"Do they get an answer?"

"No." His mouth hardened into a thin line. "Not even the psychiatrists who tried to dissect me got an answer."

"Do I get an answer?"

He moved to a rack against the wall and pulled out lengths of molding, placing one and then another against the sketch. He selected one and laid it on the table to measure it. When he spoke again his voice had steadied.

"I didn't plan it. It just happened. It happened so fast I couldn't stop it. I don't talk about it. To anyone. I told you more last night and just now than I've ever told anyone." His lips curved in a ghost of a smile. "But you're a good detective, Jeri. You just sit there, push buttons, and ask questions until you get answers."

"What happened that night?" I asked, still pushing buttons, probing for answers. Mark's face tightened and the shutters went down in his eyes. He slapped the tape measure against the table.

"You talked to the cop, didn't you? You read the newspaper articles. You know what happened."

"I know what the police found. And what the newspapers reported. I don't know what happened after you left Leo Mercer's house that Friday night, before the police arrived."

"There was an argument." His hands gripped the frame molding like a vise, his knuckles white. "They ended up dead."

"There's a large hole between that argument and murder," I said, probing harder. "What started the fight? How did it move from words to a gun?"

"Back off. Don't push me."

His voice hissed with barely contained fury. A vein throbbed at his temple and the scar showed white on his face. I said his name and his hands moved, snapping the molding he held. The crack of breaking wood echoed in the room.

His eyes had darkened with a kind of black undissipated anger, and his hands shook, each holding a jagged piece of wood. I saw that he was capable of murder. Most of us are, given the right—or wrong—set of circumstances.

I walked around the table, warming myself at the space heater. The glowing electric coils did little to cut the chill in the room. Mark looked at the broken molding in his hands, then he dropped it into a waste bin.

"I'm sorry," he said, his anger burning itself out, released in a sigh. The vein at his temple subsided.

"How did you end up here?"

"When I got out of prison, Vee said she'd set me up in business. All I had to was pick the place. I wanted to live in a small town, away from the city. A place where I could work with my hands and be accepted by my neighbors and not share my living space with another human being."

"Is that what you have?"

"I get by. I don't have a cellmate, but sometimes I get lonely. I frame pictures and work at odd jobs. It's enough to pay the rent on my shop and my apartment. I'm happy, Jeri. Whatever that means. As happy as I'll ever be in this life."

"Until I came along and disturbed your smooth little pond."

"I didn't say that."

"But it's true. I've upset your routine. Dredged up the past."

"If you hadn't, I wouldn't have met you."

"That's a mixed blessing," I said. "But it's beside the point. I came up here hoping to find your sister. I think I understand a little better why she disappeared. But I haven't found her. I guess I was wrong."

"How can I get in touch with you?" Mark asked. "Just in case you're not."

I took a card from my wallet and handed it to him. He read it before he slipped it into the breast pocket of his shirt.

"Maybe I'll call you anyway."

"I don't think that would be a good idea, Mark."

"Are you married? Involved with someone?" When I didn't answer, his mouth quirked in the same cheeky grin he'd thrown at me yesterday. "You like to ask questions, but you don't like to answer them."

"I'm divorced."

"So you have a few scars too."

"Yes," I admitted.

"Then I'll call you."

I looked into his blue eyes and wasn't sure how I felt. I liked him a lot more than I should. I was also wary of any involvement with him.

"Goodbye, Mark."

He leaned over and kissed me very gently on the mouth. Then his arms encircled me and his lips moved on mine. I slipped away from his embrace. "Goodbye, Jeri."

Cibola's streets were busier than they had been when Mark and I walked to the shop. I headed for the Murdock House. I should have been thinking about Elizabeth and the next step in my efforts to find her. Instead I was thinking about Mark Willis. I kept telling myself that this was a man who spent

123

twelve years in prison for murder, but that didn't stop what I felt when he kissed me. I was on dangerous ground, and I wasn't sure of my footing.

Fourteen

I DROVE BACK TO OAKLAND BY WAY OF STOCKTON, located on the Delta, that vast water system where the Sacramento River and the San Joaquin River join and mingle their waters before flowing into San Francisco Bay. Vee Burke had given me her parents' address and directions to the house. The Madison house, in the northern part of the city, near the University of the Pacific, was a one-story structure with an attached garage, maybe thirty years old, built of dark red brick with white trim. The street was Sunday-afternoon quiet as I parked my car and went up the walk. The dried remains of a funeral wreath still hung on the front door, a reminder that Lester Madison, Elizabeth's grandfather, had died last week.

The woman who answered the door looked a bit like Vee Burke. She had the same nose and chin, but her face was thinner. Where Vee's unruly hair flew out all over her head, this woman's gray hair was short. She wore a navy blue skirt and a plain white blouse. It looked like a uniform. A pair of wire-rimmed glasses rode her nose, magnifying her blue eyes.

"Alice Gray?"

"Yes?" She looked at me as though she'd been expecting someone else.

"I'm Jeri Howard, the private investigator working for your sister."

"Oh, yes. She called me. You want to talk about Beth. Please come in." Her voice sounded like a rusty hinge, suffering from disuse, contrasting with her neat schoolmarm exterior.

She stepped back from the door. The house was quiet, but it was an uneasy quiet, as though it were waiting for something to happen. Alice Gray glanced over her right shoulder, at the hallway that led to the bedrooms, and put a cautionary finger to her lips.

"Mother's taking a nap. I don't want to wake her."

"I understand."

I looked around me. The living room had a musty scent, as though it had been shut up too long and needed fresh air and sunlight. It was crowded with heavy dark mahogany furniture. A high-backed sofa sat in front of the fireplace, bracketed by end tables and matching wing chairs. The sofa and chairs were upholstered in a rough-textured brownish red fabric that reminded me of dried blood. The furniture looked out of place in this room, as though it belonged in another house, in another time. Several flower arrangements wilted and drooped on the mantel, on the end tables, and in the center of the low coffee table in front of the sofa.

"My father died," Alice Gray said. Her hands touched a bowl of spiky yellow chrysanthemums on the coffee table. Several petals dropped onto the shiny dark wood. She swept them into her hand and tossed them onto the ashes in the fireplace.

"I know. I'm sorry."

"We were expecting it. He'd had several strokes." She moved to the center of the room and turned to look at me. "Sit down, please. Would you like some coffee? I just made a fresh pot."

"Yes, thank you."

She walked through a doorway leading back to the dining room and kitchen. In her absence I examined the room. I didn't see any pictures, other than an amateurish oil landscape above the mantel and some floral watercolors scattered here and there in the living room and hall. Most people had family pictures, like those that crowded the mantel in the Franklins' house in Alameda. But there was nothing here to show any evidence of the Madison family. I saw a thick black-covered Bible and several pamphlets on one of the end tables. I picked one up and leafed through the pages. The fundamentalist text trumpeted doom and the impending end of the world.

Alice Gray returned with a lacquered Japanese tray bearing two steaming cups, a sugar bowl, and a little pitcher of milk. I took a seat on the sofa. The coffee was strong and bitter. I lightened it with some milk. My hostess settled into one of the wing chairs.

"Vee says Beth is missing," she said, sipping her coffee.

I nodded. "Elizabeth's husband, Philip Foster, hired me to find her. Then he changed his mind."

"Because of this story that Beth hit the child," Alice finished. "What nonsense. She wouldn't do something like that."

"Did you know she was using the name Renee Mills?"

Alice nodded. "Yes. As though a name mattered."

"Vee said she contacted Elizabeth about her grandfather's illness, but Elizabeth said she couldn't come to Stockton."

"Beth wouldn't come back here." She shook her head, a swift, economical movement. "Beth left Stockton at eighteen and never returned. She couldn't wait to get out of this town. She doesn't keep in touch with anyone except Vee, and maybe Karen."

"She lived with you for nearly two years in San Leandro, while she was going to Cal State. Why did she drop out of school?"

"Beth never stayed with anything very long." Alice's voice colored with disapproval. She took another sip of coffee. "She was interested in college for a while. Then it lost its appeal and she wanted to do something else. So she quit. It's happened before."

"How?"

"She was constantly starting things and not finishing them. Piano lessons while she was in high school. Sewing projects left to gather dust in the closet. Summer jobs that lasted midway through July. She dropped out of college. I suppose she's dropped out of her marriage now. I'm not surprised."

"Why?"

"You know how my sister and her husband died," Alice said grimly. "How do you suppose that would affect an impressionable fourteen-year-old girl? To have her parents shot down in cold blood while she was in the house." She clasped her hands tightly on her lap and leaned forward in her chair.

"It was horrible, appalling. I don't think any of us ever got over it. My parents were devastated. Beth was a very sensitive girl. She didn't rebound the way Karen did. Karen has always been very resilient. She was a very tough little girl."

She still is, I thought, recalling the very tough young woman I'd encountered Friday. Karen had presented me with a radically different view of her sister. Which eyewitness was closer to the truth?

"Beth was just entering those difficult adolescent years," Alice continued. "To have her parents taken from her so suddenly, so brutally . . . Vee and I tried to repair some of the damage by taking her to a psychologist. But after a while she wouldn't see him anymore. Another project she wouldn't finish." She stopped, looking pained.

"Did she like school?"

"She liked learning. But school was difficult for her. She was such a sensitive child, easily hurt, moody at times. She felt separated from her classmates. They didn't have her experiences to contend with, and they didn't understand. Children can be very cruel."

"I've read the newspaper accounts of the murders," I said. Alice flinched at the last word, as though the mention of murder still had the power to hurt after fifteen years. For a moment I felt as cruel as Elizabeth's long-ago classmates. "The articles don't give a complete picture of your sister's family. Tell me about George and Frances. Sketch them for me in more detail."

"I'm the oldest. Vee's in the middle. Frances was the

youngest. We called her Franny. I've always thought she was Dad's favorite. Mother—well, never mind Mother.''

She stopped talking for a moment, sipping the coffee, her face softened by memory. Then she spoke again.

"Franny was very pretty, always a little more independent than the rest of us. After high school Franny went to college at San Francisco State. That's where she met George. As I recall, they met at a reception on campus.''

My eyebrows went up slightly. Lenore Franklin had told me Franny met George in a bar in San Francisco. I wondered if Franny had sanitized the story of their meeting for family consumption.

"He'd just gotten out of flight school in Florida," Alice continued. "They had a short courtship and got married several months later. They eloped, actually. Dad was disappointed at first. Franny was so young, and Dad wanted her to finish school.''

"George didn't have any family?''

"Just an uncle who was active in state politics. When George decided he wanted to go to the Naval Academy, this uncle helped him get an appointment. George's mother died when he was quite young. His father was a farmer in the Florida panhandle. He died of cancer while George was in flight school.''

"Were George and Frances happy?''

"Every marriage has its ups and downs." She shrugged, tilting her head to one side. "I suppose they had the same joys and problems as any other couple.''

Was Alice an astute observer or one who looked through the haze of memory? "How often did you see them?'' I asked.

"Not as often as I would have liked. Navy families move around so much. They were in and out of San Diego, Pearl Harbor, Guam, even the Philippines. When they were transferred to Alameda we were delighted, with Vee in Piedmont, me in San Leandro, and Stockton an hour's drive from the Bay Area. Still, we didn't get together that often. I'm sorry now that we didn't.''

129

I heard a noise behind me. Alice Gray shifted rapidly from bittersweet memories to strained concern. I turned and saw a heavyset elderly woman. Her wrinkled black dress looked as though she had slept in it. Below her uncombed white hair she had a mulish jowly face that radiated anger and distrust at people in general. She gave me a long measuring look full of suspicion.

"Mother." Alice jumped to her feet. "I thought you were lying down."

"Heard talk." The old woman came slowly into the room, her feet sliding in a pair of too-large bedroom slippers. "About the girls. Where's the girls?"

"They're not here."

Alice seized the old woman's arm, trying to coax her out of the room. Mrs. Madison wouldn't be coaxed. She shook off Alice's hand and walked around the end table to the wing chair, one hand gripping the chair back for support. She took the seat Alice had vacated, fixing me with her watery blue eyes.

"You're not one of the girls," she challenged.

"No, Mrs. Madison." I wasn't sure if she meant her daughters or her granddaughters. Alice and I had discussed both. "I'm Jeri."

Mrs. Madison harrumphed and gave me a thorough once-over. She focused on my head and glared at me.

"Red hair," she said, pronouncing judgment. "Sign of the devil."

"Mother!" Pained, resigned embarrassment crossed Alice's face. She plucked her mother's rumpled black sleeve. Mrs. Madison ignored her and leaned toward me, so close that I backed away in reflex.

"Are you saved?" she demanded.

"I'm not sure," I said politely.

"Get right with the Lord or He will smite you." She shook her finger in my face.

"Mother, please go back to your room," Alice said. The phone jangled in the kitchen, adding to her exasperation. "Damn. I'll be right back."

130

She hurried toward the ringing phone, leaving me alone with Mrs. Madison, who was concerned about the effect of my red hair on my soul. On first glance I decided the old woman wasn't wrapped very tightly, but after the second, I thought I saw a shrewd glimmer in the blue eyes.

"Have you seen Beth? Or Karen?" I asked, giving her stare for stare.

"Yellow-haired witch," Mrs. Madison said, as though we were chatting about the weather. A flinty smile creased her bulldog face. "Prying, pawing, sniffing around. She's evil, and the Lord will strike her down. Just like Franny. Franny was evil and the Lord struck her down. We'll all go to hell unless we come to Jesus."

"I expect you're right."

She hadn't answered my question. Or had she? Karen had yellow hair, I thought, recalling her platinum mane. But so did Elizabeth. The old woman had switched from singular to plural. I couldn't tell if she was including both grand-daughters, along with her daughter Franny, in her pro-nouncement of perdition. Certainly Karen's job in the skin trade made her a candidate for her grandmother's version of hell, if Grandma knew about it. But I wondered if Grandma's opinion of poor sensitive Beth was more in line with Karen's view than those of Beth's aunts.

I took Elizabeth's picture from my handbag, the photo-graph of Philip Foster with his wife and child in front of the Christmas tree. I held it out so Mrs. Madison could see it.

"Have you seen her?" I asked again. The old woman peered at the photograph and grinned at me.

"Yellow-haired witches," she said. "Both of them."

I tucked the photo back in my bag. This old woman with her talk of yellow-haired witches wasn't exactly a credible witness. I didn't think her memory was reliable back further than a few days, if it was reliable at all. But her words in-trigued me. Had Karen or Elizabeth paid a call on Grandma Madison recently? Neither of them had actually attended their grandfather's funeral. But had one of them come to Stockton,

131

prying, pawing and sniffing around, unknown and unseen by anyone except her grandmother?

"Mother," Alice said, returning from the kitchen. "That was Mrs. Nevins. Remember Mrs. Nevins? She's coming over to see you. She'll be here in half an hour. Don't you want to change your dress?"

The old woman laughed, a delighted cackle. Alice succeeded in pulling Mrs. Madison to her feet and steering her toward the hallway. She was gone a few moments, evidently to help the old woman change.

"I am sorry," Alice said when she returned to the living room, her mouth a tight line. She slumped into the chair and put a hand to her face. "Mother's gotten worse since Dad died. She's eighty-five and sometimes she's not quite lucid. She's getting . . ." She couldn't bring herself to say the word *senile*.

"Some people take comfort in religion."

"Comfort?" Her laugh was bitter. She shot a poisonous look at the Bible and pamphlets on the end table. Her mouth twisted in a humorless smile.

"Mother was never particularly religious until Franny and George were killed. Then she fell prey to this charlatan who calls himself Reverend Jarvis. He's got some sort of off-brand church. I don't even think the fundamentalists would claim it. Jarvis got his hooks into Mother shortly after the murders, and she became almost impossible to live with. She did some rather peculiar things."

"Karen mentioned birthday parties."

"She remembers that?" Alice got up. She stood by the fireplace. Suddenly words poured from her, words she hadn't said to anyone in a long time.

"Mother did celebrate Franny's birthday for a couple of years. She'd buy a present and bake a cake. She made Karen and Elizabeth come to the party. Dad put a stop to it as soon as he found out." She grimaced and shook her head, embarrassed by the revelation.

"This wasn't the best environment for those girls. After the murders I thought they needed to get away from the Bay

132

Area, away from all the memories. But Stockton wasn't the right place. Mother and Dad weren't the right people to raise a couple of teenagers. The end result was that both girls couldn't wait to get away from here. Elizabeth left when she started college. Karen couldn't even stick it out until she was eighteen. She showed up on Vee's doorstep when she was sixteen and finished school in Oakland.''

"Karen said your mother thought God was punishing the family for a variety of sins.''

"That line is courtesy of Reverend Jarvis,'' Alice said, the minister's name a bad taste in her mouth. "God, I loathe the man. He's used a family tragedy to prey on a grief-stricken woman for fifteen years. While Dad's health was good, he managed to keep Jarvis at bay. Left alone, Mother would have given that leech more money than she already has.''

Her once-calm look turned to one of bitter frustration. She punched her fist into the palm of her other hand, as though it were Jarvis's face.

"When Dad had his first stroke about two years ago, I retired from teaching, gave up my apartment in San Leandro, and moved back here to look after things. I've been doing battle with Jarvis since then. He doesn't like me much. I'm sure he tells Mother I'm evil. These days she thinks everyone is evil.'' She stopped talking, then sighed. "I'm really running on, aren't I?''

"It sounds like you need to talk.''

"I do. Usually I call Vee to unload. Vee's the rock of this family. Nothing fazes her. But you came all the way to Stockton looking for Beth. Instead you've found a sick old woman who's lost her grip on reality. Sometimes I think I'm losing it too.''

"I've been to Cibola,'' I said. She looked at me curiously. "To see your nephew, Mark.'' A spasm crossed her face. "Vee told me he lived there. Didn't you know?'' She shook her head. The anger that fueled her words a moment ago was gone. In its place I saw fatigue.

"I don't want to know. I can't bear to think of Mark. He was such a sweet little boy. If I think of him at all, that's how

133

I try to remember him. I know Vee keeps in touch. But I can't forgive him. He killed my sister and her husband. How could he do that to his own parents? To all of us?"

I couldn't answer her questions. Nobody could.

As Alice and I said goodbye on the front porch, she looked over my shoulder and her face froze. Then the anger came back, animating it.

I followed the direction of her gaze and saw a portly middle-aged man in brown slacks and a plaid sports coat getting out of a sedan parked at the curb. He came up the sidewalk, his round face creased in a broad smile. I didn't need an introduction. Alice's eyes stared through Reverend Jarvis like a pair of lasers.

"Hello, Mrs. Gray," he chirruped. "Is Sister Sarah up and about?"

"She's sleeping," Alice said, standing squarely in front of the door. I left her to conduct the next skirmish in her ongoing battle.

Fifteen

"YOU DON'T LOOK LIKE YOU'VE MISSED ANY meals," I told Abigail, who was scolding me for leaving her alone all weekend. Cassie had kept the cat's food and water dishes full while I was gone. Nevertheless, I was treated to the full repertoire of querulous meows as I unpacked my overnight bag. The performance didn't stop until I picked up the cat and fussed over her. I carried her to the living room and stretched out on the sofa, my feet up and the cat on my stomach.

The rain had started as I drove back from Stockton, thinking about Elizabeth Willis. I felt a certain kinship with her. I had toyed with acting as she had with dance, before settling into a more secure job to pay the rent. And I'd bailed out of a marriage, though my leaving Sid wasn't as abrupt as Elizabeth's disappearing act. Why had she left so suddenly? Was it Philip, her in-laws, a lover, her past? Was the accusation of child abuse leveled against her true?

With Abigail purring on my lap I stared at the wall, seeing Mark in his shop this morning, rolling up his sleeves to show me the old burn scars, as he accused his mother of putting them there. Then I saw Philip Foster's anguished eyes as he repeated his father's accusation that Elizabeth had hurt the couple's son. Child abuse had two faces, both of them ugly. Why was I ready to believe Mark's story, yet unwilling to credit the same behavior to Elizabeth?

In both cases the accused was not present to defend herself. And my feelings about Mark were getting in the way.

I was restless. I put on a raincoat with a hood and went

135

for a walk down the hill to Lake Merritt. Despite the weather I saw joggers wearing out their Nikes on the paved path circling the lake, passing strollers with raincoats and umbrellas. I walked around the lake. I didn't think about the case, my life, or the world in general. I just put one foot in front of the other and walked, watching people and dogs and ducks, getting soaked as the rain increased in intensity.

By the time I completed my circuit of the lake it was nearly dark. The Necklace of Lights around the lake's perimeter brightened the path, the continuous string of electric bulbs reflected in the rain-pocked surface of the water. I stood for a moment looking at the glow, then I hiked back up Adams Street to my apartment.

After a hot shower I put on my butt-sprung cranberry sweats, went to the kitchen, and opened the refrigerator door. The contents didn't look promising. Sometime soon I had to make a trip to the grocery store. I pulled leftovers from the refrigerator and threw out those that had turned an interesting shade of green. I concocted a stir-fry from the remaining vegetables, listening to a David Sanborn album as I ate. Then I put the record away and assumed my favorite prone position on the sofa in front of the television set, cat on my stomach. I watched a tape of Spencer Tracy in *Bad Day at Black Rock*.

Spencer had better luck in one day than I had all weekend.

Monday morning I got on Interstate 880 and headed south. When I left Oakland the East Bay was wrapped in a cool gray mist that hinted at more rain. As I reached San Jose, the fog had burned off and the sun glimmered off the mirrored windows of office buildings along the freeway. Past San Jose the wooded coastal mountains rose, separating the Santa Clara Valley from the ocean to the west. Los Gatos nestled on the eastern slope.

I left the freeway and went looking for Philip Foster's house. I found it on a street of comfortable-looking suburban homes with kids' bikes on green lawns and station wagons in driveways. Philip's yard looked untended, and there was no one home. He must be staying with his parents.

136

Foster Senior lived about five miles away at the end of a cul-de-sac, further up the hills and the housing scale. The two-story stucco house, white with dark blue trim, wasn't exactly a mansion, but it sprawled, and there was a gardener out front grooming a hedge. I parked on the street. On my right a long driveway led to a detached double garage, with a brown Mercedes standing in front of the closed doors.

I nodded to the gardener and went up the center walk and the wide shallow steps of the porch. The doorbell sounded deep in the house. After a moment or so the door opened and I saw a young woman in a maid's uniform, her long black hair braided down her back.

"Is Mrs. Foster here?"

"She is in the back," she said, her voice flavored by a Spanish accent. "Who shall I say?"

I gave her my name and she shut the door. The woman who opened it next was athletic looking, in her late fifties, with short silvery blond hair. She wore a white tennis dress over the brown leathery skin of someone who spends a lot of time in the sun. Her face reminded me of Philip, but the set of her mouth was pure Edward.

"I know who you are," she said. "You're that private investigator from Oakland. What are you doing here?"

"I'd like to talk with you."

"There's nothing to say."

"I think there is."

"My son fired you."

"Your husband fired me."

"I heard how you talked to Edward," she said, glaring at me.

"Stood up to him, you mean."

Mrs. Foster arched one eyebrow, then she laughed, her head tilted to one side. "Stood up to him, did you? Are you standing up to me?"

"If it will get me some conversation."

"Go on, Helen," a voice said. A younger woman stepped from a doorway at the back of the entry hall. "What could it hurt?"

137

Mrs. Foster considered this for a moment. Then she motioned me inside. "All right. I'll give you a few minutes."

I followed Mrs. Foster through the back of the house and out onto a redwood deck. Once outside I inspected the other woman, a slender brunette in a lilac-colored jumpsuit, sandals on her feet. Her toenails and fingernails were painted the same frosty lavender as her eyeshadow and lipstick. Color-coordinated all the way. She saw me looking her over and smiled, smoothing her long dark hair.

"I'm Sandra Baines," she said. "A friend of the family."

The deck held a barbecue grill, a round white metal table, and an assortment of matching chairs, padded with blue cushions. Ms. Baines and Mrs. Foster had been sharing a pitcher of iced tea. They didn't offer me any. Mrs. Foster moved a tennis racquet off one of the chairs and indicated I could sit down. We regarded each other over the table.

"It's your nickel," Mrs. Foster said.

"Your son wants to find his wife."

"Not anymore he doesn't."

"I think he does. Your husband talked him into dropping the case. He told him Renee had been abusing the child. Is that true? Or did your husband cook it up to get Philip to come home?"

Mrs. Foster's mouth tightened in her tanned face. "You've got a lot of gall, young woman."

"Yes, I do. I also have another client, one who wants me to find your daughter-in-law. I need to know if your husband's story is true."

"You don't believe it?"

"Let's just say I'd like to verify it."

I heard a high-pitched burst of chatter above me and looked up. On the second-floor balcony I saw a towheaded toddler running with the awkward waddle of a kid with a diaper and training pants under his bright red shorts. He was wearing a yellow shirt, so all I could see were his chubby arms and legs. The young maid laughed and pretended to chase him, calling to him in Spanish. The little boy giggled and ran back and forth, dodging her.

138

"Let me take a look at him," I said.

"Let you examine my grandson? Why? To see if he's bruised, like a piece of fruit at the grocery store?"

It was true. Rational or not, I wanted to see tangible evidence that Elizabeth had abused the child. But it had been nearly two weeks since she disappeared.

"I'm sure the bruises have faded by now," I said, "*if* there were any to start with." Helen Foster's lips compressed into a tight line. "I'm curious about something, though. You didn't see any bruises on your grandson until after his mother left. I find that hard to believe. Philip made it sound like she's been hitting the kid regularly since he was born. How is it that no one noticed this until after your daughter-in-law disappeared? Until you and your husband decided it was good riddance to Renee?"

Helen Foster came out of her chair looking as though she'd like to whack me with her tennis racquet. "I've had enough. Get out."

"Has she been abusing him? Prove it. I'll go back and relay that information to my client."

"I don't have to prove anything to you," she shouted. "Get out. Or I'll throw you out myself."

Sandra Baines stood up. She put a hand on Mrs. Foster's arm. "Helen, please. Ms. Howard is leaving. I'll walk her out myself."

Mrs. Foster gave me a final poisonous glare and stalked into the house. "It's true," Sandra said. "Jason had a bruise on his back. I saw it."

"And I'm supposed to take your word for it?"

"I guess you'll have to." She took a pack of Virginia Slims and a gold-plated lighter from the pocket of her jumpsuit. "Who's your client?"

"I can't tell you that."

"See. We all have our secrets."

"What's yours, Ms. Baines?"

She took a drag on her filter tip and exhaled a stream of smoke. "Let's walk up the driveway. I think Helen would have a stroke if you went back through the house."

139

I followed her down the steps to a gate that led to the garage and driveway. She stopped and leaned against the Mercedes.

"Philip and I went to school together, years ago," she said.

"High school sweethearts?"

"He was my date for the senior prom, but the sweethearts part didn't happen until later, in college. Helen always thought we'd get married."

"But you didn't."

Sandra shook her head. "I married someone else. Had a baby, got divorced. Moved back to Los Gatos with my daughter. She's seven."

"Are you maintaining old friendships with the Fosters?" I asked. "Or checking out your options in case Philip turns out to be free?"

"What a way you have of putting things, Ms. Howard." She puffed on her cigarette in silence, then she spoke.

"I've known Philip since we were kids. He's kind of dull, but that's fine with me. My ex-husband was exciting and he turned out to be a creep. At least with Philip I know what I'm getting."

Yeah, I thought. Helen and Edward and the family fortune.

"Philip needs someone who can act as a buffer between him and his parents," she continued, "someone who can get along with them. Now that you've met both of them I'm sure you understand why. Renee isn't that person. Helen and Edward have never really liked her, and she doesn't like them. Oh, everyone's polite, for Philip's sake, but there's no warmth behind the courtesy. Now they're angry with Renee, since they found out she's been hitting their grandchild. They dote on that little boy."

"*If* she's been hitting their grandchild."

Sandra smiled. She took one last drag on her filter tip and dropped it to the concrete, grinding it out with her heel. She put her hands into the pockets of her jumpsuit.

"I think she has. Renee's very moody, you know. Swings

140

from high to low and back again. Sometimes I wonder if she uses drugs. It's all academic anyway. Renee's not coming back.''

"You seem very sure of that."

"I'll tell you why. She's been having an affair with someone she worked with, at the computer place in Sunnyvale. It's obvious she's run away with him."

I chewed on this piece of information for a moment. "How do you know that?''

"I saw Renee with him, in a bar, several months ago. An attractive man, with blond hair and wide shoulders. I made a few inquiries. His name's Dean Bellarus.''

"What were you planning to do with this little item?"

"I hadn't decided yet," Sandra said. "Then Renee left and I didn't have to do anything. You don't believe me? Ask that girlfriend of hers, the one who works at the same place. Tasha Something-or-other.''

No wonder Philip Foster was such a wimp, I thought as I drove out of the Los Gatos hills into the flatland of the Silicon Valley. I'd never seen a better matched set of vampire parents than Edward and Helen Foster. They had removed whatever backbone he'd had years ago.

Sleek little Sandra wouldn't be much better if she proceeded with her plan to replace Renee as Philip's wife. She struck me as a vampire too, a sneaky underhanded one. For a moment I didn't blame Elizabeth for bailing out of her marriage.

When he hired me, Philip said his wife didn't have any friends. After hearing how that sounded, he'd amended his statement, mentioning one of Elizabeth's co-workers, Tasha Loring. I located the computer firm in a business park off Highway 237 in Sunnyvale, a jumble of glass and concrete buildings that looked raw and new, surrounded by a parking lot and open fields.

It was the sort of place where I needed an identification badge clipped to my lapel to get past the receptionist. But I didn't have the requisite I.D. and I didn't want to explain myself to a lot of people, so I waited on the sidewalk in front of the double glass doors. It was nearly eleven-thirty. Maybe I could catch Tasha Loring as she went to lunch.

A few minutes later I saw a mobile lunch wagon pull into the parking lot. I walked over and bought a soda from the woman in the back of the truck, who went back to preparing sandwiches. The driver was a short bantam rooster of a man with broken capillaries in his nose and a cigarette hanging out one side of his mouth.

He liked to talk, so I let him. The mobile lunch business was his, and it was sure as hell a gold mine, what with all these businesses going in out here, away from the main corridor of Silicon Valley firms along Highway 101, away from restaurants and with no cafeteria for the employees. He assured me he knew a lot of people on sight. He lit a new cigarette from his first and flipped away the butt.

"You know Tasha Loring?"

"Who wants to know?" He tilted his head with a cagy look. "You a process server or something?"

"Me? No. She's got a car for sale. She said to meet her here at work, but I don't know what she looks like."

"Yeah, I know who she is. I seen her name on her badge. A real looker. If she comes this way, maybe I can point her out to you. Hey, Emma!" he called to the woman in the truck. "Look sharp. Here they come."

People began to trickle out of the buildings, some toward their cars and some toward the lunch wagon. I could smell grease as hamburgers hit the grill. The voluble driver chatted with the customers, greeting some of them by name. I moved away from the truck, surreptitiously checking I.D. badges as people passed.

Three women went past me. As they queued at the lunch wagon, I heard the driver say loudly, "Hey, Tasha, you still playing racquetball?" I didn't hear the woman's reply, but I turned to see the driver look at me then jerk his chin toward one of the women, a tall blonde in a lemon yellow shirt and green slacks. I mixed into the crowd around the truck and watched as she bought a chicken salad on whole wheat and a bottle of mineral water.

142

"Tasha Loring?" I asked as she turned to walk back toward the building. A quick glance at her badge confirmed her identity. The driver had called her a looker, but I thought she was rather horse-faced, with a long jaw and an equally long nose set above her wide red lips. Her yellow hair was piled in careful disarray atop her head. Over her shoulder I saw the driver examining her rear end in the tight green pants, leaving no doubt as to which part of her anatomy he found attractive.

"Can I ask you some questions?"

"About what?" Her hazel eyes looked at me curiously. She twisted the cap off her mineral water and raised the bottle to her lips.

"Renee Foster."

"I haven't seen Renee in a while."

"How long ago?"

"What business is it of yours?" she asked. "Who are you anyway?"

"I'm a private investigator."

She narrowed her eyes. "Do you have some I.D.? So I'll know you're who you say you are?" I pulled out my wallet and showed her my license. She peered at it for a moment, then lifted her eyes to my face. "OK. I guess you're for real. But why do you want to talk about Renee?"

"She's missing."

"Missing?" The hazel eyes widened in shock. "You mean gone? Disappeared?"

"That's what I mean."

"Oh, my God." She clutched her lunch to her chest. A parade of emotions marched across her face. "She wouldn't . . ."

"She wouldn't what?" I shifted position so that I was between Tasha Loring and the building. She knew something and she was going to tell me what it was.

"What about the baby?" she asked me, brows shooting up over her anxious eyes.

"Renee left the baby with her mother-in-law a week ago Wednesday. She hasn't been seen since."

"Oh, my God. I gotta sit down." Tasha looked around us, then turned and headed for a bench sheltered by an inadequate tree.

"When's the last time you saw her?" I asked.

"Four or five weeks ago." Tasha's right hand went to her earlobe and she tugged on her yellow enamel earring. "We had a drink after work."

"What did you talk about? Did she say anything about leaving?"

She shook her head, but her face took on a guilty cast, and she looked down at the sandwich on her lap. She unwrapped it and took a bite of chicken salad, chewing slowly.

"Tell me."

"I don't know if I should," she said, swallowing. "I don't want to cause trouble."

"She's already in trouble. And I don't mean with her husband. I have to find her."

Tasha chased her mouthful with a swallow of mineral water. "Renee was seeing someone," she said finally. "Someone from here at work."

"You mean recently?" I sat down next to her. "She hadn't worked here since before her baby was born."

"They started dating when Renee came to work here. It's been one of those on-again, off-again relationships. They'd fight and see other people, then get back together. I think she married Philip on the rebound."

Which is a terrible thing to do to anyone as earnest as Philip Foster, I thought, seeing the soft brown eyes of my former client. It's hell to love someone who doesn't love you back.

"When did she start up the relationship again?"

"When the baby was about a year old. I told her, you're crazy. You've got a nice husband, a beautiful kid. What do you want to blow it for? She said it just wasn't working."

"Did she say why?" I asked.

Tasha shook her head. "No. I met Philip a couple of times when she was still working here. He seemed like a nice person, but I didn't think they had much in common. Renee liked to go out, have a good time. Philip's a real stay-at-home."

"Did she say anything about her in-laws?"

"Plenty. They didn't like her, and the feeling was mutual. She said once they didn't think she was good enough for Philip."

"Renee's boyfriend—who is he?"

"A guy in marketing. He travels a lot."

"What's his name?"

"Dean Bellarus," Tasha said. The same name Sandra Baines had given me.

I stood up and looked toward the building. "Where can I find him? Is he here today?"

"No," Tasha said, shaking her head. "He's on vacation. For two weeks."

That meant Renee's disappearance coincided with Bellarus's vacation. Maybe Sandra was right. Maybe Renee had run away with her lover. That would make this easier to explain, no matter how mundane. It would also mean I was wrong about a few things. "When is he due back at work?"

"I don't know."

"Do you know where he lives?"

"No," she said, shaking her head. I pressed her further, but Tasha Loring insisted she didn't know anything more than what she'd just told me, and she wasn't willing to find out. When her friends called to her she jumped quickly to her feet, eager to get away from me and my questions. Before she left I gave her my card. I was sure she would dispose of it as soon as she got into the building.

Sixteen

I SPOTTED A PHONE BOOTH AT ONE END OF THE business park and walked over to it. Thumbing through the pages, I found two listings under Bellarus, one with the initial D and no address. The phone number was a Mountain View exchange, but there was no answer.

I'd made note of Norman Gerrity's address from the letterhead on his report to Philip Foster. Gerrity's office was in a building in downtown San Jose, a couple of blocks from police headquarters. I suspected his was a solo practice, and I was right. When I opened the door I saw a man in his late fifties seated at a desk, writing on a lined yellow pad.

"You said if I was ever down this way you'd buy me a brew."

"You're Howard?" He stood up and grasped my hand in a firm grip. "I'll do better than that. How about lunch?"

Gerrity turned on his answering machine and held open the office door. He was a solidly built man with a broad bulldog face and a nose that looked like it had been broken a couple of times. Gray hair curled on his head and his thick forearms and at the open neck of his short-sleeved knit shirt. After he locked the office we walked down the stairs and across the street to a restaurant with dark red vinyl booths and friendly middle-aged waitresses.

"Best burgers in town," Gerrity said, ordering a bacon cheeseburger, medium rare. I took his word and ordered the same.

"You look like a retired cop," I said after the waitress brought us each a cold Budweiser.

146

"It shows, huh? Yeah. Boston—twenty-five years."

"How'd you end up here?"

"My daughter married a guy from San Jose. My wife and I used to come out to visit. We liked the weather. When I retired a few years back, we decided we'd had our last Boston winter and we moved out here. Believe me, I don't miss that snow shovel. Only I got bored with retirement. So I got a license and a gun permit, and now I'm a P.I. My grandkids think it's great. My wife and daughter think I'm crazy."

"My mother feels the same way." I gave him a brief history of how I got into the investigative business. The waitress brought our food, and I doctored my burger with ketchup, mustard, and relish.

"This isn't a social call, Howard," Gerrity said, spreading ketchup liberally over his fries. "We've traded our bona fides. Now tell me what's on your mind."

I took a bite of my burger and wiped my hands and mouth with a napkin.

"The Foster case. I got fired."

"Ha," Gerrity said. "I'm not surprised. The old man show up?"

"Oh, yes. He's one-of-a-kind. He told Philip that Renee's been abusing the kid. So Philip decided to pack it in and come home."

"Child abuse. Damn, I hate that. Used to see a lot of it when I was a cop. That could explain Old Man Foster's attitude. I know how I'd feel if I found out someone was hitting my grandkids. There'd be hell to pay." He picked up his burger and took a bite, chasing it with beer. "But you're still on the case. Otherwise you wouldn't be down here."

"I have another client. Renee's aunt. She doesn't buy the child-abuse story."

"Do you?"

"I don't know. In the past few days I've found out a few things about Renee that make this look like more than a routine missing-persons case." I gave Gerrity a rundown of the Willis murders and the evidence of family violence in that household.

147

"I went to see Helen Foster this morning. She's taking care of Philip's little boy, but she wouldn't let me near enough to see if he had any marks on him. There was another woman there, a friend of the family named Sandra Baines. She told me Renee had a boyfriend, and one of Renee's co-workers confirmed it."

"Bellarus," Gerrity said.

"How'd you know about him?"

He grinned and took a swallow of beer. "Maybe I'm just an old male chauvinist. I gotta tell you my first thought was that young Mrs. Foster took off with another guy. So I nosed around that place she worked. Somebody mentioned his name."

"Was this before or after you were fired?"

"After."

"Didn't you tell me on the phone you were glad to be off this case?" I asked. "Because your gut did a tap dance on this one."

"Yeah," he admitted. "But I don't like being canned, especially by the likes of Edward Foster. Guess you could say it wounded my professional pride."

I nodded. "That's how I felt."

"I did a little background check on old Ed, by the way. He's got a reputation as a cutthroat businessman. He's also a real nut on privacy. Couple of years ago he got verbal with a photographer from the *Mercury-News* who tried to take pictures of Foster and his wife at some charity ball. Threatened the guy. Philip's his only child."

"Something tells me Philip hasn't turned out quite the way Dad hoped." I finished my burger and wiped my hands on a napkin. "Did you come up with an address for Bellarus?"

"Monte Vista Apartments in Mountain View, a couple of miles west of Highway 101." He gave me the street address and apartment number. "I went by there several times, but I came up against a blank wall. He's not there."

"According to Renee's friend, Bellarus went on vacation about the same time Renee disappeared."

148

"Sounds more and more like she left with him," Gerrity said.

"I'm not so sure. Thanks for the address. I'll check out Bellarus's apartment and see if any of his neighbors have seen him."

Gerrity insisted on paying for lunch. I told him next time we got together I'd buy. Leaving downtown San Jose, I drove north on the freeway to Mountain View. I found Bellarus's apartment complex, a collection of two-story buildings grouped around a swimming pool and clubhouse, with an office facing the street. I circled through the parking lot that surrounded the complex, looking at the numbers on the curbs. Bellarus's space was empty. I pulled into an unmarked space near a dumpster and got out of my car.

Shrubbery and palm trees masked the rectangular wood buildings. A concrete sidewalk led to the front of Bellarus's unit. Each building contained four apartments, two up and two down. The lower apartments had enclosed patios, and those above had balconies. The mailbox for 303 had a strip of white adhesive tape lettered in black ink, reading D. H. BELLARUS, and nothing inside. Either he'd stopped mail delivery while on vacation or he'd picked it up recently—nobody in this life escapes junk mail.

I found 303 on the second level and rang the bell. No answer. I peered over the railing of the balcony in front of 303. I saw a couple of folding lawn chairs and a small barbecue grill. Several houseplants in green plastic containers sat on the balcony's wooden surface next to a watering can, with water seeping out the bottom, darkening the wood. The curtains covering the sliding glass door that led from the apartment to the balcony were open, and I saw a stack of envelopes and magazines on a coffee table in front of the sofa.

Bellarus must be home from vacation, I thought as I went back down the stairs, or he'd left his key with someone who fetched his mail and watered his plants. There was an oil spot on the concrete in the middle of his parking space. I knelt and touched it. My hand came away smeared with black. The oil was fresh.

Back in my car I wiped the oil from my fingers and waited. Forty-seven minutes later a silver Datsun 280Z with a sputtering engine drove slowly through the parking lot and made a left turn into the space numbered 303. The driver got out and opened the rear hatch. He tucked a six-pack of beer under one arm, then scooped up several bulging plastic sacks of groceries and headed for the front of the building, leaving the hatch open. When he came back for a second load I was standing between him and his car.

"Dean Bellarus?"

"Yeah?"

I could see why Elizabeth had been attracted to him. He was tall, deeply tanned, and muscular, his body displayed by a sleeveless yellow athletic shirt and green shorts, a pair of leather sandals on his feet. His shaggy blond hair had been bleached pale gold by the sun, and a mat of darker gold hair covered his deep chest and his legs. The beginning of a beard partly obscured the lower half of his face. Above it his eyes were light blue. Right now he looked past me at the groceries in his car as though his ice cream was melting.

"I'd like to talk to you about Elizabeth Willis."

"Who's Elizabeth Willis?" Either he didn't know Renee's real name or he was a good actor. I decided his lack of knowledge was genuine.

"Renee Mills Foster, then."

"What about her?" Bellarus's face tightened and he stepped past me to the car.

"She's missing." I moved to one side so I could watch his face. "Since a week ago last Wednesday."

"Shit," he said.

He reached for another grocery sack. A head of lettuce escaped the sack's confines and rolled across the carpet-covered surface of the car's hatch. He retrieved it and jammed it back into the sack, all the while avoiding my eyes. With plastic sacks hanging from both arms and a gallon jug of milk in his left hand, he turned and headed for the sidewalk.

"Have you seen her?"

"What makes you think I've seen her?" He tossed the words over his shoulder. I followed him up the stairs and into the apartment, where he dumped the sacks on the kitchen counter.

"I understand you and Renee have been good friends for a long time."

"Who the hell are you?" He glared at me, then opened the refrigerator. He jockeyed the six-pack of beer and the jug of milk into place on the top shelf, then reached into sacks and shoved the perishables haphazardly onto the remaining shelves.

"I'm a private investigator."

"Yeah?"

I took my wallet from my purse, flipped it open to my license, and held it out, my elbow resting on the counter separating the kitchen from the living room. Bellarus looked at the license, then turned back to his groceries, not saying anything.

"Satisfied?" I put away my wallet. Then I took a seat on one of the bar stools on the living-room side of the counter.

"I don't know where she is," Bellarus said abruptly.

"Someone at work thought she might be with you." I leaned forward, propping my arms on the pale brown Formica surface of the counter.

"No way, lady." He shut the refrigerator door, shaking his head, and opened the cabinets, shoving in canned goods and boxes of cereal and crackers. "I've been in Ensenada for a week and a half, deep-sea fishing, sailing, and drinking beer. Just me and three other guys."

"Can you prove it?"

Bellarus shot me an exasperated look. He stalked out of the kitchen through a door that led to the bedroom. A moment later he returned, tossing a handful of papers onto the counter in front of me. While he put away the rest of his groceries I sifted through the papers. The folder on top contained a used airline ticket issued to Dean H. Bellarus, roundtrip. San Jose to San Diego, leaving twelve days ago, returning yesterday. The other items were tourist brochures and credit car receipts from restaurants and ships in Ensenada.

"That doesn't mean Renee wasn't with you."

"We sailed for Baja the day I got to San Diego," Bellarus said, sounding exasperated. "We stayed on my friend's boat. His name's Greg McCardle. He lives in Chula Vista and he's in the book."

"I believe you." I stacked the papers into a pile and pushed them to one side. Bellarus and his friends left for Mexico the same day Elizabeth Renee Willis disappeared. Another dead end, I thought. "When was the last time you saw her?"

"I saw her the night before I left, Tuesday."

"Did anything happen between you two? Argument, something like that?"

Bellarus shut the cabinet door with a bang. "Look, did her old man hire you to get something on us?"

"He hired me because she left the baby with her mother-in-law and vanished. As far as I know, he doesn't know you exist, much less that you've been having an affair with his wife. Come on, Bellarus. If you know anything that could help me find her, talk."

He frowned and scratched his fresh growth of beard as he took a bottle of beer from the refrigerator and uncapped it. Then he kicked off his leather sandals and sprawled on his brown-and-yellow sofa, one foot propped on the coffee table next to his unopened mail. He stared at the wooden shelves that held his television and sound system.

"How did you meet her?" I asked.

"At work. I've been with the same company for eleven years. She got a secretary's job there, about six years ago." He sighed. "There was this spark between us."

Renee would have been about twenty-three when she met Bellarus. His words filled in some of the gap between the time she lived as Elizabeth Willis with the musician in the Haight and her marriage to Philip Foster. Some of the gap, but not all.

"What happened when you saw her Tuesday?"

"Something was going on," he said finally, after a long pull from the beer bottle. "I don't know what."

"What do you mean?"

"She seemed really edgy."

"Why? Did she say anything about her relationship with Philip or her in-laws? Did she say anything about her baby?"

"Oh, hell." Bellarus put both feet on the floor and hunched forward, leaning his arms on his knees. "She said she'd had enough. Her marriage was down the tubes. She wanted to leave Philip. She wanted to blow this place and go someplace else."

"And what did you say?"

"I told her she was crazy. I've got a good job, a good life. I'm not going to screw it up for her."

"Why not?" I left the bar stool and crossed the living room to the glass doors that led to the balcony. "You must have felt something for her."

"Shit." He set the beer bottle on the coffee table, got up and paced, his bearded face furrowed with a frown and his blue eyes refusing to meet mine. "You ever do cocaine? Renee's like cocaine. Seductive. Exhilarating. When I'm with her I want her more and more. Sex was incredible. We'd spend a whole weekend in that bedroom, screwing and drinking."

"Does she drink a lot?" I asked, thinking of Franny Willis.

"Sometimes," Bellarus said reluctantly. "She isn't an alcoholic or anything like that. She just likes to get high. Booze, mostly, maybe a little pot. We had some good times."

"But not all the time?"

"No." He shook his head. "Coming down from the high was a bitch. Jekyll and Hyde. Manic-depressive. It's been like that ever since I met her. When I first knew her, we'd break up, get back together, break up again. Once we had a screaming fight. I almost hit her. It was like she wanted me to. She was egging me on. I walked away from it, though." He sighed heavily.

"She said she never wanted to see me again. I started

dating another lady. Next thing I know she's flashing a wedding ring at me. That poor son-of-a-bitch Philip. I'll bet he didn't know what hit him.''

He does now, I thought. "So marriage and motherhood didn't work out. And she came back to you."

"About six, eight months ago," Bellarus said. He stopped walking and reached for his beer. "I was between ladies. Renee showed up here one night after work. About three seconds later we were in bed. I tried, but I couldn't get her out of my system."

"But you don't want to run away with her."

"Stay with Renee on a permanent basis?" He looked at me as if I'd lost my mind. "Are you kidding? I'd be burned out. She does that to people."

He sounded like the moth blaming the flame for the attraction that burns, unable to admit his own complicity in the relationship. I left the glass doors and stood in front of him.

"Did Renee ever say anything about her family?"

"As far as I know, she didn't have any. She said something about her parents being dead."

"No sisters, brothers, aunts and uncles, cousins?"

Bellarus shook his head. "None that I know of."

"How about friends?"

He thought about it for a moment. I expected him to echo her husband's words that first day I met him. Philip Foster told me then Renee didn't have any friends. I thought I knew why. Everything I'd found out about her so far indicated that she viewed men as conquests and women as competitors. That kind of woman doesn't have friends. But Bellarus surprised me.

"Yeah. She had a friend. This lady in San Francisco. They talked on the phone a lot. Renee would go up and spend the weekend with her. This other lady came down here once, a few years ago. A tall, foxy blonde. Her name was Karen."

"Karen Willis?" I leaned forward.

"Yeah. I think that was the name. Willis. Isn't that the name you said earlier, downstairs by the car?"

I ignored his question, my mind digesting this new piece

of information. When I talked to Karen, she said she hadn't seen her sister in years. She told me she didn't know Elizabeth had changed her name to Renee.

I wondered what else Karen hadn't told me.

Seventeen

THE INSURANCE COMPANY WHERE PHILIP AND ED-
ward Foster worked was located in a steel and concrete tower
near Interstate 280, its mirrored glass windows reflecting the
afternoon sun. I checked the directory near the elevators and
caught the next car to the tenth floor. The reception area was
a small rectangle with pale green carpet and several dark
green chairs around a low mahogany table.

A set of double glass doors led to the inner sanctum. They
were guarded by a woman at an L-shaped counter, presiding
over a large switchboard. A tiny headset with a microphone
was perched on her impeccably coiffed gray hair, and she
wore a green silk dress that matched the chairs. Though she
was seated she managed to look down her nose at me.

"Do you have an appointment?" Her eyes flicked over my
khaki pants, red shirt, and low-heeled walking shoes. Her
tone implied that Philip ordinarily got a better class of visitor.

"Just tell him Jeri Howard is here."

She called Philip's office, announced my presence, and
listened while someone on the other end talked.

"He's in a meeting," she said imperiously, expecting me
to disappear.

"I'll wait."

A table to the receptionist's left held a coffee urn and some
cups. I poured a cupful and planted myself in a chair directly
opposite the receptionist, so she wouldn't forget I was there.
Someone had left a copy of the San Jose *Mercury-News* on
an end table. I picked it up and opened it, the pages rustling.

The receptionist gazed at me with disapproval. A couple of middle-aged men in business suits walked into the reception area. She favored them with a warm, solicitous smile.

When I finished reading the newspaper I asked the receptionist to call Philip's office again. He was still in a meeting. I had some more coffee and waited another ten minutes.

"He's still unavailable," the receptionist said after a whispered conversation with her headset.

I leaned over the counter and she drew back as though I might bite. "Tell him I'm not leaving. You got that?"

She got it. I half-expected to see the firm's security staff appear to hustle the crazy woman out of the building. But Philip himself appeared, looking pale in his blue pin-striped suit, with deep shadows under his brown eyes. He held open one of the glass doors and motioned me into the hallway.

"You have to sign in," the receptionist called to my departing back. "You have to wear a visitor's badge."

Philip didn't say anything as he led me through a maze of offices, cubicles, and work stations to a conference room with a large oval table. He shut the door and turned to me.

"My mother called. She said you'd been to the house. I thought you might show up. I've been waiting for you."

"I thought you were in a meeting.'

"I was. Whether you believe it or not."

"You're back at work," I said, a barb in the words. "Business as usual."

Philip winced. "What do you want?"

"I want to find Renee."

"You're not working for me anymore."

"I have another client."

"Who is it?" I didn't answer. "Why did you go see my mother?"

"I wanted to find out if it's true that your wife's been hitting your kid. Your mother wouldn't let me see him."

"Of course it's true. Do you think my parents would make up a story like that?"

"I think they'd do anything to break up your marriage. Including lie." I folded my arms and leaned against the con-

157

ference table. "I'm a professional skeptic, Philip. I need to see some hard physical evidence of abuse before I'll believe it."

"And then what?"

"I'll keep looking for Renee."

He looked as though he were holding back tears. "Leave it alone. Leave me alone. It's over."

"I can't. I want to find her almost as much as you do."

"I don't want to see her again," he said tonelessly, but the longing in his eyes told another story. Elizabeth had the same addictive effect on Philip as she had on Dean Bellarus.

"I think you do."

"No," he said. Then quiet bitterness filled his voice. "Did you talk to her lover?"

"You know about Bellarus," I said. "Who told you? Your friend Sandra?"

"Renee told me."

His words said everything there was to know about Elizabeth's relationship with her husband. The more I found out about her the less I liked her. But I didn't want to stop looking. I was hooked just as badly as Philip and Bellarus.

"How long have you known?" I asked Philip.

"Months. We were having an argument. She blurted it out. I was hurt." He took a deep shaky breath, looking like a man who'd been kicked in the stomach. "But I could deal with it. I put up with a lot from Renee. I'd do anything to keep her."

"Anything? So you looked the other way while she had an affair?"

"I was afraid she'd leave," he cried.

"She left anyway." What else had Philip ignored? If it was true that Renee had abused the child, had he tolerated that behavior too?

"Did she run away with him?" Philip asked, the pain of his obsession in his eyes.

"No. He hasn't seen her."

"If you find her will you tell me where she is?"

I shook my head. "You're not my client anymore. You fired me, remember?"

"I want her back."

"Why? So you can punish her for leaving?"

"I want things the way they were before."

"Your wife was sleeping with another man and you want to resume the status quo?"

"You don't understand."

"You're right, I don't."

"Oh, Christ," he said, his voice ragged. He looked ragged too, a man skating on the edge of a cliff, ready to go over. He balled his fists and came at me, as though he wanted to hit someone and I was the closest target. I stepped out of his way. He walked to the conference-room window and leaned his head against the glass. Then he banged his fists against the window, again and again, until I was afraid he'd break the glass.

"Stop it." I grabbed his arms. He shook me off. I seized his wrists and dragged him away from the window. I pulled one of the chairs away from the conference table and shoved him into it.

The conference-room door opened. I looked up and saw Edward Foster's hard brown eyes in a face twisted with fury. Two men stood behind him. Building security, I thought. They had that look.

"What are you doing here?" Edward demanded. Despite his rage his voice was even, businesslike.

"I came to see your son."

"You also went to see my wife. I understand you have another client. Who is it?"

"That's my business."

"Oh, no." Edward stepped into the room. "When you invade my home, my office, my privacy, when you harass my family, that's my business. I want you out of here. I want you off this case."

I straightened and put my hands on my hips, giving him stare for stare. "I don't threaten easily, Mr. Foster. And I'm on this case until it's finished."

159

"If you're not out of this building in five minutes, I'll have you arrested." He jerked his head in the direction of the two men who accompanied him.

I glanced at Philip, slumped in the chair, his elbows on the conference table, his head in his hands. "Goodbye," I said. He didn't respond. I walked past Edward to the door. One of the men stayed in front of me and the other at my rear as they escorted me out of the insurance-company offices.

The South Bay sunshine didn't last as I drove north on U.S. 101 toward San Francisco. Gray clouds scudded across the sky and it began to rain. My windshield wipers beat a slow whooshing pulse. Once I reached the city I got off the freeway and drove to the South of Market movie studio where I'd interviewed Karen Willis on Friday. Once inside I scoured the halls looking for Karen, but no one on or off the set had seen her. I retraced my steps to Wardrobe, where Lila stood over her worktable, dressed in a scarlet sweater and black denim jeans.

"What do you want?" she barked, glancing at me.

"My name's Jeri Howard. I'm a private investigator. I was here Friday, talking to Karen Willis. Do you know where she is?"

"I'm not her goddamn social secretary," Lila said as she picked up a pair of scissors and attacked a length of peach-colored gauze. "Beyer fired her ass."

"Who's Beyer? Why did he fire her?"

"He's the director and he's pissed. Karen didn't show up for work Saturday. He has to reshoot all her scenes with another girl."

Damn. She's bolted. "What about her boyfriend?"

"Rick Petrakis? He's gone too. They left the hotel Friday night," Lila said, referring to the place where the cast and crew were quartered. "No one's seen them since."

"Where's the hotel?"

"The Cockroach Arms? Near Ninth and Folsom. If you plan to get anything out of the desk clerk, bring money."

"Do you know where Petrakis lives?"

"What am I, Information?" Lila waved the scissors at me in exasperation. "He lives somewhere in the East Bay."

"I need to talk to Karen. If you see her—"

"I'm not likely to," Lila interrupted.

"If you see her or find out where she is, call me."

I gave Lila my card. She muttered something I took to be grudging consent and stuck the card in her pocket. I left the studio and headed for the hotel. It took twenty bucks to pry open the desk clerk's thin-lipped mouth. Karen Willis and Rick Petrakis had checked out late Friday night, and they were in a hurry.

Now Karen had pulled a disappearing act. She'd lied to me about her relationship with Elizabeth. She must have known I'd locate Bellarus and learn she was lying. Why? What was she hiding?

I got on the freeway again, now clogged with afternoon rush hour traffic, and headed across the Bay Bridge to Berkeley, contemplating a little illegal entry at Karen Willis's apartment. The rain had stopped and the sun was playing peek-a-boo games with the clouds. I parked down the block from the apartment house and watched it for a few minutes before walking down the driveway to the back of the house. I took the stairs up to the deck. The door leading to the second-floor corridor was unlocked. I stepped inside. Music played in one of the first-floor apartments, but I didn't hear anything from apartment D, Karen's neighbor. I reached for the set of picks in my purse.

A door opened and shut below me. I froze as I heard someone coming up the stairs. Then I went out the back door onto the deck just as Karen stepped into the hallway, followed by the dark-haired man I'd seen with her at the studio. She unlocked her apartment door and they both went inside.

I was going to have the opportunity to talk to Karen after all. Back inside the building, I put my ear to the wall and listened. I heard Karen and her boyfriend moving around, talking, though I couldn't make out the words.

I rapped sharply on the door of apartment C. Sound and movement ceased. I knocked again.

"I know you're in there, Karen."

The boyfriend opened the door. Over his shoulder I saw Karen, jamming clothes into a suitcase. She looked up, a strange, almost frightened look on her face. I couldn't tell if she didn't recognize me or if she was expecting someone else.

"It's you," she said finally. "The private eye." She zipped the suitcase shut.

"You lied to me when you said you hadn't seen Elizabeth in years. You knew she changed her name. Dean Bellarus says the two of you visited back and forth all the time."

A slow smile spread over Karen's face. "So I left a few things out. Big deal."

"What else did you leave out, Karen? And where are you going?"

"Look, Ms. Detective, Rick and I don't have time to stand around here and chat with you. We're supposed to be at work. I just came to get a few things."

She started for the door but I blocked her way, my hand on her arm.

"I talked to Lila. She said Beyer fired you when you didn't show up for work. Why did you leave the hotel?"

"None of your damn business." She pulled her arm away, dislodging my hand. "Why'd you come over here anyway? To pick my lock and search my apartment?" She jerked her chin at Rick. "Let's get out of here."

I reached for her arm again. She swung the suitcase at me, then shoved me hard, out of the door of her apartment and against the wall. The obliging Rick shut the apartment door and blocked me, his knee connecting with my leg, his elbows pushing against my stomach.

Over his shoulder I saw Karen at the back door. I struggled with Rick, who blocked me like a football player. He pushed me back toward the stairs until my foot hit air instead of floor. I fell, noisily and painfully, onto the landing halfway between floors. I scrambled to my feet and took the remaining stairs two at a time, ignoring my body's protests and the startled occupants of the first-floor apartments who'd opened their doors to investigate. As I ran out the front door I saw Karen's white BMW streak away from the curb.

I limped back to my car before any of Karen's neighbors called the cops. I drove back to Oakland, telling myself that the ache in my back would feel better after a hot bath. There were no customers in Granny's Attic, and Vee Burke sat at her desk drinking tea, the old Yorkie in the basket at her feet.

"Jeri," she said, smiling when she saw me. Wearing a high-necked ivory lace blouse and a long black skirt, she looked as comfortably rumpled as she had the first day I'd seen her. "Have you made any progress? Did you talk to Karen?"

"Not so far. And yes, I talked to Karen. Why didn't you tell me what she does?"

"My niece the porn star?" Vee colored, then shook her head. "It's not the sort of information one broadcasts. I keep hoping she'll realize she's being exploited by those sleaze merchants and get out. But I think she likes taking her clothes off in front of a camera."

"She says it pays well."

"That may be," Vee said, "but Karen doesn't hold on to money very long. She spends until she's overextended. She's always asking me for loans. She does pay me back, though, I'll give her that. Did she say anything about Beth?"

"Karen says she hasn't seen her sister in years. But she's lying. I talked to someone else who told me Karen and Elizabeth visited each other frequently."

"I don't know," Vee said. "Karen never talks about her relationship with Beth. Karen doesn't talk much at all."

"Did either Karen or Elizabeth know that Mark lives in Cibola?" I asked.

"I may have mentioned it," Vee said. "Did you talk to him?"

"I went to Cibola and Stockton this weekend. Neither Mark nor Alice have seen Elizabeth." I refused an offer of tea and stepped behind the counter, taking a seat on the old sofa. "Vee, I went down to Los Gatos today. I saw Philip and his mother. Philip's mother wouldn't let me see the little

163

boy, except at a distance. I don't know if Elizabeth actually hit him, or if it's a story her in-laws cooked up.''

"Of course it's a lie. It's despicable," she said, a frown tightening her mouth. "Can they hate her that much?''

"It's more complicated than that.''

She fingered a cameo brooch at the neck of her blouse as I gave her an account of my conversation with Helen Foster. Then I told her what Sandra Baines had told me.

"An affair? Is it true?''

"One of her co-workers verified it. Then I located the man." I told Vee what Bellarus had said about his relationship with Elizabeth. "He says they fought and he left the next day for a vacation in Mexico. I believe him.''

"What about Philip?" Vee sat with her hands folded in her lap, looking past me at a quilt displayed on the wall.

"Philip knew about Elizabeth's affair with Bellarus. He told me he put up with it because he didn't want to lose his wife.''

Vee winced. She didn't say anything for a moment, and I watched an array of emotions flow across her face. Then she composed herself and straightened in her chair. "I want you to keep looking. She's in trouble. Her family is all she has left. Surely she'll contact one of us.''

I was doubtful that Elizabeth would surface that easily, but I nodded. "I'll do my best. Vee, tell me about their mother, your sister Franny.''

Vee looked startled, then troubled. "What do you want to know?''

"Other people I've talked to have told me things about her.''

"Lawrence Kinney, you mean.''

"You must know that when he took Mark's case he looked into the possibility that your sister and brother-in-law had been abusing the children.''

"Lawrence had his theories," Vee said. The look on her face told me the memory was as painful now as it had been fifteen years ago. "None of them held water.''

"Someone else told me your sister drank.''

164

"No more than anyone else I know. I never saw her drunk, if that's what you mean."

I didn't think Vee would tell me if she had. "Did Franny and George have a good marriage?"

"They moved around so much, because George was in the Navy. I know that was hard on Franny. But she never said anything to me one way or the other."

"Did you sense anything?" I said, probing further.

"I don't like talking about such things."

"I know you don't. But I can't help you unless you're honest with me."

"I am being honest with you. As honest as I know how. I can only tell you what I know, Jeri. In spite of Lawrence's theories, I don't believe that my sister would hurt her children, any more than I can believe Beth would strike hers." Vee's fingers tugged at the cameo brooch.

"Franny was impatient with the children sometimes. But I never saw her hit them. I know she had a busy social life that included a lot of parties. If she drank a bit more than she should have now and then, it wouldn't surprise me. She always seemed to be in control."

Vee stood up, ending the conversation. I didn't think she was lying. She was telling me what she knew, colored by her own feelings and beliefs. I felt like a cop interviewing eyewitnesses to a car accident. Everyone had a different version of the truth.

Eighteen

WHEN I CAME OUT OF THE STAIRWELL, A MAN IN blue jeans, his hands stuck into the pockets of a leather jacket, was leaning against the wall outside my office. It was Mark Willis. I saw the corner of his mouth lift in a smile at my amazement.

"What are you doing here?"

"Someone tried to kill me last night. I thought you might be interested."

I stared at him for a moment, digesting his words. Then I unlocked the door and motioned him inside. The answering machine's light blinked red, reminding me I had messages. I switched it off.

"Tell me what happened." I took off my coat and hung it on the rack. Mark remained standing, his fingers playing with the zipper tab of his leather jacket.

"I had dinner with Virginia Newton," he said, "the woman who owns the bookstore next to my shop. We went to Salty's Café on Main Street. Then I walked her home. She lives up on the county road, where it intersects with the highway. It's about a quarter mile north of town. We talked on her porch for a bit, then I left. When I stepped out into the road this car came out of nowhere, hauling ass and heading straight for me. I jumped out of the way. The car kept going, through the stop sign and north toward Jackson."

"What kind of car?"

He shook his head. "Late model, I think. I'm not sure about the color. It was dark. Virginia's porch light doesn't reach out to the road."

"Could it just have been a reckless driver?"

"It didn't look like a reckless driver." He frowned at me. "Don't you believe me?"

"I didn't say that. Did you report it?"

"Yes, to the town constable. He doesn't believe me either."

"Did Virginia see all of this? What does she say?"

"She thinks the driver must have been drunk."

I leaned back in my chair and studied him. "It's a long drive from Cibola. You could have called."

"I wanted to see you. To see if you believe me." He looked at me intently, his bright blue eyes boring into mine. "I know how it sounds. I don't have any proof. Do you believe me?"

I couldn't answer his question. Not now. "Who would want to kill you?"

"I have no idea." He paced restlessly at the side of my desk. "I thought about it all the way down here. I came up blank."

"Is there anyone in Cibola that you don't get along with?"

He shook his head. "It's a friendly little town. I get along with everyone."

"What about San Quentin?"

"San Quentin." Mark stopped pacing and his fingers went to the scar that marred the left side of his face. His eyes turned bleak. "I try to forget San Quentin. The things that happened there. The things I had to do to survive. Of course it's hard to forget, when I look in the mirror every morning and see this."

"How did you get it?"

"One of the other inmates tried to rape me," he said matter-of-factly. "I fought back. He pulled a shiv and cut me. I picked up a chair and knocked him cold."

"Would he come after you? Would his friends?"

"That was seven years ago. He's dead. Somebody else cut his throat. I've been out of prison for three years, Jeri. If somebody I knew in the joint wanted to kill me, why wait until now?"

"So it took a while to find you."

"Maybe. But it doesn't make any sense." He slumped into one of the chairs in front of my desk.

"None of this does."

I had an idea, plucking at the back of my mind like an ignored child. But I had to consider it further before I mentioned it to Mark.

"I want to talk to Virginia," I said, picking up a pencil. "What's her number?"

He gave me her home number as well as that of her shop. "Have dinner with me," he said.

"I have work to do."

"Please."

I thought about it for a moment, then nodded. "Meet me at seven at Ti Bacio on College Avenue." I gave him the address. "Where are you staying tonight?"

"With Vee. I usually do." He looked at my wall clock. It was nearly six. "Maybe I can catch her before she leaves her shop." He reached for my hand and held it briefly. "I'll see you at seven."

When he had gone I picked up the phone and called Virginia Newton at her home in Cibola. I identified myself and told her why I was calling. She described the incident of the previous night much as Mark had.

"It surely wasn't intentional," she added. "The local kids hot-rod up and down that road all the time. Mark . . . well, sometimes Mark gets a little paranoid."

I thanked her and broke the connection. I didn't know whether to believe Mark either. Was this an attention-grabbing device? A means of deflecting my search for his sister? He already had my attention. He'd gotten it a long time ago, before I met him in Cibola, before he kissed me good night.

What if he was telling the truth? Something had happened last night in Cibola, coincidental accident or deliberate attempt, something that couldn't be easily explained. I shook my head, trying to clear it and think about this case dispassionately, trying to strip away the emotion that was clouding

168

my judgment. I sought order in work as I switched on the computer and updated the Foster file, adding another layer of paper to the sheets in the manila folder, another layer of impressions and opinions of this case that was going nowhere.

As the printer spat out words, I played back the messages on my answering machine. My theatrical friend had called. Elizabeth's dance troupe had been named *Invitation to the Dance*, after a composition by Weber. She gave me names and phone numbers of two other members of the group, adding that she didn't know whether the numbers were current. I picked up the phone. One number got me a disconnect recording and the other rang and rang but no one answered.

At a quarter to seven my stomach rumbled, reminding me of my dinner date with Mark. I locked my office and went downstairs. It had stopped raining and a cold damp mist had moved in off the bay, obscuring the neon lights of downtown Oakland, making my back ache from its awkward landing on the stairs at Karen's apartment. I thought fondly of the hot bath I'd promised myself.

The proprietor of the little Vietnamese café on the corner stood smoking a cigarette in the doorway. I said hello, then crossed the street to the parking lot, keys in hand. I heard a siren and turned in the direction of the sound. That's why I didn't hear them come up behind me. One of them caught my shoulder and spun me around, shoving me back against a car.

There were two of them, one big and one little. The big one had done the spinning and now he stepped back, letting the smaller of the two move into position in front of me. He was short and black with the muscled frame of a bantamweight fighter, the angular, pointed face of a gremlin. His companion was white, with muddy brown hair and colorless eyes. He was over six feet tall, and bulky, a pair of massive shoulders straining the seams of his black knit shirt. From the way his nose was skewed in his moon face I guessed it had been broken more than once.

"You should learn to mind your own business," Little

said, his voice a sibilant high-pitched whisper. Big narrowed his eyes above his mashed nose and looked intimidating. His eyes had a vacant look, as though some of his muscle was between his ears.

"Who sent you?" I asked, keeping my voice steady. I felt cold, and it wasn't the weather. Scenes were flashing through my head, scenes from a couple of years ago, that parking lot off San Pablo, the two men who'd worked me over and put me in the hospital.

Damn it, why hadn't I seen them? For days I'd known, somewhere on the edge of my consciousness, that I was being watched. Now that a move was finally being made against me, I was unprepared.

I took a deep breath, forcing air into my tightening chest. Don't panic, I told myself. Think, assess the situation, look for an out. My keys were in my right hand. I threaded a couple of fingers through the brass ring and maneuvered the keys so that several protruded between my knuckles.

"There you go, asking questions again." Little did the talking. Big just stood there, breathing hard and making fists with his thick-fingered hands. "That kind of shit is what gets you in trouble."

We were in the middle of the lot. My car was about twenty feet to my right, the street some thirty feet to my left. I could see the Vietnamese man through the window of his café, clearing the counter. Little stood so close to me that bolting didn't seem to be an option. I considered screaming. It was about seven in the evening. Cars and people moved along Franklin Street. There had been people around the last time I confronted two thugs in a parking lot, but none of them had come to my aid then.

"I'm supposed to give you a message," Little said, hissing like a snake. "Drop the case."

"Which case?"

"You know which case. Lay off. Bag it. Stay out of things that don't concern you."

"And if I don't?"

"You're a smart girl. You should be able to figure out what

170

happens if you don't.'' Little grinned, his mouth a rictus in his sharp-featured face. "We'll give you a taste now, so you can think about the main dish.''

He drew back a fist but I struck first, scraping his face with my fistful of keys. He squeaked indignantly as his hand moved to the scratches. I kicked at his legs and dodged to the left, toward the street. Not fast enough, though. Big seized my right arm and shoulder and dragged me toward him, pinning my arms behind my back.

Little came at me. In the light from the streetlamp on the corner I saw several scratches on his face oozing blood. He pummelled his fists into my abdomen in rapid-fire succession, driving the air from my diaphragm. I gasped and would have doubled over, but Big held my arms, forcing me into an awkward upright stance.

I stamped on Big's foot. He made a rumbling sound and tightened his grip. Little had moved back to watch his handiwork. Now he stepped in close again, the top of his head on a level with my nose. He took my chin delicately in his left hand and slapped me hard with his right. Then he backhanded me, the ring on his hand cutting the skin near my mouth. I felt something trickle slowly down my chin and tasted blood with my tongue.

When he stepped back again, I kicked out with my right leg, aiming for his groin. The blow must have landed somewhere in the vicinity, for he cried out in what I hoped was pain. Across the street I saw the Vietnamese man step out of the doorway of his café, a trash bag in his hand. I pulled air into my lungs and hollered. He looked up. Then he dropped the trash bag and shouted something in Vietnamese as he ran toward the parking lot.

Little hissed a command at Big, who dropped me into a heap on the asphalt. Little kicked me hard in the stomach. Tears sprang to my eyes and I fought to keep from vomiting as I lay shaking on the pavement.

"Something to remember me by, bitch," Little said. "I'll be back.''

I heard their footsteps rush away. Two car doors slammed

and an engine gunned as their car sped down Franklin Street. The Vietnamese man knelt beside me, his thin dark face full of concern, his hands on my shoulders. I pulled myself into a seated position.

"Police?" he asked.

I shook my head. I sat for a moment on the gritty surface of the parking lot, taking stock of my injuries. My stomach ached with a dull steady pain where Little had punched and kicked me, but I didn't think any ribs were broken. My wrists felt hot and scuffed, as though I had rope burns. The cut oozed blood. I'd feel a lot worse in the morning, but I didn't want to have to explain it all to the Oakland police.

But someone had already called them. As the café owner put a supporting arm around my back and helped me to my feet, a cruiser with pulsating red lights braked to a halt at the curb. Two uniformed men got out and hurried toward us. I didn't recognize either of them.

"Who called you?" I asked one. The name on his tag was Conwell.

"I don't know. We got it from the dispatcher a few minutes ago. Woman being attacked in the parking lot at the corner of Twelfth and Franklin. You need an ambulance?"

"No. I'll be okay."

"What happened?" the other officer asked.

I gave the officers an edited version—a mugging attempt in a dark parking lot—and a description of my assailants. I minimized the beating and left out the message the two thugs had delivered. I knew it was the Foster case I was supposed to drop and I had a good idea who sent them. But I couldn't prove anything.

Another car pulled up to the curb. A tall man got out and walked quickly across the concrete surface of the parking lot. Conwell looked up, surprised. "Sergeant Vernon."

"What are you doing here?" I asked him.

"I wanted to see if you were all right."

I frowned. "How did you know it was me?"

"That's the interesting part," Sid said, one corner of his mouth twitching under his mustache. "Whoever called nine-one-one to report this little incident mentioned you by name. Have you got a guardian angel, Jeri?''

No, I thought, a watcher. I looked up at the windows around me and saw eyes. Eyes on my back, eyes that didn't want me out of commission. Which meant that whoever was watching wanted something from me.

''Your mouth's bleeding.'' Sid pulled out a handkerchief. I took it from him and touched it to the corner of my mouth. ''What happened?''

''A couple of would-be muggers. I gave the officers a statement.'' I nodded in Conwell's direction. He and Sid traded looks, then he and the other officer moved off to take a statement from the café owner who had come to my aid.

Sid narrowed his eyes and stared hard at me. ''Don't bullshit me, Jeri. Those goons weren't after your purse. They were after you.''

''Maybe.''

''There's no maybe about it,'' he said. ''This has something to do with Foster's missing wife, doesn't it? I looked up the Willis murder case after you called me the other day. The oldest girl—Elizabeth—she'd be the same age as Foster's wife. Is Mrs. Foster Elizabeth Willis?''

I looked down at the spot of blood on the white handkerchief. ''I don't have to tell you anything. Client confidentiality, remember?''

''You and your damned cases. I'm sorry I ever gave Foster your number.''

''Why did you, Sid?'' I crossed my arms over my aching stomach.

''I told you before. It was spur-of-the-moment. I was in the office when Missing Persons called Homicide to see if we had any Jane Does matching Mrs. Foster's description. Foster said something about hiring a private investigator. I gave him your name.''

''And you had a good laugh about it later,'' I said, ''because you don't think I can find Renee Foster.''

''Is that the only reason you're doing this? To show me?''

173

His mouth quirked. "I didn't know my opinion mattered anymore."

"Oh, come on, Sid. You threw down the gauntlet. You issued a challenge. I merely accepted your invitation to play the game."

"Getting worked over by a couple of assholes isn't a game. You got off easy. Last time they put you in the hospital."

"I can take care of myself," I said grimly. It was the second time in a week someone had reminded me of what happened in the parking lot on San Pablo Avenue. First my father, now Sid.

"It's different now than when you were working for Errol. You were part of a team. You had someone to call on for backup. Now you're a woman working alone."

"And being a detective is a man's job, right?"

"A few years ago it was." Sid punctuated his words with a gesture. "I know you're an experienced investigator. I'm just telling you there's a reason cops work in pairs. It's so we can cover each other's butts. You're working alone. Your butt isn't covered."

"I take it this means you're concerned about me."

He moved toward me. His hand reached out and touched my hair. "Did it ever occur to you I might care what happens to you?"

He looked at me the way he used to, his eyes searing my skin in the cold night air. At one time I would have felt a responding heat, but I didn't anymore. At least I told myself I didn't. There was too much water under that particular bridge. That tingle was just my body playing tricks. And the look in Sid's eyes was that of a cat mesmerizing a bird. He inclined his face toward mine. I looked away before I could get caught.

"That doesn't work anymore, Sid." I walked away from him, toward the officers and the café owner.

"The hell it doesn't." The sly cat smile played over his face, then went away again. He sighed. "I do care about you. In spite of everything."

174

" 'Care' covers a lot of territory. I care about you, Sid, but not the way I did."

"My loss." He looked at me for a long moment. "Let's get back to the original subject."

"There's nothing to discuss."

"Yes, there is. Who sent the goons?"

"I have theories, Sid, but no facts. It could be one of my current cases, or something I worked on during the past year. I haven't lacked for business."

"I know. I salute your success." The light tone of his voice didn't match the look in his eyes. "You've proved that you can get along very well without me."

"That isn't the point, Sid. Our marriage didn't work out. I can admit it even if you can't. Are we finished here?"

"You'll have to check with Officer Conwell. Look, Jeri, I can tell you're hurting," he said. "Will you at least go to the hospital?"

"I'll be okay." I folded the soiled handkerchief into a square. "I'll wash this and get it back to you."

The officers had finished taking notes. I thanked the café owner for his help. He bowed slightly and went back across the street, where his wife waited in the door of the restaurant.

Sid followed me as I walked slowly to my car. I unlocked the door and slid carefully into the driver's seat. When I reached for the shoulder harness, I couldn't quite make the stretch. Sid shook his head but he didn't say anything. Instead he pulled the belt down, leaned over, and fastened it for me.

I started the car and drove out of the parking lot, using a circuitous route that took me all over downtown and North Oakland. When I was certain I wasn't being followed, I drove home.

Abigail, wanting to be fed, meowed at me as I came in the door, but I headed for the bathroom first. I leaned over the sink and washed the cut at the corner of my mouth, then dabbed it with some iodine from the medicine cabinet. Then I swallowed some Tylenol.

In the bedroom I shed my clothes, looking at my body in

the mirror above my dresser. My wrists looked chafed where the big man had held me. My stomach and abdomen glowed red, no bruises showing yet. I'd look worse in the morning.

I pulled on a robe and went to the kitchen, Abigail at my heels. I fed her, then I filled a plastic bag with ice, wrapped the bag in a dish towel, and carried it into the living room. I lay down on the sofa and pressed the ice to my stomach, feeling the chill numb the ache.

It hurt, but it wasn't as bad as the beating I'd taken two years ago. I stared at the ceiling and saw that parking lot behind a bar on San Pablo Avenue and the two men who methodically worked me over.

I moved the ice pack and took a deep breath, probing my abdomen with my fingers. The time before, that deep breath brought a sharp stabbing pain from two broken ribs. I remembered how it felt to lie on a gurney with paramedics asking for my name and address while they poked and probed and took my vital signs. And the hospital emergency room where strange hands removed my clothing and held out a clipboard and pen so I could sign myself in as a patient.

I sighed and hugged the ice pack to me. It could have been a lot worse, but it was meant as a warning. Drop the case, Little had said.

The Foste case. In addition to pissing off Admiral Franklin last week, and Karen Willis and her boyfriend this afternoon, I had also managed to antagonize everyone in the Foster family except the baby. I sorted through the possibilities. Philip could barely function. Although his mother had looked as though she wanted to bounce me like a tennis ball, I doubted she'd send a couple of apes to do it for her.

That left Edward. After looking into Edward's hard brown eyes I figured he was capable of anything. Even so, he must know that I'd consider him the likeliest author of tonight's revels.

I went back over the past few days and recalled the sensation I'd felt that night on the steps outside Lawrence Kinney's office, the feeling that I was being watched. An hour later someone had tried to break into my office. That first time I went to Karen's apartment I'd experienced the same feeling. And there was the blue car that seemed to follow me as I drove through Berkeley. Had Edward been trying to scare me off?

I lay on the sofa and thought about various ways to get even with Edward Foster, until the ice in the bag melted and I felt cold water seep through the towel and my robe, chilling my flesh. I got up, moving carefully, and dumped the remains of the ice pack in the kitchen sink. Then I went to bed, where I dreamed I was being chased through an endless dark parking lot, pursued by black and white snowmen.

Nineteen

WHEN I WOKE UP THE NEXT MORNING, I FELT LIKE
a herd of elephants had been tap dancing on my entire body.
I groped my way to the bathroom, swallowed a couple of
Tylenol, and went back to bed. The phone on the nightstand
rang and rang, but I burrowed my head under the pillow and
went back to sleep.

When I woke up a second time Abigail had curled up on
the pillow, between my ear and my shoulder, so close that
every time I turned my head I came up against a wall of cat.
I looked at the clock and saw that it was midmorning. Finally
I threw back the covers and stood, my body screeching in
protest as I pulled my nightshirt over my head.

I was downright colorful, with an ugly purple patch below
my breasts. I ran a finger along the scratch at my mouth, then
twisted my torso from one side to the other, feeling like a
rusty hinge. Pulling on a robe, I went to the kitchen to feed
Abigail, who had been more than patient under the circumstances. I showered, standing under the stream of hot water,
letting it loosen my aching muscles. The phone rang several
times again while I dressed. I ignored it, lingering at the table
as I read the morning newspaper, drank coffee, and ate a
bowl of Cheerios.

It was past noon when I left for the office. Outside the sky
was gray, matching my mood. The weather guesser on my
car radio said a front was moving in from the Pacific, due to
hit us this afternoon or evening. The red light on my office
answering machine blinked furiously. I made a pot of coffee
before sitting down to play back the tape.

Sid had called four times. With each call his voice sounded progressively more irate because I hadn't returned his previous calls or answered the phone at home. Interspersed with Sid's calls were two calls from Cassie, three from other clients, and seven hang-ups. And there was one abrupt message from Karen Willis.

"I'm sorry about yesterday," she said after identifying herself. "I have to talk to you. I'll call back."

I rewound the tape and listened to it again. There was some background noise that sounded like the diesel roar of a bus. Had Karen made the call from a phone booth, or while standing near an open window? There was no way to tell. She could have been anywhere.

I called Cassie to let her know I was in, then I got up to pour myself a cup of coffee. When I settled back into my chair the door opened and Sandra Baines walked into my office, an unbuttoned gray raincoat over tweed slacks and a white sweater. She tossed a small manila envelope onto my desk.

I picked it up and opened the flap. The envelope contained photographs, half-a-dozen Polaroid shots, all of them showing the same tow-headed little boy I'd seen yesterday at the home of Edward and Helen Foster. He was wearing blue shorts decorated with yellow ducks. The maid held him up to the camera, her dark skin contrasting with his soft white baby flesh. He had a bruise on his back, a dirty yellow blotch the size of a fist.

I spread the photographs out on the surface of my desk, side by side. Then I leaned back in my chair and looked at Sandra Baines.

"That's what you wanted, isn't it?" She sat down and crossed one leg over the other. "Proof."

"Is it? Proof?"

"Call Helen's doctor in Los Gatos. His name's Graffinger."

"All this proves is that he had a bruise, an old one at that. There's nothing in these pictures to indicate when they were taken. Or what really happened. Maybe he fell, or ran into

179

some furniture. If somebody hit him, it could just as easily have been Helen. Or Philip.''

She laughed and pulled her cigarettes and lighter from her purse. She lit a filter tip and looked around for an ashtray. I took one from my desk drawer and passed it across the desk.

"Helen adores that little boy," she said. "So does Edward, in his way. Philip certainly wouldn't do anything like that.''

"That's what Elizabeth's aunt says about her. Besides, the nicest people abuse their kids. Which brings me back to the question I asked yesterday. If someone's been hitting this kid, why didn't anybody notice it until now?''

"I don't know. Does it really matter?''

"Yes, particularly if all of you are lying about Elizabeth. Why are you doing this, Sandra?''

She took a few puffs of her cigarette. "I told you. I want Philip. I'll get him, too.''

"Just one little problem. He already has a wife.''

"Had. She left him. She's a child beater. A few weeks in Reno will wipe the slate clean.''

"There may be a little chalk dust left on the board. What happens if she shows up again?''

"She won't. I told you. She ran off with her lover.''

"I checked him out. He doesn't know where she is.''

"It doesn't matter," Sandra said, supremely confident. "It's too late for Renee. She dug her own grave. I'm merely taking advantage of the situation.''

She took a final puff on her cigarette and ground it out in my ashtray. Then she stood up to leave.

"Philip still loves her," I said.

"Maybe he does now. But I can take care of that.''

I was sure she could. Philip was used to being manipulated. One more person pulling the strings wasn't likely to bother the puppet.

After Sandra left, I stacked the photographs into a pile and looked at them again. I didn't like what I saw. The pictures were disturbing, particularly when I considered that Elizabeth may have been abused herself. I put the photographs into the envelope and stashed it in my desk drawer. The phone rang and I picked it up.

"Howard, this is Gerrity. How goes the Foster case?"

"It doesn't. What can I do for you?"

"It's what I can do for you," he said. "Helen Foster's doctor is a guy named Arnold Graffinger, in Los Gatos. He probably won't talk to you. I took a pass through Philip Foster's neighborhood this morning. One of Renee's neighbors told me she saw Renee smack the boy on several occasions."

"Thanks, Gerrity," I said, eyeing the photographs Sandra Baines had delivered. "You didn't have to do that."

"I like the cut of your jib, as those nautical types say. Besides, I'm between assignments. Things getting complicated?"

"Curiouser and curiouser, as Lewis Carroll would say. A couple of goons paid me a visit last night. They told me in word and deed to drop the case."

"Edward Foster?"

"He's at the top of my list." I told Gerrity what had happened yesterday when I went to see Philip at his office.

"You going to take the hint?"

"I wouldn't give the son-of-a-bitch the satisfaction. But at the moment I don't know which way to go."

"Wait for it," Gerrity said. Good advice, I admitted to myself after we'd ended our conversation.

It wasn't until Mark walked into my office that I remembered my dinner date with him. The attack in the parking lot had driven it out of my mind. Now he stood in front of my desk, blue eyes giving off sparks, looking like one of Mr. De Pinna's firecrackers, ready to explode. Emotions played across his face like water racing down a mountain stream, revealing stone and sand and treacherous rapids.

"You stood me up," he said.

His mouth twitched at one corner. Looking at him, I saw the same kind of anger he had displayed in his shop in Cibola, the suppressed violence that had erupted when I pressed him for details about the night he killed his parents. Only now it

181

was directed at me, over something as trivial as a missed dinner date.

"I've been trying to decide why you stood me up. You think I lied about that car trying to run me down? Just say so. If you didn't want to go out with me, all you had to do was say no."

As he spoke his face changed. The unsettling anger gave way to vulnerability and bruised ego. I felt like a passenger on an emotional roller coaster, riding blindfold, without a seat belt. The Foster case had me scrabbling through a maze, looking for a way out. I was struggling with the attraction I felt for Mark and at the moment I didn't know whether to deck him or comfort him.

"If you want to know why I didn't show up last night, all you have to do is give me a chance to explain." I stood up and winced as my body reminded me of last night's attack.

"You're hurt," he said, surprised.

I sat down again and pulled out the bottom desk drawer where I kept my first-aid supplies. Pulling out a bottle of Tylenol, I negotiated the childproof cap and shook out a couple of tablets. I picked up my coffee, which had by now grown cold.

"Cheers," I said, washing down the tablets. "Two thugs jumped me in the parking lot last night. Someone called the cops. By the time it was over, I'd forgotten about dinner."

Mark's hands balled into fists and he stuck them into the pockets of his jacket as though he didn't know what else to do with them. "I'm sorry," he said finally, his voice subdued. "I was out of line. Please forgive me. Have you seen a doctor?"

"Don't mother-hen me. I don't like it any better than I like being on the receiving end of your temper. Sit down and let's start over."

He did as I told him, sitting uneasily in one of the chairs in front of my desk. I got a fresh cup of coffee for both of us. When I returned to my desk the phone rang. I reached for it, hoping it was Karen.

"Jeri, where the hell have you been?" Sid roared at me

through the receiver. "Goddamn it, why haven't you returned any of my calls?"

Terrific, I thought. This is all I need. "I can't talk right now, Sid." I hung up.

"Who's Sid?" Mark asked.

"My ex-husband. I don't want to talk about him." I took a swallow of coffee and burned my tongue. "Yesterday I wasn't sure I believed your story about the car trying to run you down. Now I'm not sure I don't. It's possible. I'm being watched. I've felt it for days. Tell me again what happened with the car."

He sipped his coffee and went through his story again as I probed to see if he remembered any details about the car. The phone rang again. This time it was Karen. I thought I heard another person moving in the background.

"You wanted to talk," I said. "Does it have something to do with the vanishing act you and Rick pulled?"

"Yes," Karen said, sounding subdued. "It's about Lizzie. I'll tell you the whole story when I see you."

"Give me a preview."

"I wasn't where I was supposed to be."

"That's cryptic. What does it mean?"

"Not over the phone. Let's meet someplace."

"Your apartment?"

"No. Vee's shop. At six."

"Vee's at six. Fine, I'll be there."

"Who was that?" Mark asked as I hung up the phone.

"Your sister Karen. She wants to talk to me about Elizabeth."

"You think she knows something?"

"Yes. Look, Mark, I have things to do."

"I know," he said, setting the coffee mug down on my desk. "It's okay. I have to go to San Francisco anyway."

"Why?"

"As long as I'm down here I might as well stock up on framing supplies. The wholesaler's over in San Francisco." He stood up and zipped his jacket.

183

"Maybe we can have dinner another time," I said, by way of a peace offering.

Before he could say anything the door to my office swung open so hard it banged against the wall. Sid walked in looking like a grizzly bear ready to attack.

"Don't hang up on me again," he said in a deceptively calm voice, his cat's eyes glaring at me.

"I'll hang up on you if I damn well feel like it." I got to my feet and glared back. Getting yelled at in my own office twice in one afternoon was twice too often.

"Where the hell have you been? I've been trying to reach you since last night."

"I got your messages."

"So you couldn't pick up the phone and call me back? It never occurred to you that it might be important?"

"What do you want, Sid?"

Sid's eyes blazed. "I thought I might inquire about your health, after what happened last night. But you don't seem any worse for wear." Then he looked at Mark as though he were seeing him for the first time. He jerked his chin in Mark's direction. "Who's this?"

"Mark Willis."

Sid straightened. His eyes narrowed and he surveyed Mark as though he were wondering if there were any outstanding warrants on him.

"Mark, this is Sid Vernon. My ex-husband. He's a sergeant with the Oakland Police Department."

"Hello," Mark said. They looked at each other like a couple of cats with their backs up, circling each other before a fight. "I was just leaving."

"Stay," Sid ordered. "This may concern you too. If Renee Foster is Elizabeth Willis. Is she, Jeri?"

"Yes. What are you talking about?" I felt something in the pit of my stomach and it wasn't indigestion.

"The Coast Guard pulled a floater out of the Oakland estuary last night. A woman, no identification."

"Drowned?" I asked.

"Throat cut. She matches the general description Foster gave Missing Persons."

"Didn't Foster leave a photo?" I said with a calmness I didn't feel. "I've never met Elizabeth face to face, and Mark hasn't seen her in fifteen years."

"We need dental records," Sid said. "The coroner estimates she'd been in the water a couple of days. And the face is unrecognizable."

I didn't ask for details. Anything could happen to a body floating in that busy ship channel. The color drained from Mark's face and he sat down as Sid continued. "We've been trying to reach Foster at home, but there's been no answer."

"Did you call his office?"

"Yeah. This morning. Some secretary said he hadn't come in yet. I left a message for him to call me, but he hasn't. I thought maybe you'd know how to reach him. I'm not saying it's her, but we need to eliminate that possibility."

I told Sid I'd contact Philip at his office or at his parents' home. After he left I turned to Mark, who sat hunched in the chair, his face bleak.

"Vee," he said finally. "What are we going to tell Vee?"

"We don't tell her anything. Not until we know for sure. That body may not be Elizabeth. Go to San Francisco, to your supplier." He started to protest, but I silenced him with a gesture. "Meet me back here when you're finished. By then I will have talked to Philip about getting her dental records. I'll meet Karen at six and then you and I can sort things out."

He nodded and looked at his watch. "All right. It shouldn't take me more than a couple of hours. I'll meet you here at five."

When he was gone I pulled the Foster file from the cabinet. Philip had given me his parents' phone number during our initial interview. When I called Los Gatos the phone was answered by the maid. Señora Foster was not at home. I disconnected and dialed Philip's office. The receptionist rang his office and a secretary picked up the call. Mr. Foster wasn't in. She didn't know if he was coming in at all.

"Transfer me to Edward Foster," I said, and waited. Another secretary answered and asked my name. I gave it to her and she came back on the line a moment later, saying Mr. Foster was in a meeting. Convenient, I thought. Or he had no intention of talking to me.

"Interrupt him. It's important."

"I can't do that," the secretary said.

"I know Foster doesn't want to talk to me and you're only doing your job. But you tell him if he doesn't take this call I'm going to swear out a complaint against him. For assault and battery."

She gasped and put me on hold. A moment later Edward Foster himself came on the line, his voice crackling with venom and threats.

"Foster, you don't like me. Believe me, the feeling is mutual. I wouldn't be calling if it wasn't important, so shut up and listen." He sputtered into silence. "The Coast Guard pulled a body out of the Oakland estuary last night. It might be Renee, it might not. They need Renee's dental records to make an I.D."

I heard an intake of breath, nothing else.

"Regardless of how you feel about your daughter-in-law, you owe it to her—and your son—to find out if that body is Renee."

"Who do I contact?" he asked finally.

"The Alameda County Coroner's Office." I flipped through my Rolodex and gave him the number.

"I'll take care of it."

"I'm sure you will. And Foster—I wasn't kidding about the assault and battery charge."

"I don't know what you're talking about."

"I think you do. I'll be in touch."

Twenty

THE STORM BLEW INTO THE BAY AREA IN LATE afternoon, dumping a steady curtain of rain from a dark blue-
gray sky. Mark hadn't returned to my office by five. I waited
as long as I could, then at a quarter to six I left my office and
drove through snarled traffic to Vee's antique shop. I parked
on Piedmont and walked back to the shop, a cold wind blow-
ing rain into my face. The wind rattled the glass panes at the
front of Vee's shop as people bundled in raincoats hurried
past. A sudden gust caught a man's umbrella, breaking the
supports and rendering it useless.

Vee was surprised to see me. When I arrived, dripping, at
the shop's front door, she had her keys in her hand, ready to
lock up and go home.

"I'm supposed to meet Karen here at six," I told her.

"She's not here. Come dry off. I'll make some tea." Vee
locked the front door and turned out the lights in the front of
the shop. She led the way back to her office area and plugged
in the electric space heater. Soon its coils glowed red, cre-
ating a pool of warmth between the sofa and the desk. I took
the towel she offered and wiped my streaming face.

Vee put the kettle on the hotplate. When it whistled a few
minutes later, she got up to pour the hot water over tea leaves
in the china pot. She let them steep, then poured us each a
cup. I could have used something stronger. I knew Vee was
curious about my meeting with Karen and about Mark's sudden, unexplained visit to the Bay Area. I didn't know what
to say to her so we didn't talk at all. The hands of an antique
Seth Thomas mantel clock went slowly round its face. Out-

side the evening grew darker and the rain drummed steadily on the roof.

"Would Karen come to the front door?" I asked.

"She might. Or she could park in the alley behind my car. I leave the light on over the back door." Vee picked up her china cup and sipped her tea. "Maybe she's stuck in traffic."

"Maybe she's not coming."

I set my teacup on the desk and got up, moving restlessly in the small area behind the counter. The Yorkshire terrier looked up at me from its basket, then yawned and tucked its muzzle under its forepaws. I walked between the rows of old furniture to the front of the shop and stood gazing out at the rain. A grandfather clock on the left wall bonged the half-hour, followed by the softer chime of the Seth Thomas. I checked my watch. We were all in the vicinity of six-thirty.

"Did she say what she wanted to talk about?" Vee asked, unable to contain her curiosity any longer.

"Just that she wanted to talk about Elizabeth."

"Mark didn't say why he came down here?"

"Yes," I said, but I didn't elaborate.

"You're both being very mysterious. Well, I'll be glad of the company. My husband's still out of town." Vee got up to pour herself some more tea.

I stood with my elbows resting on the glass counter, chin propped on my fists. Then I straightened. I saw someone peering through the front window of the shop. In the light from the street it looked to be a woman, bundled against the rain in a tan raincoat belted at the waist. The face was obscured by a soft-brimmed rain hat. Karen, I thought. About time. I grabbed the keys Vee had left on the counter and walked toward the front door.

As I approached I realized the figure was too short to be Karen Willis. Besides, the woman appeared to be looking at the window display. Two men in raincoats, one carrying an umbrella, passed behind her. The edge of the umbrella grazed her rainhat, knocking it askew. I saw short dark hair at the nape of the neck. She adjusted her hat with a black-gloved hand, then turned and moved quickly away.

188

Through the rain-splattered windows I saw cars going by, their headlights punching holes in the rainy darkness. The bulk of an AC Transit bus stopped across the street, blocking the neon signs on buildings across the street, then went on in a roar of diesel power. The rain came down harder, a steady din on the roof. My watch read twenty to seven.

"She isn't coming," I told Vee as I tossed the keys onto the desk.

The Yorkie roused itself with a yawn and a snuffle. It stepped gingerly out of its basket and went to the back door, looked up at Vee and barked once, a gruff sound for such a small dog.

"I suppose you have to go out, Ziggy," Vee said. "And in this weather. Can't you wait until it lets up a bit?" Ziggy looked at her as if to say, Of course not. She walked over and opened the back door just enough to let the Yorkie out into the alley.

Someone knocked on the front door, rattling the glass. It was Mark. I picked up the keys and went to let him in, Vee following closely behind me. He stood on the mat just inside the front door, rain plastering his dark hair to his skull and running down his face. His jeans were soaked from the hem to the knee. He took off his jacket and let the water drip onto the mat.

"God, what lousy weather. I'm dripping all over your floor, Vee." Mark leaned over and kissed his aunt on the cheek.

"It's only water." Vee led the way to the area behind the counter and handed him the towel.

He dried his hair, then patted the excess moisture from his jacket. After hanging both towel and jacket on a coat tree near the back door, he took the steaming cup Vee offered. She turned the space heater up a notch and Mark stretched his legs out in front of it.

"You were going to meet me at my office at five," I said.

"I just got back from the city. Traffic was a god-awful mess. I was stuck on the Bay Bridge for over an hour, waiting for CHP to clear up a three-car pileup." He lifted the cup to his lips. "Karen's not here?"

"She never showed." As if to underscore that fact, the grandfather clock struck the three-quarter hour.

"Maybe she was stuck in the same traffic jam I was." He sipped the tea, cradling the warm china cup in his hands. "Assuming she was coming from the city."

"Or she's decided not to keep our appointment."

"There's something you two aren't telling me," Vee said. "Mark, you usually call to let me know you're coming. You showed up here yesterday without a word. When I asked why, you didn't answer. I thought it was just one of your moods, but something's up."

It was obvious Mark hadn't told his aunt about the attempt on his life. "Spur-of-the-moment visit," he said. "I needed supplies. And it's been a while since I've seen you."

Vee wasn't deterred. "It has something to do with Beth's disappearance, doesn't it? You know something, and you came down here to tell Jeri."

Neither of us answered her. I couldn't meet her eyes in the uncomfortable silence so I stared at the front window of the shop. On the other side of the glass the rain came down in sheets, smearing the colors of the neon signs. Something was wrong and I couldn't sort it out. Karen wasn't coming. Or she'd been prevented from coming.

I looked past Vee and Mark toward the back door and my eye fell on the empty dog basket. It had been more than ten minutes since Vee let the Yorkie out into the alley to do his business. The little dog hadn't come back. It hadn't even scratched at the door, asking to be let in from a dark rainy alley.

I rose swiftly from the sofa and pulled open the door. Vee had left the light on above the back door, thinking Karen would park in back of the building. Several other doors along the alley had lights above them, but the pools of light they provided didn't extend very far into the alley.

"The dog," I said, stepping out into the rain.

"Ziggy?" Mark came up behind me and laid a hand on my shoulder. "What about him?"

"He hasn't come back. Vee let him out awhile ago."

"He doesn't like the rain. He's probably under a car or something."

"Why hide under a car when you can scratch at a door and come back to your nice warm basket?"

He looked at my face and frowned. "It's not about the dog, is it?"

"No. Stay here." I moved to the left, but he grabbed my arm.

"You're not going out there alone."

"I know what I'm doing. Stay here." He shook his head. "Okay. You go right, I'll go left. Be careful."

"What am I looking for, besides Ziggy?"

"I'm not sure," I said.

The cold rain quickly wet my hair and shoulders. Vee's car, a Cadillac, hugged the wall immediately to the left of the shop's back door, but the alley was wide enough for another car to pass it. I knelt and looked under the Caddy, but there was no sign of the Yorkie.

I straightened and continued down the alley. Twenty yards farther an open door led to the kitchen of a small restaurant, throwing a rectangle of light onto the puddles and gravel. I peered in and saw a man in white pants and shirt working at a stove. Under the wet scent of rain I caught the aroma of hamburgers, grease, and onions.

The alley provided access to houses and apartment buildings on the street that ran behind Piedmont. I saw openings in the fences at intervals, some with cars wedged into them, some with trash barrels. One such opening led to an apartment-building parking lot. As I walked toward it, a car pulled out of the lot. It turned and headed away from me toward the side street, its headlights illuminating another car parked farther down the alley. The parked car was white, and in the brief flash of light I thought I saw a BMW emblem on its hood.

I walked toward the car, feeling dread in the pit of my

stomach. I could see something lying along the wall of the building, in front of the tires, something black and shiny that looked like a sack of garbage, but wasn't. It was a raincoat. Crumpled under the raincoat I saw legs and a pair of feet, one shoe on and the other in a puddle of water nearby.

Something moved as I walked up to the car. The Yorkie was huddled next to the right front tire, about six inches from Karen's head. I knelt and looked down at her. Her eyes were open, her surprised unseeing stare directed up at the night sky. The long platinum hair was pinned up under a rain hat of the same shiny black material as her raincoat, knocked askew as she fell.

Her right hand rested in a puddle. I knelt and reached for it. The little dog growled and barked at me, but made no move to attack me as I felt for a pulse. There was none. I reached out and took the lapel of the raincoat gently between thumb and forefinger and pulled it aside. What had been a shirt made of some pale silky material was now dark and sodden with blood. Karen's throat had been slashed from ear to ear.

I pulled my hand away and watched the rain wash the blood from my own flesh. Then I heard footsteps in the gravel behind me. I straightened and turned to face Mark.

"I thought I heard Ziggy," he said, ... ien he saw her. Horror flashed across his face as he looked down at Karen's body.

"Call the dog," I said quietly. "We don't want him in the way."

Mark knelt and whistled. The Yorkie whined, then skirted the body and rain to Mark, who scooped the wet, shaking animal into his arms. Just then we heard Vee's voice, calling us. I saw her step from the back door of her shop into the alley.

"Oh, God," Mark said.

"Can you tell her, or do you want me to do it?"

"I will."

Together we walked back up the alley and shepherded Vee into the shop. Mark set the dog down, put his arms around

192

Vee, and told her Karen was dead. As her face dissolved into grief, my stomach reeled. I picked up the phone and called 911, giving the dispatcher the details. Then I left Vee huddled on the sofa, Mark with his arm around her, and went back out into the rain to wait for the police.

The rain had eased a bit by the time the patrol car drove up the alley. It parked behind the BMW. Two young cops in uniforms walked to where I stood, near Karen's body, and started asking questions. Then another vehicle pulled in behind the patrol car. My stomach tightened as I recognized the car, a black Mercury Cougar. The passenger door opened and a short stocky man with a receding hairline got out. His name was Wayne Hobart. He'd been Sid's partner for years.

Wayne looked at me glumly, then over at the driver's side of the Cougar. The door opened. Sid got out, his arms resting lightly on the top of the car door as we faced each other in the alley. Then he moved away from the car, slamming the door shut.

"Who is she?" Sid asked me, looking down at the body.

"Karen Willis."

Sid's eyes flickered at the name. He gazed at me, all business. He and Wayne listened as I told them how I'd discovered Karen's body. When I mentioned Mark and Vee, I looked back in the direction of the shop. I saw Mark standing like a shadow under the single light bulb.

Sid followed my glance. "Go wait in the shop. Tell your friend to stay put. I want to talk to him. And his aunt."

Dismissed, I walked slowly back to the shop. I passed the back door of the restaurant. The man I'd seen cooking at the stove now stood in the doorway, smoking a cigarette as he watched. The alley was bright with red-and-white lights as more police vehicles arrived. Curious onlookers from the apartment buildings across the way peered from driveways and balconies.

When I reached Vee's shop, I stepped past Mark and saw Vee slumped on the sofa, wiping the tears from her face with the same towel she'd given Mark to dry his hair. Ziggy was coiled tightly in his basket. Mark knelt and stroked the dog's head.

"Do you think he saw what happened?" he asked.

"The dog? I doubt it. I think he wandered down the alley, found her body, and stayed with it until we missed him."

"I see your ex-husband took the call."

"Luck of the draw." I leaned tiredly against the wall. "He'll be in to talk to you and Vee as soon as he and his partner finish out there. It could be a while." I moved restlessly around the office area.

Mark pulled out his cigarettes. He rummaged on the desk surface and found a cracked saucer to use as an ashtray.

"She knew something," I said. "She was going to tell me. I should have insisted on seeing her right away, when she called."

"Maybe it wouldn't have made any difference where or when you saw her," Mark said quietly. I examined his face, with its scar and the deep lines left by his frown. He looked troubled but controlled.

I walked to the doorway. Rain was still coming down, though not with the same intensity as it had earlier. It had washed away a lot of the evidence while Vee and I had sat and waited for Karen, while all the time she'd been lying dead in the alley. I saw strobes flashing as a police photographer took pictures of the scene. Cops with flashlights ranged up and down the alley, looking in garbage cans, looking for the murder weapon.

As I stood there I felt angry, angry with myself. I'd been here in the antique shop drinking tea while out in the alley someone killed Karen. I hadn't even realized anything was wrong until the damn dog didn't come back. Her hand was cold when I picked it up to check the pulse, whether from rain or time I didn't know. What I did know was that I'd been in the shop for almost an hour, and Karen, attempting to keep her appointment with me, was murdered in the alley less than fifty yards from where I sat, teacup in hand. The thought of it filled me with anger, despair, frustration.

Time dragged by. Mark paced a rut in front of the display

counter, filling the saucer with ash and butts as he smoked one cigarette after another. I made some more tea for Vee. She'd stopped crying now, but her face was as white as paper, and every few moments she bit her lip. Finally Sid loomed out of the darkness. He stepped past me into the shop and gave Mark a cool once-over. Then his eyes rested on Vee, sitting on the sofa.

"This is Vera Burke," I said, "Karen's aunt."

"Mrs. Burke, I'm Sergeant Vernon, Homicide. I'd like to talk with you."

Vee straightened and pushed a strand of hair back from her face. She folded the damp towel in her lap, then threaded her fingers together and placed her hands on top of it. She nodded at Sid.

"Have a seat, Mr. Willis. You too, Jeri. I have a few questions."

Mark moved to a spot near the sofa but remained standing, his hand resting lightly on Vee's shoulder. I stood leaning against the desk, my arms folded across my chest.

Sid took a notebook and pen from the inner pocket of his jacket and poised a pen over a blank page. The pen glittered in the light. It was a gold Cross, engraved with his initials. I'd given it to him on our last anniversary together. In a cold professional voice Sid asked Mark where he lived.

"Cibola, near Jackson."

"What are you doing in the Bay Area?"

"I heard my sister was missing," Mark said.

"So you decided to help Jeri look for her?" Mark didn't answer. "When did you arrive?"

"Yesterday afternoon."

"And where are you staying?"

"With my aunt."

Sid turned to me. "What are you doing here, Jeri?"

"I had an appointment to meet Karen Willis here at six," I said.

"Why?"

"She called me this afternoon and told me she had some

information. She suggested the time and the meeting place, and I agreed.''

"So as far as you know, she was coming here to meet you.''

"That's right. She was late. I thought she'd been delayed by traffic, or that she wasn't coming.''

"Did you know about this meeting, Mr. Willis?'' Sid turned his gaze to Mark.

"I was in Jeri's office when Karen called.''

"When did you leave?''

"Right after you did. I didn't look at the time.''

"Where did you go?''

"San Francisco. On business.''

"What kind of business?''

"I'm a picture framer. I had to pick up some supplies.''

"So you're combining business with your concern for your sister. Where is this supplier located?''

"South of Market. Near Eleventh and Folsom.'' The same area as the studio where Karen had worked. I looked hard at Mark as he pulled his wallet from the hip pocket of his blue jeans and extracted a buff-colored business card. He held it out.

Sid took it and glanced at the engraved print. "What did you buy?''

"Moldings and mats, a few other things. They're in the back of my Blazer.''

"Where is your vehicle?'' Sid asked.

"Parked on the next block, near the corner of Forty-First and Howe.''

"What time did you leave the city?'' Sid's voice was deceptively calm.

"Four-thirty, four-forty-five.'' Mark sounded calm, but I saw his face tense.

"And what time did you get here?''

"Sometime after six-thirty, I think. I'm not sure.''

"You're not sure.'' Sid's bushy eyebrows went up. He turned his gaze on Vee, sitting on the sofa with her hands knotted in the towel. "Do you know what time your nephew got here, Mrs. Burke?"

"I think it was around a quarter to seven," she whispered, her agonizing eyes going from Sid to Mark.

"What about you, Jeri?" Sid burned a look at me. "Can you confirm what time Mr. Willis got here?"

"Six-forty, give or take a few minutes. Where is all this leading?" Trouble was, I knew damn well where Sid was headed and I didn't know how to derail his train of thought.

"So, you left San Francisco at four-thirty or a quarter to five, and you got to Oakland at approximately six-forty. That's roughly two hours for a trip that normally takes half an hour."

"It takes longer than that in rush hour," Mark said evenly. "There was an accident on the Bay Bridge, on the cantilevered section just past Treasure Island. Traffic was at a dead stop for forty-five minutes to an hour, then it crawled all the way to Oakland. I'm sure CHP can confirm it."

"I'll check." Sid shut the notebook. "That still doesn't tell me when you got to Oakland. I think we'd better go downtown and talk about it some more."

I pushed away from the desk and stepped between Sid and Mark. "You've got nothing," I said.

"Don't I? He could have killed her anytime before he got here."

"You're reaching, Sid. Why would he kill his sister? He hadn't seen her in years."

"He killed his parents fifteen years ago, for no apparent reason," Sid said. "That makes him a damn good suspect as far as I'm concerned. Besides, there's another body in the morgue with a cut throat."

"Am I being charged with murder, Sergeant?" Mark's face hardened into a mask, the scar standing out as the skin drained of color. He held himself very still, but I saw a pulse beating at his temple. Vee watched them with wide, horrified eyes as she realized what was happening.

"I'm taking you in for further questioning." Sid tucked away the notebook and pen.

"Then cut the bullshit and let's go." Mark swept up his damp jacket and moved toward the back door.

I grabbed his arm. "You don't have to do this."

"Don't I?" He shook me off and stepped out into the alley. "Take Vee home."

"Don't answer any more questions, Mark. I'll be right down, Sid. With a lawyer." Sid shrugged and followed Mark into the alley.

"He couldn't have done it." Vee stood up and took a step, as though she planned to follow Mark. I caught her arms. She was shaking.

"I'll take care of it, Vee. I have a friend who's a lawyer." Vee scooped the little dog out of his basket and cradled him in her arms as I picked up the phone on her desk.

"Karen Willis has been murdered," I told Cassie when she answered. "Elizabeth may be dead too. Sid took Mark downtown for questioning. Will you meet me there?"

"Oh, Lord, I'm in my bathrobe. Let me throw myself together. I'll be there in half an hour."

Twenty-one

SID WAS CONVINCED THE FLOATER IN THE MORGUE was Elizabeth Willis, although the woman who'd been pulled from the estuary had not yet been identified. Mark was a convicted murderer, Sid pointed out. Both women—his sisters—had died in the same manner. And he didn't buy Mark's story about being stuck in traffic on the Bay Bridge.

"You don't have a case," I said. We were in the glassed-in lieutenant's office, glaring at each other over the desk. "You don't even know if that Jane Doe is Elizabeth Willis."

"If it is I'm gonna be asking Willis some hard questions. Even if it isn't, I've got the other sister in the morgue and your friend with a shaky story."

"You told me the coroner estimated that body had been in the water two days. I saw Mark Willis in Cibola two days ago."

"The coroner's estimate is just a guess. Cibola's maybe three hours from Oakland. He could drive here and back in a night. Besides, why did he show up here yesterday?"

"He came to see me." I decided to omit Mark's story about the car that nearly ran him down in Cibola. That was a tangent I didn't care to explore right now.

Sid ignored my explanation. "Willis had plenty of opportunity to kill both women."

"No motive," I argued. "And no murder weapon."

Cassie's arrival ended the conversation. Her idea of throwing herself together was full lawyer regalia, a severe charcoal gray pin-striped suit with a pale gray blouse, black pumps to match her black briefcase, and little gold studs in her earlobes. She swept into the noisy, smoky room that housed Homicide Section, getting appreciative stares from the night shift.

Cassie and I went out into the hall. "Has Mark said anything?" she asked. "Since he got here, I mean? They can't hold Mark if he won't cooperate. Sid will have to arrest him and it sounds like he's not ready to do that."

I shrugged. "They've got Mark stashed in an interview room. He answered Sid's questions at the shop, but I told him not to say anything more."

Cassie squared her shoulders. "Let's go talk to Sid." I held the door open for her. Cassie sailed back into Homicide Section and set her briefcase on the desk with a thump, favoring Sid with a cool smile.

"You're holding my client, Sergeant Vernon," she said sweetly. "Mark Willis. Are you going to charge him?"

"I want to question him further, Ms. Taylor. I'd advise you to tell him it's in his best interest to cooperate."

"You asked him plenty of questions at the scene, all of which he answered without hesitation. You want cooperation? What if he agrees to talk to you tomorrow morning? With counsel present, of course. That will give you time to contact CHP to verify the details of that accident on the Bay Bridge. And to contact the framing supplier."

"I think I have ample reason to hold Willis," Sid replied, matching her smile with one of his own, one that didn't quite reach his eyes.

Cassie laughed, a gentle tinkling sound. "Don't jerk me around, Sid. Charge him or let him go."

Sid gazed at her for a long moment, considering. I watched his eyes, but they gave no clue of what was on his mind. I wasn't sure he'd go for Cassie's proposal. But he didn't have much choice.

"All right. Talk to him. If he agrees to come in tomorrow, I'll cut him loose. Ten o'clock, this office."

Sid led the way to the interrogation room, where Hobart waited near the door. The partners conferred for a moment and I saw Hobart shake his head. Either he didn't like the idea of letting Mark go or he was confirming my guess that Mark had refused to answer further questions. I looked past them. Mark stood at the back of the room, in a corner where he could see all of it. His hands were stuck deep into the pockets of his leather jacket.

Finally Sid and Hobart came to some agreement. They motioned Cassie and me into the room. Mark's eyes went from my face to Cassie's, questioning. "Cassie's an attorney," I said.

"Sergeant Vernon has agreed that it would be far more sensible to ask his questions tomorrow morning," Cassie told him. "With me present. Will you agree to that?" Mark thought about it for a long moment. Then he nodded. "Good. We need to talk, then."

"Anywhere but here," Mark said. He zipped up his jacket and walked out of the room.

It had stopped raining while we were at police headquarters, but the streets still shone wetly. We drove to Biff's, an all-night coffee shop near Twenty-Seventh and Broadway, Cassie in her own car, and Mark in the passenger seat next to me. He didn't say anything as we drove. My eyes flickered between the wet pavement and my rearview mirror, at a pair of headlights that had followed me all the way up Broadway from police headquarters. The car made the turn onto Twenty-Seventh several lengths behind me, then went past as I pulled into the coffee-shop parking lot. It was a sedan, but I couldn't tell the make, model, or color and I didn't see the driver. I parked my car, shut off the engine, and unlatched my safety belt.

"I didn't kill her," Mark said, sitting motionless. Then his hand reached for his belt latch. "I didn't kill either of them."

"I know." But I didn't know, not for sure. I just wanted to believe it. "We don't know that Elizabeth's dead. Cassie's a good lawyer. Trust her."

We went inside and settled into a booth. The waitress kept the coffee coming while Cassie probed and questioned Mark, preparing for tomorrow's session with Sid. I excused myself and called Vee from a pay phone. After the police had taken Mark away I had followed Vee's Cadillac as she drove home to the house on Monticello. I worried about leaving her, but the housekeeper, named Nellie, looked unflappable. She listened to my blurted explanation and took Vee upstairs, the Yorkie trailing forlornly behind.

Now Vee answered the phone, her voice tremulous but calm. I brought her up to date. She told me she'd called Alice Gray in Stockton, and that she was trying to reach her husband at his medical convention in Baltimore.

I went back to the booth. Cassie had been making notes on a yellow legal pad, but now she'd set aside the pen and was sipping her coffee. Exhaustion painted Mark's face with deep shadows.

"How are we doing?" I asked.

"We're doing fine." Cassie looked so assured and confident I almost believed her. She stowed the pad and pen in her briefcase. She pulled a couple of bills from the wallet and covered the check. "I'll pick you up tomorrow morning at nine-thirty, Mark. Where are you staying?"

"I don't know," he said dully, staring into his coffee cup. He looked up with a brief, apologetic smile. "I was staying with Vee, but I just can't go back there. I'll find a motel."

He looked like a man who didn't need to be alone. "My place," I said. "I've got a sofa bed."

The waitress collected the check and we walked out to the parking lot. After Cassie left, Mark and I got into my car. I drove to Forty-First and Howe, where he'd left his Blazer. All the way there I checked my rearview mirror, but there was no sign of the car that had followed us earlier. If it had been following us.

I waited while Mark started his engine and switched on the lights. He pulled the Blazer out of its parking place and followed me closely as I drove home. I pulled my car into my parking space. Mark found a spot farther down the street. He walked toward me as I unlocked the front gate and checked my mailbox.

Abigail started to make a racket as soon as we hit the door.

I picked up her food and water bowls. While I opened a can of cat food, Mark knelt and scratched her ears. She butted her head against his blue jeans and purred.

"What's her name?"

"Abigail. You should feel fortunate. She doesn't usually take to strangers."

"Did I tell you I was going to be a vet?" he said softly. "That's why I wanted to go to UC Davis. They have the best school."

"I'm sorry," I said, thinking of lost hope, lost dreams.

"I have a cat, sort of." He straightened and stood in the doorway of the kitchen. "It's a stray that hangs around the shop. I feed it."

"It's trying to adopt you. Why don't you take it home?"

"I don't know. Maybe I'm afraid of the commitment."

I smiled. "Hey, cats are easier than people." I scooped some cat food into Abigail's dish and set it on the floor. She attacked it with vigor.

Mark was in the living room, looking at the furnishings and the pictures on the wall. He ran his hand over the oak sideboard that had belonged to my grandmother. "This is a beautiful piece."

"Grandma Jerusha left it to me. She was the one from Jackson."

He looked at the books in the bookcase without really seeing them. Then he sighed, a long shuddering sound.

"I thought I was all right," he said. "I thought I'd done a good job of putting my life back together after I got out of prison. Of course, you can't really put anything back together after it's broken. The cracks show. You have to create something new."

"You have."

"I wonder. The cracks started showing when you walked into my shop Saturday. Asking questions about that old life. Making me think about things I'd decided to ignore. You see, Jeri, I thought if I ignored my past it would go away. Instead it's staring me in the face. I didn't think I'd be in

Oakland tonight, with the police breathing down my neck. Karen dead, and Betsy . . .''

"Maybe I set this all in motion," I said, "with my questions. But I told Vee I'd find Elizabeth. I had to check out the available leads."

"Available leads." He laughed. "Of all the women I've met in the past three years, you interest me the most. To you I'm an available lead."

"That's not true."

"Yes, it is. We'd never have met if it hadn't been for your damned case," he said. "I don't imagine it's a good idea for a private investigator to get emotionally involved in a case."

"A lousy idea," I agreed. But I was already emotionally involved in this one. I walked past him to the front door and slipped the chain lock into place. I'd left the light on in the kitchen. Now I switched it off. "Let's talk in the morning."

I went to the linen closet in the hall, intending to get sheets and a blanket so I could make up the sofa bed. Mark followed me. He shut the cupboard I'd opened and turned me around the face him. He threaded his fingers in my hair and kissed me, the pressure of his mouth at first gentle, then hard and urgent. I moved as if to pull away, but his hands left my hair and he wrapped his arms around me, pressing my body hard against his. I kissed him back.

"This is not a good idea," I murmured against his mouth. In the back of my mind I heard a voice telling me why I shouldn't be doing this. It wasn't professional. He killed his parents fifteen years ago and he might just have killed his sister tonight.

But my mind was out of synch with my body. My hands left his tangled dark hair, stroked his shoulder blades through his knit shirt, his buttocks through the worn seat of his faded jeans. I slipped my hands between denim and skin as I pressed him close, feeling the hard lines of his body against mine. The tip of his tongue explored the roof of my mouth as his hands tore at the buttons of my shirt. He slipped it from my shoulders, down my arms to drop unheeded on the floor. He found the fastener of my bra and unhooked it, tossing it aside. His fingers moved delicately over the exposed flesh of my breasts.

Then he saw the bruises on my abdomen and looked up. "Is this what happened last night?" he whispered.

I shook my head. "It doesn't matter." He looked troubled as he kissed me again. His mouth left mine and traveled down the sweep of my neck, his lips gently seizing first one nipple, then the other. I gasped and caught my breath, unsteady on my feet as sensations rippled through me.

We swayed together in the hallway, then moved in a clumsy two-step through my bedroom door. I heard drumming on the roof as the rain started again. Light from the surrounding apartment buildings filtered through the blinds. Mark pulled his shirt over his head. My hands brushed the hard planes of his chest. His skin had a slight musky scent. It was smooth under my tongue, with a salty tang. My hands moved to the fly of his Levi's and unfastened the metal buttons. I pushed him to a seated position on the edge of my bed and pulled off his shoes and socks and pants. Then he watched me with an intensity I could feel rather than see as I took off the rest of my clothes.

We stared at each other for a tiny space of time. Then I reached out and pulled down the comforter on the bed. I lay back on the sheets, cool against the growing heat of my own body. Mark stretched beside me, his own flesh warm and silky, then damp with perspiration as we explored each other's bodies with hands and mouths. The rain outside fell against the roof in a steady rhythm.

Twenty-two

THE ONLY THING CLEAR THE NEXT MORNING WAS the weather. I sat on the sofa with my legs tucked under me, wrapped in my thick white terrycloth bathrobe. I had showered and washed my hair. Abigail curled into a smooth ball of cat on my lap, her face covered by her paws, her tail lying just so along her flanks. I'd been sitting here long enough for my hair to dry while I sipped my way through a large mug of coffee. I wanted another cup, but I didn't want to get up, at least not yet. Abigail had spent so much time arranging herself I hated to disturb her.

I thought about Mark, still asleep in my bed, about the urgent, swept-away rush of passion tempered by the awkward reality of fumbling in the medicine cabinet for condoms and diaphragm. Sex is a dangerous thing. I don't mean getting pregnant or catching diseases. It's the emotional baggage that goes along with the physical act. Lately I was used to sleeping with a cat instead of another human being. With the intimacy of bodies came the intimacy of emotions, nakedness of a different sort. Apart from fearing that my thighs revealed my weakness for pasta and my lack of sensible, regular exercise, I wondered if I had shown Mark too much of myself. It made me feel vulnerable, and right now I didn't need to be vulnerable. I had too many questions without answers, and too many things to do.

I heard a noise from the bedroom. Mark came out, barefooted and barechested, his jeans low on his hips. He ran one hand through his dark hair, then over the stubble on his chin, regarding me with sleepy blue eyes.

"Coffee?" he asked, hope distilled into one word.

"In the kitchen. Get me another cup, will you?" I held out the mug and he took it without a word. He disappeared into the kitchen and returned with a mug in either hand, balancing them carefully. I took mine, then watched as he took a mouthful of coffee, holding the mug with both hands as though the brew were necessary to life. He took another swallow and a slow smile spread over his face as the caffeine did its work.

"Hello." He leaned over and kissed me gently on the forehead. "I'm not very coherent first thing in the morning."

"Neither am I. I've been up awhile, though."

"I know. I missed you." He sat at the other end of the sofa, leaning on the arm, his legs stretched out in front of him. "I woke up earlier and you were there. Next time I woke up the cat was on your pillow, so I went back to sleep."

I raised the cup to my lips, recalling the pleasant tangle of limbs, the hard comfort of his body against mine as we made love and as we slept nestled together, all the feelings I'd been dissecting as I sat here on the sofa.

"Are you thinking of all the reasons you shouldn't have gone to bed with me?" Mark's eyes searched my face.

"Yes," I admitted. "Logical, hardheaded, practical reasons."

"There's nothing logical about sex."

"No, there isn't."

"Want to talk?"

"Not now. It's likely to be a long conversation. We don't have time. Cassie's picking you up at nine-thirty. There's a disposable razor in the medicine cabinet, so you can shave." I shifted the sleeping cat from my lap to the sofa and got up, leaving my coffee mug on the end table.

While Mark showered I put on a pair of pants and a knit pullover. Then I went to the kitchen and scrambled some eggs. Neither Mark nor I had eaten anything last night. I wasn't sure about Mark, but I knew I didn't want to face this day with an empty stomach.

Mark came into the living room, newly shaved and his hair still damp. "Smells good," he said. "I'm hungry."

"So am I." I handed him a plate and filled another for myself.

"Tell me about your ex-husband." Mark picked up his fork and dug it into the eggs.

"There's not much to tell." I looked down at my plate. Picking up my toast, I buttered it and washed down a bite with some coffee. "Sid and I were married for three years. It didn't work out. I still like him. But it's not enough to sustain a marriage."

"Why did you split up?"

"Our idiosyncrasies didn't mesh," I said lightly. I'd used that line on my mother. She gave me the same look Mark was giving me now. "Neither did our jobs. Private investigators and cops have different ways of looking at right and wrong and things in between. We had a few disagreements about that."

"He seems determined to pin Karen's death on me."

"Not if your story checks out. Cassie's a good lawyer, Mark. Just listen to her, do what she says."

Cassie arrived as Mark and I were washing the dishes. I buzzed her through the security gate at the front of the courtyard and she hurried across the flagstones and up the steps to my door. She wore a dark blue suit with pearls and a determinedly cheerful expression on her face.

"Half a cup," she said, when I offered her coffee. I handed it to her and she drank a quick mouthful. "I checked with CHP first thing this morning. That three-car accident yesterday on the Bay Bridge was reported to them at four-fifty-five. Traffic was screwed up for the rest of the evening commute." She waggled a finger at Mark. "If your frame supplier confirms that you left his place between four-thirty and four-forty-five, I think we're home free. There's no way you could have gotten onto the freeway and across the bridge ahead of that accident."

I walked with them out to the street. Mark opened the

208

passenger door of Cassie's red Honda. "Where can I find you later?" I asked him.

"Assuming your ex doesn't arrest me for murder? I'll be at Vee's house. She was in pretty bad shape last night. I should go see her."

He got in and fastened his seat belt. Cassie gunned her engine and headed down the block to the stop sign at the corner. As she turned right, I saw another car pull away from the curb, a dark blue Ford that made a running stop and turned right.

A tail, I thought. I wondered if it was the same car I'd seen following us last night. Sid must have put a tail on us last night when we left police headquarters. It was a prudent thing to do from his standpoint, but it irritated me to think of a cop sitting outside my apartment building all night, reporting to Sid that Mark had spent the night at my place.

I turned toward my own car, thinking of the times over the past week when I felt I was being watched. The first time was that evening outside Kinney's office, a prelude to the attempted break-in at my own office. There'd been a blue car following me the next day when I left Karen Willis's apartment building in Berkeley. At least it looked that way until I lost sight of it. Then Monday night, when some anonymous tipster called the cops to report that Jeri Howard was being attacked. It was almost as though the watcher wanted me to know I was being watched.

I drove to Alameda. Lenore Franklin was in the front yard of her house on Gibbons Drive, kneeling on the damp grass with trowel in hand as she dug in the soil of a flower bed. A wooden flat beside her contained petunia sets, their bright velvety petals a riot of yellow, red, pink, and purple. When she saw me coming up the walk, she stood up, grass stains on the knees of her tan slacks. She took off her gardening gloves and smiled at me uncertainly as she said hello.

"I need to talk with your husband, Mrs. Franklin."

"He's playing golf," she said with a little shrug of her shoulders. "He plays golf every morning."

"A little damp, isn't it?" I said, surveying the still-spongy lawn. "After all that rain."

"That's nothing to a true fanatic."

"Which course?"

"Why, the Alameda municipal one. At Harbor Bay Island. Is something wrong?"

"Karen Willis has been murdered."

"Dear God." Shock filled her eyes as she raised one hand to her mouth. "Why do you want to talk to Joe?"

I didn't answer. I left her standing in the yard. Harbor Bay Island is really a peninsula between Oakland Airport and Alameda proper. What used to be marsh is now landfill covered with houses, condominiums, and golf links. I drove across the steel-surfaced drawbridge on Otis Drive and took a right on Island Drive. The golf course sprawled on my left, an expanse of lush emerald grass, sandtraps, and ponds populated by geese and ducks. I made a left turn up the road leading to the clubhouse and parked my car in the lot. At the caddy shack I asked about Admiral Franklin. One of the caddies said he'd just seen Franklin and his partner at the tenth hole. I set out in the direction he'd indicated.

I found the Admiral at the twelfth hole. His partner was a short man with a round belly stretching his bright yellow golf shirt and a cigar stuck in his mouth. Franklin was taking his stance, a golf club in his hands. I hung back in the shelter of a tree and watched him swing his club at the ball, knocking it far down the fairway. He handed his club to the caddy as the short man assumed the position in front of his own teed-up ball.

As Franklin poured himself a cup of coffee from a thermos, I examined the caddy. He was about five-six, with dark hair and a slender build, clean-shaven, and wearing blue jeans and a short-sleeved shirt. He laughed at something the Admiral said, then reached up and scratched his head with his right hand. I saw the blue lines of a tattoo running from his hand to his forearm—a flock of butterflies.

Franklin's companion finished his shot and twirled his club before handing it to the caddy. The caddy hoisted the golf bags as the party prepared to leave. I stepped away from the tree into the morning sunlight and Franklin saw me, a frown clouding his face.

"We need to talk, Admiral."

He drew himself erect as though he were addressing a seaman recruit. "I have nothing to say to you."

"Really? We could start with breaking and entering. Your caddy fits the description of the guy who tried to get into my office last week. Right down to the tattoo." I drilled the younger man with a look. He went white under his tan. "I don't think it would take much effort on the part of the Oakland police to get him to roll over. On you. So let's talk."

Franklin's eyes blazed with fury but he didn't deny it. He turned to his partner. "Go on ahead. I'll catch up with you as soon as I dispose of this matter." The short man looked avidly curious as he and the caddy trundled away in the direction of the balls. When we were alone Franklin faced me.

"What the hell do you want?"

"It's about your daughter."

"Ruth?"

"Karen Willis," I said. "She's dead. Somebody cut her throat in an Oakland alley last night."

Joseph Franklin stared at me with a mixture of shock and grief. Then his face and body sagged, his straight-backed military posture slipping. He looked around as though searching for a life raft and spied a wooden bench under a tree. He walked slowly to it and sat down, hunched forward with his hands on his knees.

"How did you know?" he said.

"Mark told me. He had it figured out years ago."

He gave a harsh laugh. "I was so concerned about the adults finding out I didn't consider the children."

"Is that why you sent Tattoo over to burgle my office? So your wife wouldn't find out you were sleeping around twenty-five years ago? I have a feeling she's known all along."

"I wanted to find out what you knew."

"I know plenty. You can tell me more. About Franny and George and their relationship with their children."

His eyes held the same anger he'd shown when he asked me to leave his house a few days before. "I refuse to believe that Franny could have abused her children."

"You may refuse to believe it, but I have evidence to the contrary. I know Franny drank. There was an incident at the officers club when she climbed up on a table and started disrobing."

"Gossip. Blown out of proportion."

"You seem very determined to protect the reputation of a woman who's been dead for fifteen years."

"Her reputation is all she has left." Franklin's mouth tightened. "Perhaps she was a strict disciplinarian. I know George was. So am I."

"Did you ever burn your kids with the lighted end of a cigarette?"

"I don't believe it."

"I saw the scars, Admiral. On Mark Willis's arms."

"She was murdered, damn it. Both of them shot down in their own house. Slaughtered. Nothing excuses that."

"Of course nothing excuses it," I said. "But don't you want to know why? I do. Because I think that will tell me why Elizabeth disappeared, and why Karen was murdered."

He looked away from me, across the green in the direction his golfing partner had gone. He was still handsome, despite his years. His gray hair and the lines in his face made him look distinguished. He must have been quite a looker twenty-five years ago, when he and Franny Willis caught each other's eyes.

"You had a long-term relationship with Franny, lasting several years. When did it start?"

"I'd been attracted to Franny for a long time," he said reluctantly. "She was vital, sensual."

"Did she feel the same way about you?"

"Obviously she did." He folded his arms across his chest. "She wasn't very happy. She and George were a mismatched couple. He was very stolid, phlegmatic. She told me once they got married because she was pregnant with Mark. People did that in those days, married and owned up to their responsibilities. Nowadays they just have abortions.''

The admiral's sense of morality seemed to have a large blind spot when it came to sleeping with his neighbor's wife.

''When did it start?''

''A couple of years after Beth was born. Lenore and I were having some problems. George and Franny were very understanding. I used to go over and talk. Sometimes when Lenore and I would fight, I'd end up spending the night. In the den, of course.'' He paused. ''After a while it was obvious that Franny felt the same attraction I had for her. One thing followed another.''

''Was it a steady relationship, or once in a while?''

''We both knew it was wrong,'' he protested. ''We tried to break it off. We didn't even see each other for a year while I was in the Philippines. But every time we were together we felt that pull.''

''Did you ever think of leaving your wife for Franny?''

He shook his head. ''No. At that time the Navy was a lot more traditional than it is now. Divorce was frowned upon. How would it have looked if I left my wife and children for a fellow officer's wife?''

''The threat of a black mark on your fitness reports. Is that the glue that held your marriage together?''

''Of course not.'' Indignation colored his face. ''I care for Lenore. She and I grew up together, in the same town. She's the mother of my children.''

''Not all of them. When did you find out Karen was yours?''

''We were living in the same neighborhood in San Diego,'' he said, the words coming slowly. ''I was on staff duty at the air station and George was on a carrier. He was out to sea. Franny came to see me one evening, while Lenore was out. She told me she was pregnant, that it was my child. She wanted me to leave Lenore.''

''But you didn't. For all those high-toned moral reasons. How did she feel about that?''

213

"She was angry. We had a terrible quarrel. She threw a vase at me. Later I told Lenore I'd knocked it off a table. Franny said she and George had nothing in common, that they were just going through the motions. She wanted to . . . how did she put it? Cut her losses and start over. I told her it was out of the question. I had orders to Pearl Harbor and Lenore was having some medical problems. I broke it off."

"You went to Hawaii and left Franny holding the baby, while George was out to sea. You're a real piece of work, Admiral."

He shook his head. "You don't understand. Leaving my wife and children for a fellow officer's wife wouldn't have solved any problems. It would have been disastrous, for everyone."

"Disastrous for your career, you mean. When did you see Franny again?"

"George got orders to Pearl Harbor. As my wife told you last week, we seemed always to be stationed in the same places. We remained friends with the Willises."

"Did you resume your relationship with Franny?"

"Not exactly," Franklin said, turning his head away. I moved into his line of vision.

"What's that supposed to mean? Either you did or you didn't."

"We were together a lot. Franny took up golf. By the time we came to Alameda she and I played together regularly."

"Did you sleep together?"

"You're disgusting." He stood up and glared at me, trying to intimidate me with his stare.

"You don't exactly smell like a rose, Admiral." I leaned into his glare. "You're the one who sent the caddy to break into my office. I know you're running for the state senate. That tells me this has very little to do with protecting your family with the knowledge of your affair with Franny Willis. You're covering your ass so you'll look good to the voters."

Franklin sputtered at me in rage. I pressed home my point.

"If the cops haul in the caddy he'll talk. And I'll press charges. You'll definitely get some pointed inquiries from

214

the newspapers about where you fit into all of this. I think you'd better answer my disgusting questions. Did you and Franny Willis resume your sexual relationship after Karen was born?''

"No," he said, controlling himself with an effort. "There were times when I thought we were headed that way. I would have been willing to resume it. But she always brought me up short."

"She teased you, then."

"Yes. I suppose you could call it that."

An interesting sort of revenge, I thought. Franny got next to the admiral, only on the golf course instead of in bed. It must have made for some tense mornings on the fairway.

I didn't have any more disgusting questions for Admiral Franklin. I left him at the twelfth hole, looking as though he'd like to keelhaul me. He insisted that Karen didn't know he was her father, but if Mark had figured it out, Karen may have too. Of course, Mark was nine years older than Karen and the affair between his mother and Franklin had been going on under his nose.

Karen knew something, I thought, hearing her say she wasn't where she was supposed to be. That something got her killed.

Twenty-three

I FOUND CASSIE IN HER OFFICE, ON THE TELE-
phone. I helped myself to a cup of coffee from the law-office
pot and waited in the reception area until Cassie finished her
call. I was nearly to the bottom of the cup when she appeared
in the doorway and beckoned me into her office.

"What's the story on Mark? How did it go?" I asked,
taking the seat in front of Cassie's desk. She settled into her
own chair before answering.

"The framing supplier says he thinks Mark left his shop
at four-forty. But he's not sure. The accident on the bridge
happened about ten minutes later. It's likely Mark got stuck
in that traffic mess."

"Likely," I repeated. "That doesn't sound airtight."

"It's not." Cassie looked thoughtful. "Mark could have
made it onto the bridge in five minutes, which means he
could have made it past Treasure Island right before that
accident. Sid's still convinced Mark killed Karen. His case
is circumstantial, but you know how pigheaded he can be. I
don't think he'll make an arrest until he's got more evidence.
He let Mark go for now, but told him not to leave town."

"What about the body they pulled out of the estuary?"

"Edward Foster did call the coroner's office. He's having
Elizabeth's dental records sent up for comparison. When I
talked to the medical examiner, the records hadn't arrived
yet."

I got to my feet. "I don't think Mark killed anyone, Cassie. Maybe not even his parents."

"But you're not sure," Cassie said seriously. "You like him a lot, don't you, Jeri?"

"Yes, I do."

"Well, for whatever it's worth, I don't think he killed anyone either. And I'm the lawyer."

"I'm counting on you. Where's Mark now?"

"I dropped him off on your street so he could pick up his Blazer. He said he was going over to his aunt's house."

I headed for Piedmont. Mark's Blazer was parked along the curb outside Vee's big house. I parked behind it and walked up the long driveway. Nellie, the housekeeper, greeted me at the front door and directed me to a large country-style kitchen full of blue-and-yellow tile, with copper pots hanging on the walls. Mark stood at the stove, a wooden spoon in hand, stirring something in a more plebeian stainless-steel saucepan.

"Hi," he said. "I'm fixing Vee some soup. She's still pretty ragged. She talked to Uncle Charles in Baltimore. He's got a flight into Oakland tonight."

"I talked to Cassie before I came over here." I leaned against one of the tiled counters and looked into his blue eyes.

"Then you know I'm still the prime suspect. Your ex would like nothing better than to pin this on me. I didn't kill Karen. Or Elizabeth."

"I don't think you did."

"There's a world of difference between think and know. You've considered the possibility that I murdered one or both of my sisters."

"All right, I have. I've considered a lot of things. Does that make you feel any better? Or worse? You may have had the opportunity. But I don't think you had a motive. Did you, Mark?"

He turned off the gas under the saucepan and transferred the soup to a waiting bowl. "No."

"Why do I feel you're not telling me everything?"

I didn't think he would answer that question. He didn't have to. Vee entered the kitchen, looking tired and wan, but more composed than she had when I'd brought her home last night. She wore another of her caftans, this one a subdued brown-and-gold print.

"Nellie told me you were here." She took my hand. "Mark said things went well with the police this morning."

I looked at him and he shook his head. Evidently he'd given Vee an edited version of his session with the police, leaving out the fact that they still considered him a suspect.

"Your soup's ready." Mark carried the steaming bowl to a breakfast table at one end of the kitchen. He set it on a placemat and pulled out a chair.

"I'm not very hungry," Vee said.

"I insist. Nellie said you didn't eat any breakfast. I made some sandwiches too." Vee took the chair he offered and picked up a spoon. Mark removed a dishcloth from a platter on the counter and carried it to the table.

"I've got the kettle on and you'll have some tea in a minute. Jeri, sit down and have a sandwich. There's turkey and roast beef." He opened the refrigerator and took out two bottles of beer, waving one at me. I nodded and he opened them both. He returned to the table with the beer and a couple of plates. I picked up a turkey sandwich and took a bite.

"Vee, you told me you didn't see Karen often."

"No," Vee said, dipping her spoon into the soup. "She knew I didn't approve of what she did for a living. We'd talk on the phone every couple of months. I'd call her, not the other way around. I tried to keep the lines of communication open. But that has to be a two-way street. With Karen it seemed that I was making all the effort."

"Did she ever give any indication of what was going on in her life? Would she have told you if she was having money problems, or difficulty in a relationship?"

Vee thought about it for a moment, then shook her head. "No. If she needed money, all she had to do was ask. But Karen is . . . was always independent. When we talked, it seemed to be all surface, very little substance. She'd ask about the family, I'd give her a report. That was it. She always closed by saying we'd get together for lunch. Of course we never did.''

The teakettle on the stove whistled and Mark got up, turning off the burner beneath it. He poured hot water over a tea bag and carried the cup to Vee. She patted his hand when he set it down at her place. "Thank you, Mark.''

"When was the last time you saw her?''

"Thanksgiving. That's over four months ago.'' She looked sad. "I invited her for Christmas, but she said she had other plans. I wish she had come. Mark was here.''

I looked at Mark, who resumed his seat at the opposite end of the table. "You hadn't seen her since—''

"The night my parents died,'' he finished. "No. The last time I saw Karen she was nine, headed out the door to her friend's house, the next street over.'' He tilted his beer bottle back and took a swallow.

"When she called yesterday to set up our meeting, she said she wasn't where she was supposed to be. I think she meant the night of the murders. Do either of you have any idea what she was talking about?''

Vee looked mystified as she fished the teabag out of her cup and set it on her plate. "She went to a slumber party. There were three or four little girls there, in sleeping bags in the den. Karen said they played games and watched television before they went to bed. I don't know what time they finally got to sleep. Karen was nowhere near my sister's house when it happened.''

I looked at Mark. He leaned back in his chair, cradling the beer bottle, staring down at the half-eaten sandwich on his plate. When he lifted his head his face was thoughtful. His eyes met mine.

"I don't know what she meant,'' he said quietly. Once again I had the feeling he wasn't telling me everything.

"What about Karen's relationship with Elizabeth?'' I asked Vee.

"They didn't get on very well when they were growing up,'' Vee said. "Karen was lively, into things. I think in some way she resented Beth for the attention Beth got.'' That

219

tallied with what Karen had told me last Friday. Vera sipped her tea, then picked up her soup spoon. "I'm sure Beth thought Karen was a bratty little sister."

"She was," Mark said. A shadow of memory passed over his face.

"After the girls left Stockton," I asked Vee, "did they keep in contact with one another?"

"At first they did. While Beth lived in San Francisco."

"And when Elizabeth changed her name and moved to Los Gatos?"

Vee shook her head. "I don't know."

I heard the doorbell chime at the front of the house. A moment later Nellie entered the kitchen.

"Mrs. Gray is here," she told Vee. "With Mrs. Madison."

"I'll come out. Put Alice's things in the corner room and my mother's in the room next to her." Vee pushed back her chair and left the kitchen with the housekeeper.

"You haven't seen Alice since the murders either, have you?" I said to Mark.

"No." He got up and cleared the table, wrapping the sandwiches before putting them in the refrigerator. He stacked the dishes in the dishwasher, then he stood leaning against the counter as he finished his beer. "I'm not sure I want to. From all reports, she doesn't like me very much."

I heard loud grumbling from the foyer and concluded that Grandma Madison was being difficult. Nellie confirmed this a moment later when she came to the kitchen and refilled the teakettle.

"I'm supposed to repent my sins and bring her some tea and cookies," she said, shaking her head.

"I gather my grandmother's not too lucid." Mark opened the cabinet under the sink and pitched his empty bottle into the trash can.

"I think she sees more than she lets on."

While the teakettle heated, Nellie bustled around the kitchen. She filled a bowl with vanilla wafers from a box in the pantry and set it on a wooden tray. When the kettle whistled she poured hot water over a tea bag and carried the tray out to the foyer and up the stairs.

"Might as well get it over with," Mark said. He led the way to Vee's living room at the front of the house. The room showcased Vee's antiques. Grouped around the fireplace were a sofa and two matching chairs, each with a high curved back, covered in pale blue brocade. A tall glass-frosted oak cabinet on the opposite wall displayed crystal and china. I walked across the soft blue carpet to a baby grand piano in the back corner of the room. I fingered the keys, playing a scale. Mark moved restlessly about the room, his hand toying with a vase on the mantel, then with the shutters that covered the lower half of the front window. A moment later we heard voices as Vee and Alice descended the stairs.

"I've got her settled down a bit," Alice said. "These days she hates to leave home, even for a short ride to the doctor's office." She stopped when she saw Mark standing at the window. He turned and nodded to her in an awkward gesture of remembered manners. Alice's lips compressed into a thin line as she stared at him. She turned to Vee. "What happened? You weren't very specific on the telephone."

"I told you Karen had been murdered." Vee's eyes took on a painful cast.

"I know. Was she mugged? What was she doing in that alley behind your shop?"

"She was on her way to see me." As I spoke Alice turned and stared at me, the intruder at the back of the room. I left the piano and walked to stand next to Vee. "We had an appointment to meet at Vee's shop at six."

"But why?"

"I don't know. I think she had some information about Elizabeth's disappearance."

Alice shook her head, barely controlling the emotion in her voice. "This is unbelievable. First Dad, then Karen. Do the police have any suspects?"

"They suspect me," Mark said.

His words had the effect of a slow-fused bomb let loose in

221

Vee's elegant living room. Alice wheeled and her eyes raked over him. "Why do they suspect you?"

"I don't have an alibi. At least not a very good one."

"Did you kill her?"

"Of course he didn't," Vee said.

Vee's protest went unheeded by Alice, whose eyes fixed on Mark's face. "Did you kill her?" she persisted, throwing the words at him like stones.

"No, I didn't. Why would I kill Karen?"

"I have no idea. I couldn't even venture a guess. Any more than I could when you killed Franny and George."

Mark winced. Then his face tightened into the same mask it had worn last night while Sid questioned him, and his voice took on a faint tinge of sarcasm.

"I see. Since I'm a convicted murderer, it's only natural to suspect me whenever there's a stray body in the area. You're not alone in your feelings. Sergeant Vernon of the Oakland Police Department seems to agree with you."

Anger suffused Alice's face, deepening the furrows between her brows and leaving two red spots burning at her cheekbones.

"If the police suspect you I imagine they have good reason. Yet you stand here being flippant about it. I can't believe you're my sister's child."

"I'm your sister's child, all right," Mark said with a short humorless laugh. It underscored the difference between the Franny he'd described to me and the Franny Alice remembered.

Mark's laugh made Alice even angrier. "They should have kept you locked up forever. I can't imagine you'd shelter him, Vera," she snapped. "I won't stay in the same house with him." She made a half-turn as though to head for the stairs.

"I'll save you the trouble," Mark said, his words stopping her in midstep. As he walked past us into the hall I saw that he was angry too, a cold hard anger that contrasted with the heat of Alice's words. He went up the stairs and came back a moment later, an overnight bag in hand.

"I want you to stay," Vee said, a quiver in her voice, as

she and I joined Mark in the foyer. She glanced over at Alice but her older sister stood in front of the fireplace in the living room, her back to us.

"I can't. It'll just make it worse."

"Where will you be?" I asked.

"I don't know. I'm not leaving town. Your ex-husband told me not to. I don't want to antagonize him further. I'll find a motel somewhere and leave word on your answering machine." He turned and walked out the front door. I heard the engine of the Blazer come to life as he started it and drove away.

"All right, he's gone." Vee addressed Alice's rigid back. "Are you satisfied?"

"That makes me the villain, doesn't it?" Alice turned to face her sister. "For God's sake, Vera, he killed his own parents. You act as though it never happened. You visited him in prison. When he got out, you set him up in business. And now you defend him, with Karen lying dead in the morgue."

"I believe him when he says he didn't kill her. As for as the rest," Vee said, her round face somber, "I can forgive him. I'm sorry you can't."

Alice opened her mouth to retort but I stepped between the two sisters. "You can finish this quarrel later, if you really want to. Right now I'd like to talk to Mrs. Madison."

"Good God, she can't tell you anything," Alice said, exasperated. "You saw her on Sunday. You talked to her then. She's senile."

"I'm not so sure. Something she said made me think she's seen one or both of your nieces recently."

"Time doesn't mean anything to her. She could have been talking about something that happened ten years ago."

"Maybe. Karen and Elizabeth both dyed their hair blond. How long has it been since they were brunettes?"

"Karen started coloring hers in high school," Vee said thoughtfully. "Beth . . . I think it was when she worked in Sunnyvale."

"I don't follow you at all," Alice said.

"It's a long shot. Let me talk to your mother. Alone."

Alice grumbled some more, but Vee led the way upstairs to the bedroom where they'd settled Grandma Madison. The old woman sat up in bed, drinking tea from the ceramic mug, wearing a plain black dress like the one she'd worn the day I first met her. She'd spilled tea on the bedclothes and the front of her dress. A tuneless song issued from her smiling mouth. One wrinkled hand reached for a vanilla wafer. She popped it into her mouth and hummed around it.

"Hello, Mama," Vee said.

Mrs. Madison smiled, then spotted me and frowned. "Redheaded witch."

Alice compressed her mouth in a matching frown. "Would you like some more tea?" Vee asked.

The old woman nodded and held out the mug. "More cookies," she said, bits of vanilla wafer falling from her mouth to the front of her dress.

Vee took the mug and the bowl. "Let's get Mama some more tea and cookies," she told Alice. Alice shook her head, but she followed Vee out of the room, leaving me alone with Mrs. Madison.

"I'm Jeri, Mrs. Madison." I took a seat on the edge of the bed and looked into the stubborn old face, hoping to find a glimmer of the here-and-now. She watched me like a cat watching a mouse hole. "I met you on Sunday. You thought I was one of the girls. You remember the girls, Karen and Elizabeth. You said, 'Yellow-haired witch. Prying, pawing, sniffing around.' "

"She's evil and the Lord will strike her down," Mrs. Madison said, just as she had that afternoon.

"Right. Did you see one of the girls? Can you tell me which one, Mrs. Madison?"

She grinned at me, looking crafty, the change in her face enough to make me wonder if the senility was a pose. I was sure there was more going on behind the rheumy blue eyes than anyone suspected.

"Tea?" she asked.

"Vee's bringing your tea. Let's talk while we wait for her. Where's Mr. Madison?"

"Gone to Jesus." She looked sad. "Good man."

"When was that?"

She thought about it for a moment. "Two weeks." It was not quite two weeks since her husband's death, but she was in the ballpark. Besides, Lester Madison had been in the hospital before he died. I took the photograph of Elizabeth I'd been carrying in my purse, now creased at the corners, and showed it to Mrs. Madison again.

"Have you seen Elizabeth since Mr. Madison left?"

She hummed a tune. I recognized the hymn "Shall We Gather at the River?" She didn't even look at the photograph. Her eyes were closed as she hummed. In a quavery soprano she sang a few bars. "Where bright angel feet have trod . . ." Then she opened her eyes and said, quite clearly, "Came to the house."

"Who came to the house? Was it Karen or Elizabeth?"

"Looked around. Pulled out drawers. Prying. Pawing through stuff." Mrs. Madison brushed cookie crumbs from the damp bodice of her dress. "Asked me if I knew where she was."

"Who looked around, Mrs. Madison? Who was she looking for?"

"One looking for the other."

"Which one came to the house?" I asked, but didn't get an answer. I cajoled and pressed, but the old woman ignored me. Her eyes sparkled and her wrinkled face creased in a sly smile. She started singing again, about the river that flowed past the throne of God. She sang hymns until her good humor passed, then she said I was a redheaded spawn of Satan and told me to go away. She lay down on her side, her back to me, and refused to say another word.

I went slowly down the stairs to the living room. One looking for the other implied two of a kind. Two sisters, I thought, Karen and Elizabeth. One did not know the other's whereabouts and had gone looking at the house where they'd both grown up. When I talked to Karen last week, she said she knew Elizabeth lived in Los Gatos. But it was possible she didn't know where. With the death of their grandfather, maybe she expected Elizabeth to show up in Stockton for the funeral. Or perhaps the sister Grandma Madison had seen was Elizabeth, looking for Karen. That would make sense, given Karen's short tenancy in the Berkeley apartment.

Vee and Alice sat on the sofa, Mrs. Madison's tea and cookies on the coffee table in front of them. "Well?" Vee asked.

"I asked her if she'd seen Karen or Elizabeth recently, after Mr. Madison died. She said one of them came to the house, looking for the other."

"That's absurd." Alice shook her head. "You can't believe anything she says. Besides, how could one of the girls come to the house without my knowing it? I'm with her all the time."

"Not every minute," Vee said. "Not right after Dad died. He died Friday morning and the funeral was Monday afternoon. We were at the mortuary and the church several times over the next few days, making arrangements for the funeral. We were gone several hours at a stretch. You had the next-door neighbor's daughter keep an eye on Mama. But she didn't exactly stay with her. Someone could have slipped into the house and talked to Mama."

"All right, it's possible." Alice conceded the point grudgingly. "But just because Mama said it happened doesn't mean it did. She says anything that comes into her head. The fact that you asked a question about the girls is enough to make her say she saw them."

"I know she wouldn't make a credible witness in a court of law," I said. "But I have a hunch she's telling the truth. Whoever came to the house looked around and pulled out drawers. Do you keep an address book, Mrs. Gray?"

"Yes. I have a desk in my room. The book's in the top drawer."

"Do you have a current address for Karen or Elizabeth in that book?"

"No." Alice shot Vee a black look. "Neither of the girls

226

bother to communicate with me. Vee's the only one who knows where they live."

"One looking for the other," I said, almost to myself. "But which sister, and why?" One person might be able to answer that question, if I could find him.

Twenty-four

    I HEADED FOR SAN FRANCISCO IN SEARCH OF SOME answers. The sunshine visible in the East Bay had not yet penetrated the city's fog. At the South of Market studio I climbed the stairs to Lila's domain.

    She leaned over her worktable, a needle and thread in her hand, her short black hair standing up in spikes and silvery pink eye shadow surrounding her large brown eyes. Over her baggy plum-colored jumpsuit she wore a large green apron with pockets full of thread and sewing utensils. A gauzy red costume was spread out on the worktable, a three-cornered tear near the hem. Lila frowned with concentration as she repaired the tear with tiny stitches.

    "I haven't seen her," she said, clipping the thread with a pair of scissors.

    "She's dead. Murdered last night in Oakland."

    Lila looked at me as though she were trying to decide whether it mattered. "So," she said finally. I couldn't tell if it was a question or a comment. "Was it drugs?"

    "Could have been. Was she into drugs?"

    "She did some coke. Doesn't everybody?" When I didn't answer, she shrugged and reached for a hanger. She hung the costume on the rod with the others. "There's a lot of drugs in this business."

    "Coke costs money," I said. "Did Karen have that kind of money?"

    "She made good money here. Enough to live well." Lila's mouth quirked. "That's why we're in this racket. The pay's good."

"Karen was twenty-four. She told me that was old for making skin flicks."

Lila nodded. "That's true. Karen had a great body and she knew how to use it. But in this business they like them young and dumb. Karen was neither."

"The director, Beyer. Was he thinking about phasing her out? Using somebody else?"

"Hell if I know. Ask him. If he'll talk to you."

"I will." I took Elizabeth's picture from my purse and held it out to Lila. "Did you ever see this woman? Talking to Karen, or with Karen, any time in the past couple of weeks?"

Lila took the picture and studied it. "No," she said, shaking her head. "Not that I remember, anyway. Who is she?"

"Karen's sister, Elizabeth. Karen called her Lizzie." Something crossed Lila's face, just a flicker. "You've heard that name before. When?"

"I think it was a couple of weeks ago. Karen came up here to use the phone. She was always using my phone. It was a long-distance call. I remember because she dialed more than seven numbers. I bitched at her and she bitched back, like she always does . . . did. She told me to mind my own business and get out. Ordered me out of my own workroom." She grimaced at the absurdity. "Of course I wouldn't leave. She turned her back and talked real low, but I heard her call the other person on the line Lizzie."

"What else did you hear?" I asked, leaning forward.

"They weren't having a friendly conversation. Karen seemed to be threatening this other party. It had that tone about it, at least from her side."

I wrote down the workroom phone number. If a check of the number's records showed a call to the Philip Foster residence in Los Gatos that would confirm Lila's story. But what did Karen know that was a threat to her sister? Was she planning to tell Philip about his wife's past? Or something else?

"What do you know about Rick Petrakis, Karen's friend?"

"He's a grip. Or was."

229

"How long has he been seeing Karen?"

"About a year. Of course I only see Karen when we're working. She may have had other guys on her dance card. Or girls, for all I know."

"How often do you work?"

"Beyer cranks out about six of these epics a year. Karen's been working for him steadily for three or four years." Lila shrugged. "She was okay, a cut above the rest of these bimbos. I never thought she'd wind up dead, at least not this way."

"I need to talk to Rick," I said.

Lila made a face. "You don't think he had anything to do with it?"

"No. But maybe he can tell me where she was this weekend." Lila was silent for a moment, her hands in the pocket of her green apron.

"After I talked to you I got Rick's address from one of the guys on the crew." She pulled a slip of paper from the pocket and handed it to me.

"Thanks, Lila."

"Yeah, well . . ." She dismissed me with a wave. "I've got work to do. Go pester somebody else."

My efforts to talk with Beyer, the director, came up against the closed steel doors that led to the set. He was shooting a scene. A surly underling told me I could wait, though it was no guarantee Beyer would talk to me. When I pressed him he started making noises about having me thrown out of the building. Not that he could do it himself. He was six inches shorter than me.

I was debating whether to wait or to simply sic Sid Vernon on Beyer when I glanced down the corridor and saw a dark-haired man wearing jeans and a denim jacket, carrying a motorcycle helmet. He took a step in my direction, then stopped when he saw me.

"Petrakis," I said.

He turned and headed back the way he'd come. I followed, dodging people in the hallway. He disappeared through a doorway on the left. It was the men's room, but that didn't stop me. I pushed open the door, startling an older man who hastily buttoned the front of his coveralls and got the hell out of there.

Petrakis was at the window that led to the roof of the building next door, the helmet on the floor at his feet. The window was open about six inches, and he was trying to wrench the opening wider so he could get through. I crossed the soiled linoleum floor and grabbed his jacket, spinning him around, shoving him back against the wall. The helmet rolled against my feet and I kicked it away. Petrakis struggled, balling his fists.

"Karen's dead, Rick."

He froze and dropped his hands to his sides. "What?"

"Somebody cut her throat in the alley behind her aunt's shop, when she was on her way to meet me."

Petrakis sagged against the wall, fear and something else flickering over his face. He rubbed his hands over his eyes.

"She didn't come back last night." His words sounded disjointed. "I wondered what happened. I stewed about it all night. I knew she was going to meet you, so this morning I called your office and got the machine. Called her aunt's shop. Nobody answered. So I thought I'd come over here, thinking maybe somebody heard something. I didn't know what else to do."

"You'd better tell me what you know."

"I don't know anything," he said, panic in his eyes.

"Sure you do, Rick. You and Karen left the hotel Friday night and neither of you showed up for work the next morning. Why? Where were you?"

"My place in El Cerrito," he stammered. "Karen said we had to stay out of sight for a couple of days. The only time we left was that day we went over to Karen's apartment to get some of her things. I didn't mean to push you down the stairs. I was just trying to give Karen time to get to her car."

"What about the weekend before last?"

He looked at me as though I was crazy. Maybe he had trouble remembering back further than a week. He frowned and shook his head, bewildered. "We worked. We were here all weekend."

"Karen didn't go to Stockton? For her grandfather's funeral?"

"Hell, no. She didn't say anything about a funeral. We were here. Just ask some of the crew."

Rick's words confirmed what I had suspected. It was Elizabeth who'd gone to Stockton, pawing through drawers, looking for Karen's address. Elizabeth was the yellow-haired witch Grandma Madison had seen.

"You're doing fine, Rick. Now let's talk about the night you left the hotel." I leaned toward him, my eyes catching his and refusing to let go. "Why did Karen say she had to stay out of sight? Did it have something to do with my visit?"

"I don't know," Petrakis insisted.

"Then tell me what happened Friday night."

"We left here about seven. We stopped by the hotel so Karen could change. Then we went up to Chinatown and had dinner."

"Who's we? Just you and Karen?"

"No. Some other people from the crew went with us."

"What happened when you got back to the hotel?"

"We went up to our rooms," he said, then he stopped.

"You remembered something."

"Yeah." He nodded slowly. "There was this woman waiting in the lobby. She was sitting down when we walked in, but she stood up, walked over, and said hello to Karen."

"Did Karen say anything?"

He thought about it for a moment. "She said something like, 'I expected to hear from you sooner.' Karen told me she wanted to talk, so I went up to my room. I don't know what they talked about, but fifteen minutes later Karen knocked on my door and said we had to split. I argued with her, said Beyer would fire us if we didn't show up for work. But she said we had to get out of there."

"She didn't say why?"

"No. She kept telling me she'd explain, but she didn't."

"Describe the woman," I demanded. "Short or tall?

Blonde, brunette, or redhead? You must have noticed something about her."

Petrakis huddled inside his clothes as though he were making himself smaller, trying to get away from this crazy woman who had him backed against the wall in the men's room. "She was shorter than Karen. And slender, like a dancer. Short hair, brown, I think. She had on a tan coat with a hat that matched."

A woman in a tan raincoat with a matching hat over her cropped dark hair, moving with the gliding walk of a dancer. I'd seen her last night, outside Vee's shop, peering in the window. And last week, walking along the street in front of Karen's apartment. Elizabeth wasn't dead. She was stalking me, and I'd led her straight to Karen.

A man pushed open the door of the men's room, then backed out when he saw Petrakis and me.

"When I talked to Karen Friday afternoon," I said, "she told me she hadn't seen her sister or talked to her in years. I know she was lying. She kept in touch with Elizabeth, even visited her. Karen called her Lizzie. What do you know about her?"

"I don't know anything," Petrakis insisted again. He turned his head to one side to escape my eyes. "Just that Karen didn't like her very much."

"Karen was thinking about the future, about what would happen when she got out of this business. She made good money. Did she have a nest egg put away?" He shook his head.

"I didn't think so. Karen went through money pretty fast. That nice new BMW. And the drugs. Maybe Karen was going to make a big score."

"How would she do that, Rick? Karen's sister is married to a man in Los Gatos. He's not rich, but he has money." I saw a quick flash of knowledge on Rick's face and I bore down on him.

"Karen knew a few things about Elizabeth that Elizabeth's husband didn't know. Was that it, Rick? Was she trying to tap her sister for some cash?"

"I think so," Rick whispered.

Blackmail, I thought. Karen blackmailing Elizabeth, at a time when one more thing going wrong in Elizabeth's life was just enough to send her house of cards tumbling. Karen knew about Elizabeth reinventing herself as Renee Mills. Was that enough to propel Elizabeth out of Los Gatos to Stockton, to pump her senile grandmother for information on Karen's current whereabouts? Was it enough to propel Elizabeth into murder?

"Karen called me yesterday to arrange a meeting," I said. "Were you with her when she called?" He nodded. "She said something about not being where she was supposed to be. Does it have something to do with the night her parents were killed?"

"She never told me details," he said. "Just that her parents were murdered and her brother went to prison for it. I made all the sympathetic noises and she told me not to lose any sleep over it. Said it was ancient history. Only like a lot of history it wasn't written the way it happened."

"How did she know? She was at a slumber party at a friend's house."

"She said she got mad at her friend and decided to go home, barefoot, in her PJs. She climbed over the back fence into the yard and got all the way to the porch when she heard the shots. She got scared and ran back to her friend's house."

A cat in the bushes, Joseph Franklin had said, describing the noise he heard in the Willis yard when he went to investigate the shots that killed his neighbors. Instead it was a frightened nine-year-old girl who'd seen—what? Her brother with a gun in his hand? Her mother's body in the doorway between the living room and kitchen?

"What did she see, Rick?"

"I don't know," he insisted. "She never told me. I honestly don't know."

Maybe she hadn't seen anything at all, just heard the shots. Whatever it was, Karen was going to tell me last night. But someone stopped her. I could think of only two people who had a stake in what happened the night of the Willis murders.

234

Twenty-five

I STOPPED AT MY OFFICE TO CHECK THE MESSAGES on my answering machine. Mark had called to let me know he was staying at the Boatel, on the estuary at the end of Broadway. I called, but there was no answer in his room, so I left a message at the desk.

Sid was upstairs in the Homicide Section at Oakland Police Headquarters, looking disgruntled as he helped himself to a cup of coffee. He took a sip of the poisonous-looking brew and grimaced, whether at me or the coffee I wasn't sure.

"Mark Willis is at the Boatel," he said.

"I know."

"Nice of him to stay in touch. Since I have a few more questions to ask him."

"What did the framing supplier say?"

"That Willis left the shop around four-forty. Which still doesn't tell me whether he made it over the bridge before that accident stopped traffic."

"Circumstantial evidence, Sid. You can't prove he got onto the bridge before the accident."

"Circumstantial cuts both ways, Jeri. You can't prove he didn't."

"What about the floater?"

"Coroner's checking dental records now."

"By the way, I spotted your tail."

Sid scowled at me. "You think we've got the manpower for a tail? Besides, we answered a homicide call in East Oakland right after you left."

"We were followed when we left here last night. I spotted the car again this morning when Mark and Cassie left my place. A dark blue Ford sedan."

"Are you sure it was tailing Willis and Cassie?"

"I know a tail when I see one."

"Any ideas?"

"A few. I've been over to San Francisco this afternoon. Karen Willis made porno movies, at the Folsom Studio. I talked to a woman named Lila, who works in Wardrobe, and Karen's boyfriend, Rick Petrakis."

"And you alerted them that the cops would drop by to ask some questions," Sid said with disgust. "Thanks one hell of a lot, Jeri."

"Just shut up and listen. I went to see Karen last Friday, to ask her some questions about her sister. She talked, but I found out Monday that she was lying about a few things. When I went back to the studio, I discovered she and Petrakis took a powder. Friday night they left the hotel in San Francisco where the cast and crew were staying."

"So where does all this tie in?" Sid's question was calm enough, but his yellow cat's eyes flashed.

"Karen was blackmailing her sister."

"That's a real stretch, Jeri."

"Maybe not. Petrakis said when he and Karen got to the hotel Friday night, a woman was waiting in the lobby for Karen. He went upstairs while Karen talked to the woman. About fifteen minutes later, Karen came to his room and insisted they had to clear out of there. Karen was afraid of something. I think it was the woman in the lobby, and I think that woman was Elizabeth."

"I'm still not convinced," Sid said. "Where's the motive for this alleged blackmail scheme?"

"When Karen called me yesterday to arrange a meeting she said something about not being where she was supposed to be. I didn't know what she meant. I think she planned to explain when we met. Today when I talked to Petrakis, he said Karen told him she wasn't at her friend's house the night

236

her parents were murdered. She was on the back porch when it happened.''

Now Sid looked interested. He turned to Wayne. ''Call our friend Inspector Cavalli over at SFPD and ask him to drop a net over that studio until we get there. I hope you haven't scared Petrakis off, Jeri.''

''He lives in El Cerrito,'' I said, handing him the address Lila had given me. ''Five-ten, dark hair, mustache. Rides a motorcycle.''

Sid glanced at the slip of paper. ''We'll talk later about you withholding evidence from me.''

''I just told you, didn't I?''

''You could have told me some of it last night, instead of waiting until—'' He looked at his watch. ''Five o'clock this afternoon.''

''I didn't have it figured out last night.''

''*If* you have it figured out.'' He waited until Wayne got off the phone, then they left.

Back at my office I called the Boatel, but there was still no answer in Mark's room. I dealt with the day's mail and returned a couple of phone calls. Then I switched on the computer and updated the Foster file, writing an account of the last two days. While the printer whirred across the paper, I fielded another phone call. As I put the file back into place, my eyes fell on a case at the back of the file drawer.

The box contained my gun, the one my father wished I would carry, bought when I first joined Errol Seville's firm as an investigator. I didn't use it very often. In fact, over the years I'd congratulated myself on how infrequently I'd used it. I preferred to get my information through my own resourcefulness, blending into the background, asking the right questions, being creative. I practiced regularly at the firing range, but I'd never had to use the weapon in the course of business. There were other tools of the trade, tools I used effectively, tools that made a gun seem unnecessary.

My hands moved to the case. I opened it and took out the gun. It was clean and oiled, ready for use. Did the situation warrant it? There was always the chance those two goons

237

would be back. Besides, Karen Willis was in the Alameda County Morgue. I checked the gun, loaded it, and stuck it into my shoulder bag. Then I locked up and headed for the Boatel.

The evening was clear, in contrast to last night's storm. The sky had faded from bright blue to cobalt, streaked pink and gold by the setting sun. I drove to the end of Broadway, where it crossed the Embarcadero and dead-ended a short block further in a series of shallow steps leading down to the estuary. I turned right on the Embarcadero, then left onto Washington, which led me into the Boatel's parking lot.

This section of the Oakland waterfront was called Jack London Square, a mix of restaurants and shops, offices and marinas. It was in the midst of a development phase that left several streets torn up and a half-finished structure across from the Boatel shrouded in darkness. Still, the area attracted a lot of trade, even on this weeknight. As I got out of my car, I heard people talking and saw a foursome walking toward Scott's seafood restaurant, on the other side of the steps. Light spilled from its dining room and glassed-in patio onto the pier jutting over the estuary. People sat on the benches at the center of the pier, or strolled along the walkway that roughly paralleled the shore.

When Mark answered the door of his second-floor room and saw me, he smiled and kissed me gently on the forehead. He'd been drinking.

He stepped back and let me into the room. His overnight bag sat on the bed, unopened. It looked as though he'd just checked into the room and had made no impact on it. The curtains and the sliding glass door leading to the balcony were open. A breeze blew in from the dark water of the estuary and the boats that gave the hotel its name.

"I called several times. You weren't here."

"I spent the afternoon in that funky little bar on the square. You know the one, the Last Chance Saloon, the log cabin with the slanted floor."

"Have you had dinner?"

"Not unless you count Jack Daniels and pretzels."

He came up behind me and put his arms around my waist. His lips moved against my ear and made my nerve endings shiver.

"Have dinner with me, Jeri," he whispered. "You owe me one. Let's walk down to that Italian restaurant on the other side of the marina and have pasta and a bottle of wine. Let's lose ourselves for a couple of hours."

"We can't." I moved away from his arms and turned to face him. "I need some answers, Mark."

The smile left his face. "Such as?"

"I went to San Francisco after I left Vee's house. I talked to some people Karen worked with. She was blackmailing Elizabeth."

He leaned against the dresser, crossing his arms against his chest. I watched his face. His blue eyes stared into mine, then looked away, as though he were looking into himself.

"You think Betsy killed Karen," he said, his face devoid of emotion.

"I think she wants to kill you."

"Why?"

"Maybe she thinks you and Karen are together in this blackmail scheme."

"But that's impossible. Why would I—" He stopped. His face closed. I wanted to pry it open.

"Karen wasn't where she was supposed to be," I said, using Karen's words. "Not at the slumber party, at least not for a while. I think she left her friend's house and climbed the fence into your backyard. That she was on the porch when she heard the shots. She must have seen what happened."

A look of horror transformed Mark's face. "What did happen, Mark?" I asked, knowing the answer.

He pushed himself away from the dresser and flung open the door, walking quickly out into the hallway. By the time I got into the hallway, he'd pushed open the door at the end, headed down the stairs. I caught up with him outside the Boatel, his head down, his hands in his pockets, striding

239

down the steps that led to the water. He stopped at the edge. I caught his left arm and pulled him around to face me.

"I haven't said anything, all these years . . ." He stopped.

"Level with me. I think I know, but I want you to tell me."

"I promised." In the light from an overhead lamp I saw his mouth work. "I haven't broken that promise."

"Liar."

The word was filled with venom. It didn't come from my mouth or his. I'd been expecting her to make her move and now she had. Light glinted off the gun she held in both hands. She was above us on the steps, walking with the same gliding step I'd seen before, outside Karen's apartment and Vee's shop. She wore the same tan raincoat, belted at the waist, the matching hat protruding from a pocket. The shoulder-length blond hair in the Christmas picture had been dyed dark brown and cut short and close to the head, giving her a sleek, boyish look.

"Betsy?" Mark turned, his back to the water, and stared at her.

"She isn't Betsy anymore," I told him. She wasn't Philip Foster's Renee or Vee's Beth. All this time I'd called her Elizabeth. As I looked at her face and the gun she held I wasn't sure who or what she was.

She wasn't paying any attention to me. Her gaze was directed at Mark, and so was the barrel of the gun. I glanced around me, assessing the situation. There were people on the pier above us and to my right. Couples walked along the street behind Elizabeth, oblivious to what was going on below them. My right hand moved slowly toward the flap that closed my purse.

"Don't move." Elizabeth shifted the gun in my direction.

"You've been watching me, haven't you?" I asked.

"Of course. I didn't know where to find Karen. She never would tell me where she had moved to. I went to Stockton, but Karen wasn't at Grandpa's funeral. I couldn't find any addresses in Alice's book. So I followed Vee back to Oakland after the funeral. I figured sooner or later she'd lead me to

240

Karen. Then you showed up, looking for me. All I had to do was follow you around." She laughed. "Did Philip hire you?"

"Yes. He was genuinely interested in finding you, until he found out you'd been beating your son."

Her face clouded. "I didn't mean to do that. I really didn't. Everything was falling apart. Things with Philip, things with Dean, my baby. Then Karen called."

"I should thank you for calling the cops the other night."

"I couldn't afford to let those men put you out of commission. I was counting on you to lead me to Karen. You did once, but I lost her when she left the hotel. I figured you'd connect with her again. And Mark."

His face filled with pain. "It was you in that car, trying to run me down. Why? I never told anyone."

"You liar," she spat at him. "Karen wanted money, lots of money, or she'd tell. How could she know unless you told her?"

"Karen figured it out all by herself," I said. "Either that, or she saw you pull the trigger. Not Mark. You. That's why she called you Lizzie, after Lizzie Borden. You killed Franny and George."

"It wasn't like that," Mark said.

"The hell it wasn't. She killed them and you took the fall."

He didn't deny it. The anguish in his eyes told me it was true. He stared at his sister, comparing the Betsy he wanted to remember and the reality that stood before us with a gun in her hand.

Elizabeth smiled. She looked girlish and quite mad. "It doesn't matter. Nobody else is going to tell. I'll go away where no one knows me. I'll change my name. I've done it before and I'll do it again. But first I have to kill both of you."

"Right here? At the foot of Broadway, with all these people around?" I moved my arm, encompassing the activity around Jack London Square.

"Walk," Elizabeth said, considering the wisdom of my

241

words. "Past the motel, toward where all that construction is."

Mark and I slowly climbed the steps to street level, both of us conscious of the gun. North of the Boatel and the unfinished building, away from the streetlamps, the waterfront was more industrial, a region of darkened warehouses and empty lots. Elizabeth could shoot us and disappear. Our bodies wouldn't be found until the next morning—if she didn't roll them into the estuary. As we walked past the sidewalk leading to the Boatel lobby, I saw a black Cougar parked in front. Sid got out of the car and started toward the door. Then he spotted us and changed direction.

"Where'd you get the gun, Elizabeth?" I said conversationally. Sid heard me and stopped, reaching for the gun in his shoulder holster.

"At a place on East Fourteenth. I told the guy I needed it for protection." She laughed, giddy with her success. "Now everybody needs protection from me."

I took Mark's arm and stepped off the sidewalk between a couple of parked cars, giving Sid a clear view of Elizabeth.

"Get back on the sidewalk," she ordered, tightening her grip on the gun.

"Police," Sid said, his gun out. "Drop your weapon."

Elizabeth turned and fired, the noise reverberating around us. The bullet caught Sid in the shoulder. He looked surprised as his own gun clattered to the sidewalk. I shoved Mark aside and tore open my bag, seizing my gun. Elizabeth whirled like a dancer and ran back in the direction of the steps.

"Stay with Sid," I told Mark.

I ran after her, hearing Mark's voice behind me, shouting for someone to call the police. Elizabeth ran past the steps, dodging and shoving through a group of strollers. She ran onto the pier that jutted over the estuary. My own feet thudded on the decking, gaining on her.

There were two openings in the railing. One slanted up, a boardwalk along the back window of the restaurant. The other led down, a ramp to the E-shaped floats for guest boaters. A group of people blocked the way to the boardwalk. Elizabeth altered course, running down the ramp to the floats. A sailboat was tied up at the far end, bobbing in the shimmering water of the estuary. Elizabeth reached the end of the float and realized her mistake.

"There's no way out," I called from the ramp. "It's a dead end."

Without a word, she raised the gun and fired at me. The shot went wild, shattering the plate-glass window at Scott's. I heard screams from inside the restaurant as people scrambled away from the broken glass that showered their tables. I shouted at her to stop and took aim with my gun. She fired again, a second before I squeezed the trigger. Her bullet grazed my right arm and my shot went astray, thudding into a piling behind her.

Elizabeth looked up at the boardwalk, but there was too much space and water for her to bridge. I ignored the sting in my arm and launched myself at her, grabbing her legs, pulling her down. She fought like a cornered cat, scratching and spitting, her fury propelling us backward, until my foot hit air instead of planking. We tumbled into the cold black water of the estuary.

After a long moment in the chilling darkness my head broke the surface and I gasped for air. Spitting out water, I shook my head and saw Elizabeth struggling in the water, trying to climb into the boat. I heard sirens and saw red lights flashing, reflected on the windows of Scott's. People milled on the floats and the boardwalk, some of them in uniform, carrying flashlights and coming toward us.

I swam to Elizabeth and grabbed her by the belt of her raincoat. The fight seemed to have gone out of her as I pulled her with me toward the pier. A dozen hands reached out to pull us onto the planking, a dozen voices spoke in a barrage of questions. I got to my feet and searched the faces around me. Finally I saw Mark, shoving through the crowd. I walked toward him, a question on my face.

"They took him to the hospital," Mark said. "He's going to be all right."

Twenty-six

SID LAY IN A PRIVATE ROOM AT MERRITT HOSPITAL. The night before the doctors had removed the slug from his right shoulder and listed him in good condition. Under his hospital gown I could see the white bandage against his brown chest. A flower arrangement sat on the nightstand and there were several others arrayed around the room.

"Is there anything you need?" I asked.

"Not unless you've got some booze in your purse." He formed the words with an effort, as though all his energy was diverted into his glowering look. It was a weak version of his standard bad-cop expression.

"I called Vicki last night."

"Damn it, Jeri. I don't want her to worry."

"She's your daughter. She needs to know."

"How'd she take it?"

"Like her father's child." My ex-stepdaughter had taken the news fairly well, though I had to dissuade her from hopping on a plane to Oakland. "She's okay, Sid. She'll call you today." I reached out and smoothed the hair away from his forehead. "What were you doing there anyway?"

"I came to tell Willis the floater wasn't his sister. The dental charts confirmed it. I saw the three of you walking, but it didn't register until I heard you say her name. I should have had her," he said angrily. "I had a clean drop on her and she shoots me. I'll never live it down."

I grinned. "Didn't I tell you when we were married that you're not perfect? At least she's in custody. That's the important thing."

"She admitted killing her parents *and* Karen, without batting an eye. Of course, after the headshrinkers get through with her she probably won't do any real time."

"I think she will. Crazy's no excuse these days." I looked at my watch. "I've got to go."

I leaned over to kiss him on the forehead. He moved his head and my lips met his. His hand caught mine and squeezed it.

"Hey," he said. "Come see me tonight."

"I will."

I went back to my office, feeling tired. I'd spent the rest of the previous night at the Oakland Police Department and the hospital, falling into bed past midnight only to discover I couldn't sleep. I had gone back to Homicide Section first thing in the morning, talking to Wayne Hobart until visiting hours started at the hospital.

Edward Foster was waiting for me in the hallway outside my office. We exchanged looks. Neither of us said anything as I unlocked my door. I went in and sat down. He stood in front of my desk.

"Something on your mind, Mr. Foster?"

"I came up here hoping she was dead."

"Why don't you just take satisfaction in knowing you were right about her all along?"

His hard brown eyes blinked. "My daughter-in-law's in jail and my son's a wreck. I blame you. If you'd left this alone . . ."

"Those were your messengers Monday night, weren't they?"

"You don't scare easily." He gave me an unpleasant smile. It was the closest he would ever come to admitting it.

"No, I don't. Things like that just make me more curious. I don't think we have anything else to say to each other, Mr. Foster."

After he left I made a pot of coffee and sat down at the computer to update the Foster file. I typed in an account of last night's events and printed it. The case was almost at an end. When it was over I would write a report. In this business

245

the client pays the money and gets a report, a distillation of the investigator's toil. What the client does with the end result is his or her business, not mine.

But this case was different. In a way I was my own client. True, I'd been working for Philip Foster, then for Vee Burke, but I'd also been working for myself, getting the answers to satisfy my own curiosity. Jeri Howard the client wanted one more answer before Jeri Howard the investigator could close the Foster file.

I got up to pour myself another cup of coffee. My door opened and Mark walked in.

"I was wondering when I'd see you," I said. "How about a cup of coffee?"

"Thanks." I got up, poured him a cup, and handed it to him. He took it and held it in both hands. I resumed my seat leaning back, watching him.

"How's Vee? And Alice?"

"I don't know about Alice. She doesn't talk to me." He sipped the coffee. "Vee will be all right. She's a tough lady. Besides, Uncle Charles is back. She can lean on him." He sipped the coffee.

"Mark." He looked up. "I want to know what happened the night your parents died."

He set the coffee mug on my desk and put his hands in his pockets, walking to the window. He looked out at the sunny March morning. Then he took a deep breath and expelled the air in a sigh.

"All right," he said. "I'll tell you." He turned and faced me.

"I had dinner at Leo's house. He and I were going to a party. I went home first, to change clothes. When I got there Betsy was in the living room, reading and listening to the stereo. I went upstairs. When I came down a few minutes later, Franny was picking on Betsy about something. I'm not sure what it was. It doesn't matter now." He shrugged, moving away from the window.

"Betsy was white and shaking. I knew she was scared. It had happened more often in the previous months, Franny

246

going after Betsy rather than me, like the time she burned Betsy's arm with the cigarette. I told you I was afraid of what might happen when I left for college.''

Mark came back to the desk and picked up the coffee, sipping the black brew. His face tensed as he spoke, as though the events he described were happening again, right before his eyes.

"I told Franny to leave Betsy alone. She turned on me. Me, her old antagonist. She was enjoying the prospect of one last fight. I could tell by the look in her eyes. She said, 'Where are you going?' I told her I was going to a party. She said, 'No, you're not.' I told her, 'Go to hell. I'm eighteen and I'm out of here. I don't have to listen to your bullshit anymore.'

"I started for the front door. George was in his recliner, nursing a gin and tonic. He said, 'Don't talk to your mother like that.' I said, 'Is that bitch my mother? Could have fooled me. I thought she was a whore.' ''

Mark's hand shook and he quickly set the coffee down. He stared down at the cup, then lifted his eyes to my face.

"George came out of the chair," Mark said, "and hit me across the face. He said he was tired of my lip. He was between me and the front door. I backed off. 'I don't want to argue with you,' I said. 'I just want to leave.'

"I turned and went toward the doorway that led from the living room to the kitchen. Before I got there Franny snatched Betsy's book out of her hands and threw it across the room. She grabbed Betsy's arm and yanked her to her feet. She yelled at Betsy. Betsy started crying. Franny slapped her so hard Betsy stumbled back against the sofa. Franny laughed. That really got me. I stopped. I told Franny, 'Don't do that again. I'll kill you if you do that again.' I was so angry I could feel it, like a hot wave moving from my feet all the way up to my head.

"Franny laughed again. Then she slapped me. She said I didn't have the balls to do anything. I lunged at her. I think if I'd gotten my hands on her I would have strangled her. But I didn't. George got between us somehow. He pulled me

247

away. Franny was screaming at me, flailing at me with her fists.''

He stopped and looked down at his hands. Then he folded his arms tightly across his chest.

"I'm not sure when Betsy got the gun. George kept it on the top shelf of the hall closet. I knew it was there. I knew it was loaded. Betsy knew it too. All of a sudden she was standing there with the gun in her hand. Her face was white. She was shaking so hard I thought she'd drop it.''

He was quiet again, for a long moment.

"Everything stopped,'' he continued. "It was like we were frozen in place. Nobody moved, nobody spoke. It seemed like a long time, but I'm sure it was only a few seconds. Then everything exploded, moving, arms and legs and heads. I heard Franny screaming, George bellowing. Then I heard two shots, one after the other. George was on the floor in the living room. Franny managed to crawl a few feet before she died.''

Mark stood still for a moment, then he sat down in the chair facing me, slumping, as though all the energy had gone out of him.

"Betsy was holding the gun. I took it away from her. I said, 'Go to your room. You don't know what happened.' She didn't argue with me. She just nodded and did what I told her to do.''

"Why, Mark?'' I asked, leaning forward in my chair. "How could you take the rap for her?''

"She was only fourteen, Jeri. She had her whole life ahead of her.''

"So did you.'' I shook my head. "You wanted to protect her. All her life people have been protecting her. You did her more harm than good. If she'd faced the consequences then, none of this would have happened.''

"Maybe. It's pointless to sit here and speculate what might have happened.'' Mark spread his hands out on the surface of my desk. "I made a decision, Jeri. Once I made it, there didn't seem to be any way to turn back. It was a long time

248

ago. Somebody paid for the crime. It doesn't matter anymore.''

"It matters to me. You weren't guilty of murder.''

"Maybe I was," Mark said. "I don't know whether I wanted to save them or kill them myself. Doesn't that make me an accessory to murder?''

That was a question that neither of us could answer.

"I thought about killing them," Mark said. "I fantasized about it. I even talked about it to Betsy. I told her one day they'd go too far. I'd get that gun from the hall closet and blow them away." He stopped and looked at me, his burden of guilt etching lines in his face.

"Betsy picked up the gun. But I planted that seed. I have to share the responsibility.''

".I don't believe that.''

"I do," he said quietly. He stood up.

"Karen's funeral is tomorrow. I'll stay for that, then I'm going back to Cibola. I don't like the big city. I prefer my well-ordered life in the mountains." A smile lit his face. "I hope I'll see you again, Jeri.''

"You might.''

I got up and reached for his hand. He pulled me to him and held me for a moment. Then he kissed me briefly on the lips and released me. After he left I picked up the Foster file and put it back into the cabinet.

About the Author

JANET DAWSON is a legal secretary who lives in Alameda, California. She is at work on another Jeri Howard mystery.